Memories of a Mischling

Memories of a Mischling

Becoming an American

Marianne Gilbert Finnegan

To order additional copies of this book, contact:
Xlibris Corporation
1-888-7-XLIBRIS
www.Xlibris.com
Orders@Xlibris.com
11952

Contents

MEMORIES OF A MISCHLING

Author's Note

This book has been almost as many years in the making as the events it covers were in the living. I have remembered as clearly as I could, talked with remaining family members to expand my knowledge of family lore, and read relevant history of the era to set our stories into a larger factual frame.

Because I am now the only one left who holds these stories in mind, I have felt some urgency in setting them down to preserve them. On a personal level, I hope that my children and grandchildren will someday want to know this part of their history. In a larger context, I believe that the dislocation and adaptation of the generations in this one small family group may represent many similar experiences during the era of the second world war.

The Japanese have a saying, "Small things are small. Large things are large. But small things are also large, when seen close up." I was a child during the years of the Third Reich and my own experiences were small indeed but my memories of flight and confused identity, when set into the family stories that surrounded my growing up, have shown me that history isn't just distant and past, but moves within each of us, intimate and immediate. Compared to the millions who suffered and died during those huge and terrible events in Europe, the Jewish side of my family was lucky. They got out. I am here in America because they got out. But the arrival of Hitler and his storm troopers scattered our family across the globe like fragments from a huge bomb blast and the family, as a family, was never restored. My mother's relatives remained in Berlin but not all of them survived the war. My father's relatives escaped to foreign countries, but their children, like me, grew up there and did not return to Germany. All our lives were changed forever.

What I have written may not be the whole truth but it is my own truth insofar as my memory and those of others have made possible. I have retained the names of all my family members as accurately as conversations and records permit. To spare others any possible embarrassment, I have changed the names of those persons beyond my immediate family whose actual identities are not essential for my eventual readers.

MEMORIES OF A
MISCHLING

I

***

Getting Out

I was born in a house divided. Germany, the country of my birth, was swirling in the storms of hatred stirred up by Hitler and his henchmen. The division, though not the hatred, penetrated my family. While not religious, my father was a Jew. My mother came from a strict Lutheran family. This made me, in Nazi parlance, a *Mischling*, a half-breed or mongrel, and placed me in the same danger as persons fully Jewish.

Too young to know all the details of fascism's advance through Germany, I only knew, from hearing the adults near me worry, that things were a lot better before I was born and went to hell right afterwards. I knew that before my arrival there had been mansions, money, parties and laughter, and that all that pleasant life had vanished. As children will, I assumed a good deal of personal responsibility for this situation. Clearly, my birth had not brought anyone good luck and, in fact, had even caused a major rift between my parents.

"Your father never wanted children," my mother used to tell me, "but I did. He warned me, 'If you have a child, I'll leave you.' For years I waited, but he didn't change his mind. Then I thought if there was a real baby he would like being a father and I finally decided to go ahead and have you."

Her act of defiance backfired. When I was a year old, my father left the house to buy a pack of cigarettes and didn't return for four years.

Many years later I began to suspect that my infant presence might not have been the only reason for my father's extended search for cigarettes and that rather than being the cause of the household's disruption, I might actually have been one of my mother's many attempts to hold him. The particular stratagem that gave rise to me ultimately worked no better and no worse than others she tried. As it turned out she couldn't go against nature because my father was a wanderer. Not only was a pretty Fräulein waiting for him at the time he left, but he continued all his life to wander into and out of the arms of pretty women.

Every family has its stories. First heard in my childhood and echoing through my life, the stories in my family were all grounded in the time of the Nazis. Like a deep magnet, like a sullied Trojan War, that time attracted and redirected all experience so that everything either foreshadowed, centered on, or turned back to it. The villains, those who inflicted Hitler's demonic visions upon the world, remained constant in each story. The other characters shifted with the teller's viewpoint, sometimes seen as admirable, sometimes as deeply flawed. A few did not survive and some did not recover.

Though the details didn't always agree, these stories of dangers and escapes entered my mind like an oral tradition, one that I did not want to recall for a long time. As a young person in America, I, like my parents before me, wanted to escape from history and define myself apart from former times and places. But when I became secure enough to reopen the book of my childhood, there they were, all those stories. Some were intact in my memory, others were fragments I had to piece together from documents or conversations with remaining relatives. No doubt many stories have been lost, but I feel an unexpected obligation to record those that remain.

After my father bolted, my mother made the best of things. Having embarked on motherhood she saw it through. When Hitler was elected Reich Chancellor in 1933 she, like thousands of others, left the country. She took me to Paris to wait for better times, persuading herself that my father would return to her because she was not only pretty, she was talented and smart. With her blonde hair, her green eyes that had little golden flecks around the pupils, her scent of powders and perfume, her wonderful clothes and pearls, and her singing voice like dark velvet, I thought her the most beautiful and gifted creature in the world. She didn't feel exactly the same about me.

"I suffered terribly with your birth. Two whole days. And then they had to use forceps," she told me. "When they brought you to me at the hospital, your little head was misshapen and still had marks from the forceps. I had never seen such a homely baby." Then seeing my solemn face, she patted my cheek, gave a little laugh and added, "but I loved you anyway."

My mother, the eldest of three sisters, was born in 1900 and christened Marie Louise Elizabeth Geldner. Throughout her childhood she was called Elspeth, a nickname she detested. The three little girls, Elspeth and her two younger sisters, Charlotte and Irmgard, were taken to church regularly and raised to be soberly middle class. Nevertheless, by age ten, Elspeth had the convictions of a communist or at least a failed aristocrat. One afternoon in 1910, Kaiser Wilhelm II was returning from travels in Austria-Hungary to his palace in Berlin and the city had prepared a royal welcome. The Geldner family joined thousands of Berliners along both sides of Unter den Linden, the wide elegant avenue leading to the palace. They arrived early to station themselves as close as possible to the palace so as to get a good view of the imperial procession, and waited in the raw weather. Elspeth's father turned up the collar of his greatcoat; her mother's hands were hidden in a large fur muff. The three little girls jumped up and down, stamping their feet. A powdery snow filmed the air and swirled across the avenue. Elspeth shivered, first with excitement, then with increasing chill. Finally they could hear trumpets in the distance, then a regular thudding as if the city's great heart were beating. With a clacking cascade of hooves, the cavalry of prancing horses rode into view, bearing straight-backed helmeted soldiers uniformed with gold buttons and braid. Marching ranks of the Imperial Guard followed, stern-faced men with waxed mustaches and large epaulettes, their bodies braced beneath the banners they bore, their legs in stiff rhythm to the booming drums. The crowd roared, *"Hoch! Hoch!"* The royal carriage was approaching. "Look, look, there he is. There's the Kaiser!"

Ten year old Elspeth watched the gleaming gold-encrusted carriage drawn by four plumed black horses. Inside rode an elderly man with a great mustache. He wore even more gold braid and a helmet with a spike on top. He nodded gravely from side to side in response to the cheering crowds. As the carriage passed with more retainers at the rear, the crowd moved slowly into the street to follow the end of the procession and the Geldner family joined the promenade. The mood was festive, like a big outdoor party.

As they approached the palace gates, the pace slowed. Elspeth watched the last mounted rear guards ride through the gates. Then a line of Berlin policemen stationed themselves across the driveway to prevent the citizenry from advancing further. The golden carriage was out of sight. The palace gates swung shut. The celebration was over. Gradually, people turned away and began to disperse. Elspeth was outraged.

"Why do they let those soldiers inside the gates and not us?" she complained.

"Because they are the Kaiser's own guards," her father shushed her firmly. "They belong there with him."

Elspeth was not mollified. Why should that old man get to ride in a golden carriage while I have to stand here with my feet cold, she thought. Why should he have a palace when I have to share a room with Lotti and Irma? The anger that flared during that afternoon's outing smoldered all her life. It fueled her politics, infused her personal relationships and ran like a sparking wire along the contours of her character.

The Kaiser didn't get to keep his palace much longer; his empire ended with Germany's defeat in the First World War. But the reversal in his fortunes didn't mean a golden carriage for Elspeth. In fact even the petit bourgeois security of her childhood came to an abrupt end. When she was twelve, her father, Otto Geldner, became ill and had to enter a sanitarium where he died two years later. Desperately short of money in the days before life insurance, her mother, Hedwig, was forced to sell their house and return with her daughters to her parents' home. The three girls had to leave school and go to work as each turned sixteen.

Elspeth hated her mother's subservient position in the cramped and repressive home her grandparents provided for the fatherless family, and she resented the narrow conformist routine imposed on her by poverty. She wanted a more glamorous identity and a more exciting future. She saved what money she could from her job as an apprentice draftsman to sew stylish clothes for herself. Her good looks and flair attracted the attention of Dr. Gorodiski, the family's middle-aged dentist, who proposed marriage. Determined to get away from home, Elspeth accepted and married at nineteen. The marriage meant that she could stop working but idleness was not what she had in mind. She had no intention of becoming a *Hausfrau* called Elspeth. Now that she had some money, she began lessons in singing and dancing to prepare herself for a career as a singer. At singing lessons in 1921 she met my father, Robert Winterfeld, who was studying voice to better perform his own songs. Robert composed music and lyrics for songs and operettas, thereby following his father's successful career.

"He used to have his lesson just before mine," Elke remembered, "And watching him made me laugh. He was so serious, and between songs he would mop his face with a huge handkerchief. And I liked his big ears."

Robert noticed her too, she recalled. "One day as I was leaving after my lesson, he was waiting for me. He introduced himself, very formal, 'I am Robert Winterfeld,' he said, 'and I would like to meet you.' He was so nervous. I liked that, and I thought Winterfeld was such a beautiful name."

They began to meet regularly. He said she was too glamorous to be an Elspeth and re-named her Elke. At last she had a name that suited her. Robert suited her too, as did his witty friends from Berlin's theatrical circles. Inevitably outclassed by youth, love, and wit, Dr. Gorodiski, the dentist, was quietly divorced.

At that time in Germany most middle-class Jews felt comfortably assimilated into mainstream German society, but the persistent undercurrent of anti-Semitism was intensifying. My father had been raised in a home devoted to books and music, but his Jewish origins distressed my mother's grandparents even more than his ties to theatrical circles they saw as frivolous and amoral. The opportunity to outrage them and reject the strict moralism of her Lutheran upbringing pleased Elke. In addition, Robert had inspired her with the ideals of the communist revolution in Russia which saw religion as a tool of oppression and declared it to be "the opiate of the people." In 1923, the year they were both also twenty-three, Elke and Robert renounced the religious affiliations of their birth and were married in a civil ceremony. They were never afterwards moved to establish ties with any formal religion. But their youthful attempt to escape their origins and define themselves anew was futile. Instead, history took a vicious turn and revised the lives they had planned.

My grandfather, born Max Winterfeld, started out in Hamburg as conductor of an outdoor band that played afternoon concerts at the Zoo. In 1910, he wrote "*Püppchen, Du Bist Mein*

Augenstern" (Baby, You're the Twinkle in My Eye), a song which became an international hit of such unprecedented proportions that music reviewers referred to him as "the Napoleon of the Gramophone Record." In those days, people also bought sheet music that featured the song's title and the author's name. My grandfather's agent warned, "You'll never get anywhere with a name like Max Winterfeld. You need something more glamorous, maybe something French." Max decided to blend a French first name with the surname of a famous predecessor in operetta music. And so the name Jean Gilbert (pronounced Zhan Zhilbere) accompanied my grandfather's musical career and subsequently passed on to my father who wrote as Robert Gilbert.

Robert was born in 1899 and his brother Henry was two years younger. Until their father's success in 1910, the family was poor. Robert later remembered winters when there was not enough money to heat the house and his mother, Rosa, lay in bed to keep warm while sewing hats to sell. All that changed with "*Püppchen*." Soon Jean Gilbert moved his wife and the two boys, as well as his sister and her son, Maggi, to an estate in Wannsee, a wealthy lakeside suburb of Berlin. He also adopted the son of a friend, a boy named Fritz Loewe (later well known in America as the composer Frederick Loewe). Henry all his life cherished memories of the Wannsee estate where the four boys grew up affluent and insulated from the hardships of the First World War. Robert was the adored elder son and played piano with ease. Henry had no musical talent but could write. All four boys wrote and performed amateur theatricals, practiced boxing, and sneaked out to nearby pubs on weekend evenings to meet and flirt with girls. Though nominally Jewish, the family had few religious ties. Their friends were in the musical theater; their talents and interests centered on the secular culture of Germany at the time.

After the First World War, Robert attended the conservatory where he studied composition, and classical piano with Claudio Arau. But his talent, like his father's, was for light music and he soon joined his father in writing songs and musical shows. In the

1920s he wrote the lyrics for the operetta *White Horse Inn,* a popular success for many years, and songs like "On Sunday I'll Go Sailing With My Sweetie" and "This Must Be a Bit of Heaven" that sold sheet music and records wherever German was spoken or sung. Lyrics and popular music supported Robert's lavish tastes through the 1920s, a decade of inflation and unrest in Germany. Unaware that its author was Jewish, Hitler even used the title of one of my father's love songs, *"Das Giebt's Nur Einmal"* (This Happens Only Once), to describe the advent of the Third Reich.

When Robert and Elke were married, they were both eager for independence. They moved into an apartment in Laubenheimerplatz, a neighborhood that housed artists and writers, and entered the lively cultural and political life of young people in Berlin. But Robert never forgot his early years of poverty, and Elke had also grown up poor. Both were both moved by the plight of unemployed German workers and inspired by the Russian revolution that sought to empower the working class. Increasingly alarmed by the Nazi's gains in power through the 1920s, they joined the Spartacist League, an anti-Stalinist wing of the German communist party founded by Rosa Luxemburg and Karl Liebknecht. Robert and Elke attended workers' meetings, distributed leaflets, and protested against the spread of fascism.

Robert contributed much of his income from popular songs to the party and, unlike his father, he also added more somber tones to his work. Using the pseudonym of David Weber, he became a crossover artists and wrote many socially critical songs performed at leftist and communist cabarets such as the *"Katakombe."* As David Weber, in the gruff ironic Berliner dialect, he wrote *"Stempellied"*, a poem in the voice of a man without work or hope, with no money and only a stamp in his pocket. Set to music by Hanns Eisler, *"Stempellied"* became widely known throughout the country. He and Eisler collaborated on songs and choruses for working men to aid in their struggle for decent wages and living conditions, believing that, as Eisler put it, "even our singing must be fighting." Robert also started writing satirical skits against Hitler for the Berlin cabarets and, by the early 1930s, poems of mourning and dread like, "Harrowing the Nation," and "Unshaven and Far From Home."

As it turned out, the alliance of intellectuals and artists with workers could stop neither Stalin's perversion of communist ideals in Russia nor Nazism's advance in Germany. Many years afterwards Robert said, "When I was young, my friends and I thought we could change the world. Instead we realized later, we didn't change the world; the world changed us."

When Hitler was appointed Reich Chancellor in January 1933, the fact that my father was Jewish would have been enough to target him, but his political activities put him not only generically but specifically on Hitler's hit list. When Hitler began to seize and confiscate the houses and property of wealthy Jews, my grandfather among them, the Winterfeld family was smart enough to see that things were only going to get worse. Reluctantly, they decided to leave the country. The premiere in Vienna of my grandfather's popular operetta, "Chaste Suzanne" provided the pretext. He requested permission from the new Nazi government to visit Vienna so that he could conduct the orchestra. He did not intend to return, but could not afford the crippling confiscatory taxes imposed on Jews who wanted to emigrate. With most of his property already confiscated, these taxes would have stripped him of the rest of his assets. Therefore he requested an exit visa limited to the show's rehearsal time and premiere in Vienna. The permission was granted.

The touring cars in his garage (as well as the garage itself and the entire Wannsee estate) having been seized by the new Nazi government, my grandfather hired the most ostentatious limousine he could find and arranged for a liveried chauffeur. On the appointed day he placed himself like a pasha garbed in furs and lap-robes in the middle of the limousine's wide rear seat. On either side of him rode his two sons, Robert and Henry, both without exit visas since the family had agreed that simultaneous visa applications would attract dangerous attention. At the German border, when questioned about the missing visas, my grandfather regally informed the guards that he, Jean Gilbert, world-famous composer, needed the support and services of his sons to bring his hugely popular and authentically *German* operetta to waiting Viennese audiences.

"We were all terrified," Robert later recalled. "Everything depended on the mood of one or two border guards. If they were bored, or wanted to impress their girl friends, or if you didn't have money for bribes, they could stop you just on a whim. And with my record, I'd have been arrested and taken off to God knows where. People were taken away all the time and you didn't see them again. But we sat there in this huge car, smiling and joking with the guards, singing snatches of *"Püppchen"* with them, while my father waved an enormous cigar and passed out Deutchmark like bonbons."

The border guards were impressed enough to raise the barriers. The entourage crossed into Austria. Robert's poem, "Parting in April" recreates the suspense and sadness of such moments:

> . . . Customs. Currency exchange. Passport control.
> Oh. They've let me through; it's worked. I've made it.
> My last German brook is murmuring . . .
> Lo, there a rose is blooming.
>
> Poplars seeming like gallows stand in line.
> Germany, farewell.
> Who knows, who knows when we will meet again
> By the green banks of the Spree.

Years later, I wondered about this departure and asked my uncle Henry why the Winterfeld men glided out of the country together in their hired limousine, and left their wives and children to fend for themselves.

"But you see, we were the ones in danger," he explained. "We were Jews. The women were not Jewish and could still travel freely. And in 1933 the Nazis hadn't yet started to investigate who had *Mischling* children."

My mother had already left with me for Paris. My grandfather's first wife, my Jewish grandmother, Rosa, had left the country at the time of their divorce some years earlier. My grandfather's second wife, Gerda, and their three daughters as well as Henry's wife and their ten-year old son Thomas, traveled by train from Berlin to Vienna, crossing the border without interference. Other remaining Jewish family members—unmarried great-uncles and aunts—left Germany one by one as best they could. All began several years of wandering through Europe before scattering to England and North and South America. They were among fifty thousand refugees, mostly Jews but including many Christians persecuted for their liberal politics, who fled Germany that year. (The exodus continued at an average of twenty-five thousand per year until 1938 when forced deportations to concentration camps in the east began.)

Once in Austria, the exiles tried to believe that the German people would soon come to their senses, oust Hitler, and restore more liberal politicians to office. Their talk and hopes centered on plans to return to Germany. Instead, by the end of that year, 92% of German voters supported the Nazi party.

My grandfather stayed in Austria for a while with his second family, but his German royalties were confiscated and finances were getting difficult and they were able to emigrate to England. Robert and his younger brother Henry, both writers whose work centered on their native language, decided to remain in Austria, the only other German-speaking country. Robert continued his political activities, often taking risks by acting as a courier, delivering underground communiqués from Germany to party members in France and the Scandinavian countries. Henry, then and afterwards, was a contrast to him in physique and temperament. Whereas Robert was burly, mostly bald by age thirty, and gregarious, Henry was slim, dark and somber. Robert's music brought him affluence and popularity; Henry was not musical, had little money and few friends. He envied Robert's success, but the brothers remained close and sometimes collaborated on show librettos. Non-religious as was the rest of his family, Henry had also married a Gentile woman in the early 1920s. His wife, my aunt Else, was a dainty blue-eyed blonde set on stocky legs which she covered with long skirts. Neither Henry nor Else were active in politics, though they watched the ominous events with fear and dismay. With their activities increasingly circumscribed, they stayed close to home and concentrated on raising their son Thomas, born in 1923, and Henry began to write stories for children.

By this time hatred of Jews in Germany had escalated into the discriminatory Nuremberg Laws of 1935 which declared Jews non-citizens. Marriages (and extramarital relations) between Jews and citizens "of German or related blood" were forbidden. Marriages contracted despite the law were invalid. Jews were denied the right to vote, could not hold public office, and were increasingly ostracized. In towns and villages notices appeared, such as "Jews not wanted," and "Bathing prohibited to dogs and Jews." Shops and restaurants began to exclude Jewish customers. Jews were barred from most professions and forbidden to act in theaters or perform at concerts. Even municipal park benches bore signs marked "For Aryans Only."

The laws were not specific on who was a "full Jew" and after intense debate, legal experts issued an addendum defining a full Jew as someone who had three or more Jewish grandparents. Those who had fewer were labeled as *Mischlinge* or mixed-breeds and for them the classifications were also precise. They were divided into *Mischlinge* first degree (those with two Jewish grandparents), and *Mischlinge* second degree (those with one Jewish grandparent). In most cases, first degree *Mischlinge*, like me, were considered and treated as full Jews. In a few years such classifications became decisions of life or death.

In Austria hatred of Jews was masked by dirndls, lederhosen, and funny hats but was, if anything, more virulent than in Germany. Austrian admiration for Hitler knew no bounds. They quickly passed new laws prohibiting Jews from most types of employment and the police checked payrolls to make sure they contained no Jewish names. Each month, my Uncle Henry recalled, the family received a weekday visit from the police who checked to make sure that the adults were at home and not out working. Nor were Jewish families eligible for any government financial assistance. These contradictory regulations created a serious dilemma since they denied Jews most sources of income. Both Robert and Henry were able to gain a little leeway by working in the flourishing film industry where they were paid off the books in cash.

Henry's son, my cousin Thomas, was then a twelve year old pudgy boy who wore glasses. With dark hair, dark eyes and Semitic features, he looked nothing like his blonde blue-eyed mother. Unbeknownst to him, when she walked with him on the street, she began to hear passerby's mutter comments.

"What's a pretty girl like you doing with a Jew brat?"

"You're a disgrace to decent people walking with that little Jew."

Else tried to shield her son from such taunts, but Thomas himself came to a bitter awakening one morning in the schoolyard when he overheard a classmate, who had been his friend, give a long harangue against Jews.

"We shouldn't have to attend school with Jews. We don't want them near us. They shouldn't be allowed to sit in the same classrooms."

The group of boys turned to look at Thomas. One of them darted to his side and pushed him. Another took hold of the leather book bag strapped to his back and spun him around. Delighted with this maneuver, the boys formed a circle and kept spinning him around till he fell down. At that point the school bell rang and they ran off toward the building.

From that time on, whenever his schoolmates caught Thomas alone, they grabbed hold of his book bag and spun him around till he was dizzy and staggered or fell down. He began to walk to and from school by circuitous routes and spent more and more time inside at home.

My own first vivid memory from around that time is of a living room, probably in Paris, where I sat on the floor playing while my mother was sewing at a table nearby. I was three or four years old. Marie, the maid who looked after the house and often let me tag after her, was away for her day off. It had been raining for days and I was bored. I was tired of all my dolls and blocks. I wanted to go outside, but the rain pelted the windows. Dissatisfied with my lot, I decided to stir up a little action.

"What would you do, Mutti, if I made pi-pi right here on the floor?"

"Oh, you wouldn't do a thing like that," she said steadily.

"Maybe I would, what would you do?"

My mother put down her sewing and looked at me. "I'm sure you wouldn't do that," her voice carried a warning. The imminent danger brought some excitement to the dreary day. Watching my mother's face, I squatted and began to pee, feeling the hot wetness penetrate my blue terry cloth overalls. The puddle spread beyond my shoes on the shiny wooden floorboards. My mother got up, snatched me up, gave me a single sharp smack across the bottom, then flung me aside onto the sofa. Then as I watched she went to the kitchen, got a mop, ran water into a pail, went back to the living room and mopped up the puddle, rinsed out the mop in the pail, went to the bathroom, emptied the pail into the toilet, returned to the kitchen, put pail and mop away. She never looked my way. Clearly, my mischief had caused a lot of work. Peeing on the floor didn't seem like such a good idea anymore. In suspense, I waited. Surely, more was going to happen. A single smack wasn't enough punishment for having made all that trouble. Probably I was in for a real spanking. But my mother kept moving around the apartment without looking at me. She got her purse from the bedroom and then went to the closet in the front hall and started putting on her coat. An enormous fear rose in my chest. I ran over to her.

"Where are you going?"

"I'm going away," she said, her mouth tight. "I'm not going to live with such a disgusting child." She put on her hat.

"No, Mutti, no. Please don't go away. I'm sorry, I'll never do it again." I was crying, sobbing, clinging to her knees, but through my struggles to hold on to her she fastened her coat, took her umbrella from the stand, and pushed me off.

"I'm sorry Mutti, I'm sorry. Please don't go," I kept wailing as the heavy apartment door closed behind her. My wet overalls were now clammy and cold, but I was too distraught to move away from the front door. My mother was gone. I had no idea what to do or what would become of me. Terrified, I sobbed on and on in the horrible silence of the empty apartment till I finally curled into a gasping sleep on the floor beside the closet. Some time later, I awoke to the sound of a key in the lock and my mother, raindrops glistening on her fur coat and streaming from her umbrella, was restored to me.

Perhaps she wasn't gone for more than an hour, but to me it was an eternity of abandonment. I wasn't curious anymore. I knew that when I did something really bad, people wouldn't spank or shout at me or send me to my room; they would simply leave me alone in an icy silent universe.

With my father absent, I began to worry about my mother. "Are you going to die soon?" I asked her.

"No, of course not," she was taken aback. "Why should you think that?"

I wasn't sure when or why I had begun to worry about her death. I just knew that people died when they got old. Everybody did.

"But I'm not old, Mausli (my pet name of 'little mouse') I'm still a young woman. You won't have to worry for a long time."

I was still uneasy. "How old are people when they die?"

"Most people don't die till they are over seventy."

That sounded all right. Maybe she was right and I didn't have to worry, but I still wasn't sure. "Some people die younger, don't they?"

"Yes, but they are sick. I'm not sick and I'm a long way from being seventy. Now stop fussing, there's nothing to worry about. I'm only twenty-six."

My fears quieted; even to my childish understanding, twenty-six didn't sound very old for a grown-up. A decade passed before I learned that my mother had glibly taken ten years off her real age that day. She claimed the subtraction had been simply to reassure me, but she quite enjoyed her newfound youth and continued with the lower number until she stopped using exact numbers altogether and admitted only to "twenty-one-plus."

After his escape from Germany, my father lived in Vienna with Adelheid, the young lady who had lured him there. When my parents had lived in Berlin, Adelheid had been the building janitor's daughter. She had been eager to improve her position, and Robert was always democratic, especially toward women. The two decided to set up a new household. Adelheid, who could travel freely because she was not Jewish, went to Vienna first; Robert joined her after his escape from Germany. Friends kept Elke informed of the situation and she waited in Paris for him to come to what she considered his senses. But when time passed and he showed no signs of doing so, she decided to wage a more active campaign to get him back. In 1937 she also moved with me to Vienna and after a few months, was successful. Robert returned to her in a kind of second honeymoon, though he remained on good terms with Adelheid. Elke must have decided that their reunion would be more stable if I were temporarily out of the picture. And so, at age six I was sent to *Tratzerberg*, a boarding school in the nearby countryside. At the time, I was not told of Adelheid's existence. The reason my mother gave for sending me away was that I was sickly and wouldn't eat. She said she worried and arranged to surround me with other children eagerly cleaning their plates so that I would be similarly inspired. I believed this story without conscious questions. Parents are gods and their explanations of the world penetrate like divine truth. Now the gods are gone and the truth is hard to locate, especially since political events larger than my childish refusal to eat, or even my parents' romantic difficulties, were increasing the anxiety that pervaded our lives. In contrast to these events, I was small as a gnat in a windstorm but even such a speck of consciousness encounters the world. My sense of it was of an unpredictable place where the familiar could vanish at any moment.

Nevertheless, after the first homesickness faded, I had a good time in boarding school as one of many children. I learned to read and write, played tram conductor with a toy ticket punch and, an unaware and unrecognized *Mischling*, I even played the lead angel in the Christmas play, glorified in a frothy pale blue costume with silver wings. But this was just before the *Anschluss*, Hitler's eagerly awaited annexation of Austria, and Austria was no longer safe. Further flight was the only recourse, but travel was strictly policed. My parents decided to split up once more, feeling that they might stand a better chance to get out of the country separately. To avoid attention, they packed only a few clothes and my father's manuscripts, and left their apartment, leaving behind most of their possessions. My father went into hiding, sleeping in a different place every night (some hiding places found with Adelheid's help). He was seeking some way to escape to Switzerland, the only safe haven within reach. As a Gentile, my mother was still free to travel, though it meant concealing her marriage. The sticking point was me, the child of that by-now-forbidden mixed marriage. Getting out of Austria in 1938 with a six-year old *Mischling* was a potentially dangerous mission.

The school nurse came to wake me at night in my dormitory crib, and helped me to dress and pack a small bag because my mother had come for me. When I was brought down to the office where Elke waited, she smilingly told us all she had been given an unexpected week off from work and was taking me for a holiday to the Italian seacoast. Bright smiles all around as we left, my mother promising to bring me back in a week. Since I wouldn't be gone long, most of my clothing and my beloved flowered quilt were left at *Tratzerberg* but I was allowed to carry out my favorite doll. We got into a waiting taxi and rode to the train station. At midnight, we walked the length of a platform and boarded a train amid clouds of steam that puffed across the platform lights.

Despite the excitement of this late night adventure, I soon fell asleep in the train compartment. I woke up hours later when the train stopped and two uniformed border patrol guards entered the compartment, loudly demanding "*Papiere.*" We were at the Swiss border. One after another the travelers silently handed over passports and visas for inspection by the guards.

Nothing in Elke's identity papers revealed her religion; only Jews were so marked. But she couldn't be sure that she wasn't on a list somewhere as Robert's wife. Were the guards to know who she was, they might detain her to question her about his whereabouts. She never knew specifically where he was on any evening, but the Gestapo wouldn't believe that. And the implications for her child if she were detained were too alarming to contemplate. The guards took her passport and her Austrian residency papers and glanced down at her.

"Why are you traveling to Switzerland?"

"For a holiday," she answered. "Might do a little skiing in St. Moritz."

"We have beautiful mountains right here in Austria. And excellent skiing near Innsbruck."

"Oh yes," Elke agreed quickly, "Very beautiful mountains."

The guard nodded without expression, handed back her papers, and moved on. I watched my mother. She sat very still, giving no sign of relief. Somehow I knew that this was not the time to ask about the vacation in Italy.

The guards left the compartment, their repeated demands for "*Papiere*" growing fainter as they moved on down the corridor. The train stood still for some time longer till all the papers and baggage had been inspected. Finally, we could see a dozen or so guards walking along the platform; they had finished their work. The passengers settled back into their seats without speaking or looking at each other. The conductor waved a lantern. The steam hissed, and the train moved slowly out of the station. Within a few minutes, we crossed into Switzerland.

My cheek felt sore and hot from the scratchy plush I had slept on. "Are we almost there?" I whimpered.

"Not too much longer," my mother said. "Let's go wash your face." Probably fearing further questions in public, she took me to the washroom at the end of the car.

"When will the vacation start?" I wanted to know.

"It's started already, " my mother explained, "only it's not going to be in Italy. We're going to stay in Zurich for a while."

"Will I get back to *Tratzerberg* from there?"

"You won't be going back. You'll be living with me in Zurich and go to school there. Then when Papa can come, we'll all live together again."

"Couldn't we just go back to get my blanket?" I missed the flowered quilt that had always been on my bed.

"No, Mausli, we can't go back now, it's too dangerous. And they might not let us out again. We only got out this time because they weren't paying attention and because I told them it was just a vacation trip."

"Why is it dangerous?"

"Because Hitler is coming to Austria and there are Nazis everywhere."

I knew about the Nazis. I'd learned from listening to the

hushed stories about troops marching through the streets, about people being seized and taken away, and about my grandfather's home being taken. Everyone was afraid of the Nazis. Especially the Jews. And, though I didn't know that I myself might be in danger, I knew the Nazis were after my father,

"How come Daddy can't go with us right now?"

"Because he hasn't got the right papers," my mother sighed. "But he'll get them somehow, and as soon as he can, he'll come. Meanwhile, we'll have to wait in Zurich."

Her tone convinced me that further protest would be useless. I tried not to think about my blanket. Overall, I was happy to be with my mother again.

The train chugged on through long valleys between mountains too tall for me to see the sky. Here and there a house flashed by, or a cluster of cows wearing bells around their necks. Then the houses got closer together and the mountain slopes were replaced by apartment buildings and city streets. We had reached Zurich.

In Switzerland, we waited for my father to be able to leave Austria. My mother went to the American Consulate to start the process of applying for entry to the United States and began telling me stories about America. She told me what a rich and free country it was, and how they didn't have Nazis there. Someday, she said, maybe all three of us could go to America to live there, in the same country where Shirley Temple lived. She cut pictures from magazines for me of Shirley and of ocean liners and sky scrapers. Meanwhile, she found a job in a cosmetics shop and rented rooms for us in a pleasant boarding house next door to my new day school. Our life in Zurich soon settled into a comfortable routine. We made some friends and I played with the neighborhood children. Zurich was a compact city and, small as I was, I could ride the trams by myself to buy delicious sweets at *Sprüngli*'s, the famous cafe on Paradeplatz in the center of the city. I was particularly fascinated by the imitation chestnuts, green prickly marzipan shells with chocolate centers. Sometimes I would forgo the tram rides and walk back and forth, spending the fare to buy an extra chestnut.

Once in a while, my mother would take me for a thrilling outing to ski at one of the mountains that surrounded the city. Outfitted with warm clothes and rented skis and boots, I played with other children on the beginners' slope while my mother went higher for more advanced skiing. Usually I managed quite well, sliding and shrieking down the white hill and climbing back up sideways, one ski step after another. But one day, I grew impatient for my mother's return and decided to find her by skiing down a side trail that led toward the ski-tows. But on the way I missed a turn, skied into a snow bank and found myself immobilized, the front half of my skis embedded as if in cement. Though I struggled, I could neither free the skis from the packed snow, nor get my boots off. Planted there like a shrub, I waited for my mother to come and rescue me. Time passed, but she didn't come. It seemed a long wait as, without motion, I grew colder. Occasionally, someone would ski past too quickly to notice that I was not just standing there, but stuck. Too shy to shout for help, I tried to keep from crying but soon couldn't stop the tears. At last, an older boy trudged past, carrying his skis and poles, and noticed my plight. He dug vigorously at the snow bank for a few moments and I was freed just as my mother appeared, on her way back to get me. In my haste to reach her, I slid into a heap at her feet, where she, having no idea of what had happened, also had no idea why I was crying so hard from such a minor spill.

"What are you doing here?" she wanted to know.

"I wanted to come to the hill where you ski." I sobbed. "Next time can't I just go there with you?"

"No, you're still too small. That hill is just for grown-ups."

"But I want to be with you, I don't like it so far away from you."

"No, Mausli," my mother bent down close to me to emphasize her point. "We do different things sometimes. We are two separate people and we can't be together all the time. I don't go to school with you, you don't go to work with me. You see? We don't do everything together. You have your life and I have mine."

I didn't know how to refute this since I couldn't conceive of a life of my own apart from hers, but I was to hear "you have your life and I have mine" many more times in the years ahead.

For the most part, our daily life in Switzerland seemed normal and routine. A small country surrounded by preparations for war, Switzerland maintained its independence and neutrality by serving as an international bank. The country still provided safe haven not only for refugees fleeing from Hitler but also for Nazi officials on skiing holidays in the Alps. There hunters and hunted mingled for some time in uneasy truce. But the Swiss soon grew alarmed at the swelling stream of people seeking refuge. Several months after my mother and I reached Switzerland, the country closed its borders to German émigrés. This meant that my father, still trying to get out of Austria, could no longer hope to join us in Zurich.

Until the *Anschluss* in March 1938, my uncle Henry remained in Vienna with his wife and son. Henry's books for children were becoming popular, with some being translated into English and French. Shortly after the Germans arrived, Henry was able to persuade his French publisher to bribe an official in the French Embassy to issue visas into France for the family, including his brother, Robert. Even with the visas, getting out of Austria wasn't easy. The Austrians had quickly adopted many of Hitler's policies. Before the mass deportations that would come later, Austrian Jews were forbidden to travel out of the country. With desperate courage, Henry and Else packed two suitcases and with Thomas in tow boarded a train heading to Switzerland. At the border, they were confronted by guards who examined their papers and were ready to turn them back. Henry managed to confound them by calling attention to the visas for France and calmly indicating his knowledge of the travel prohibition against Austrian Jews. Matter of factly, he claimed that he and his family were not affected by the prohibition because they were not Austrian Jews, they were *German* Jews, thereby exempt from Austrian travel regulations. This specious argument confused the guards long enough to let them through into Switzerland. Once there, their visas to France permitted them to proceed directly to Paris. There they registered with the Hebrew Sheltering and Immigration Society (HSAIS), which supplied money and shelter to refugees and sought visas from countries that would accept Jews fleeing from Europe.

On November 7, 1938 in Paris, Herschel Grynszpan, a seventeen-year old Jewish exile from Silesia, protested German mistreatment of his parents by assassinating an official in the German Embassy. The Nazis seized on this event as an opportunity for violent reprisals against Jews. During the infamous November 9th *Kristallnacht*, so named for the shards of broken glass that littered streets throughout Germany, SS troops destroyed more than 7000 Jewish shops and burned 191 synagogues and 171 apartment houses. By morning, 91 Jews were dead and 20,000 had been seized, most being sent to Buchenwald prison. Reviewing the damage afterwards, Hermann Goering commented, "I wish you had killed 200 Jews instead of destroying so many valuables."

It wasn't until eight months after the *Anschluss* that my father was able to get out of Austria. By then, Hitler was purging the Third Reich of Jews by sending them eastward to camps in Czechoslovakia and Poland. Many fled to Palestine and other countries, but almost every Jewish family who succeeded in getting out of Germany or Austria had to brazen, bribe or scuttle their way through a gauntlet of dangers. Those without money, foresight, or connections couldn't navigate the maze that might lead to freedom. Everyone had to have proper identity papers to travel out of the country. For German and Austrian citizens, these included statements that one had paid one's taxes and was not wanted by the police. My father couldn't hope to get the required statements. Jews as non-citizens were not allowed to pay taxes and furthermore he *was* wanted by the Gestapo, the most feared branch of the German secret police, for his anti-Nazi writings and underground activities. And with the Gestapo now everywhere in Austria as well as Germany, he was running out of places to hide without endangering friends who took him in.

He studied the railway schedules and watched for likely escape routes by pretending to see people off on departing trains. In this way, he noticed that one non-stop train to Paris frequently left with an unoccupied sleeping car. Chatting with the train conductors, he learned that no passengers were admitted to that car until the train reached Paris. Without other opportunities, Robert decided to risk bold action, scraped together a substantial sum and bribed one of the conductors to let him hide in the empty sleeping car until the train left Austria. At the Swiss border, as expected, several border patrol guards entered the train, walked through each car and examined all passengers' passports and identity papers, while others on the platform guarded all exits. In terror, my father lay rigid along the inner edge of an upper bunk. The conductors had assured the guards that the sleeping car was empty as usual, and they walked through with only cursory pokes at the edges of the bunks' closed curtains. After a seemingly interminable interval, the border police left the train and it chugged slowly out of the station. Robert was safe.

Having no visa for Switzerland, he stayed on the train till it reached Paris in early November of 1939. There he was at last able to telephone my mother to tell us he was safely out of Austria. She tried to get us to Paris as soon as possible. But *Kristallnacht* the year before had set off a wave of persecutions and the French had also closed their borders to German émigrés, including those who sought to enter France from Switzerland. We had to wait four more months until formal approval came through of our visas for the United States. This allowed us to travel through France in order to embark for America from Cherbourg.

A year after my parents had separated to get out of Austria, my mother packed our things, we boarded a train for Paris and left Zurich behind. As we descended from the train at the Paris station, I caught sight of my father waiting for us on the platform. He had been gone so long that I had almost stopped believing he would come back again. But there he was, in his long navy blue coat, walking toward us, waving with his hat and smiling. I tore loose from my mother's hand. Screaming "Papa, Papa," I ran toward him and he swept me up in a hug, his face scratchy and cold against my cheek. He kept hold of me as he and my mother embraced while I kept on shrieking "Papa." After a few moments, he tried to calm me, "Ja Ja, Mausli, I'm really here."

"Now quiet down," my mother urged, "everyone's looking at us." But my joy and relief at seeing him again were so intense that I couldn't stop screaming for a long time and finally my parents began to laugh in their own release from tension. In a glow of pure happiness, we walked along the platform to the station. To this day, somewhere in my memory I can still hear my own childish voice shrilling "Papa, Papa," on and on.

My parents and I were able to emigrate to the United States because the American Immigration Service gave preferential treatment to those with relatives in the United States who agreed to sponsor the new arrivals. My father's mother, Rosa, and her sisters Flora and Irma, had migrated to America several years earlier and were eager to help other family members reach safety, but regulations prohibited them from sponsoring more than one family unit per year. Because my father seemed in the greatest danger, all agreed he ought to be the first to come. Several days after we were reunited in Paris we were able to embark for America on the last Atlantic crossing of the ocean liner *Aquitania*. We had some suitcases, a trunk of my father's manuscripts, and $300 to start a new life. By then, I had learned that one should not get attached to more things than could be crammed into a suitcase, in case quick departure proved necessary.

Our ocean crossing took five days on a ship the size of a small city in the middle of a vast ocean. The passengers had nothing to do except attend various festivities organized around great quantities of food and wine, and then recuperate during hours spent reclining on deck chairs, reading and chatting with new shipboard acquaintances. One sunny afternoon, I stood clutching a doll beside my mother's deck chair in the midst of such a gathering while talk and laughter drifted around me. Suddenly, one lady looked in my direction and then giggled, "that is the ugliest doll I've ever seen." All eyes turned my way and adult chuckling pinioned me. Stricken, I looked at the doll I had loved for such a long time. Instead of finding accustomed comfort, I saw it with new eyes. It was naked, its rubber body gray from much handling. It was nearly bald; its head which once held luxurious masses of blonde doll hair was now a scalp of minute holes with a few putty-colored tufts. One China-blue eye was missing. It was indeed an ugly doll. I felt mortified at having loved such an ugly thing. In a rage of humiliation, I threw the doll in a wide arc over the edge of the deck into the ocean. Then I dashed away from the suddenly quiet group and fled, bereft and furious, back to our cabin. There I huddled on my bunk, isolated in my shame, until my parents came in to get dressed up for our dinner seating.

Though the group's careless amusement afflicted me, no one had intended harm. They were merely trying to pass with light diversions those days when they were suspended between the lives they had left behind and their uncertain futures, while the ship steamed on to America. Probably all of them had been cast out of places and stripped of possessions they had valued. Even more painfully, this voyage of grim necessity was separating them from people they loved. My father worried about his brother Henry's family waiting to embark for America, about his father who had reached London but was in poor health, and about friends and colleagues still trying to get out of Europe. My mother feared for her family—her mother Hedwig; her sister Lotti and her husband and their son Heinz; her youngest sister Irma and her husband—all of whom were still in Berlin. Though they were not Jewish and thus not in personal danger from the Nazis, they lived in a country rapidly heading into war.

On a misty morning in March 1939, the *Aquitania* entered New York Harbor. All the passengers gathered on deck and watched in solemn silence our approach toward the Statue of Liberty. Those refugees who now fly over her by plane can never know that full tide of relief, gratitude, and hope inspired by the sight of her across the water, massive, regal, her torch held high to welcome us to safety.

II

***

Arrival

Puzzled, the immigration officer shook his head as he shuffled documents. My parents tensed. What could be wrong? What could happen to us at this last moment? We had just reached the front of one of the long lines of passengers in the ballroom of the ocean liner *Aquitania*. It was March of 1939, Hitler was invading Czecho-slovakia and we were among 60,000 German immigrants who had come to the United States since 1933. The ship's ballroom had been set up as a temporary processing center for immigrants waiting anxiously for permission to enter the United States. They were used to waiting, having escaped from a Europe full of barri-ers, bureaucrats and border police. They didn't mind waiting on this ship so long as the result was approval to enter the country. The immigration officials had boarded the *Aquitania* as she docked in New York Harbor and were now reviewing passports and identity papers. Their judgments could mean the difference between life and death and even one slight hesitation or raised eyebrow heightened fears that this last refuge might be denied.

I stood between my parents as they watched the man study their papers. I didn't understand English yet but I knew my mother was nervous when I felt her hand tighten on mine. Afterwards, they translated the exchange into German for me.

"You got two names here," the official said to my father. "The birth certificate says Robert Winterfeld. The passport and visa say Robert Gilbert. Are we dealing with two people here? Which one are you?"

"I explain," my father said, trying to look relaxed while speaking in stiff high school English. "I am author and composer, so for that I have a name, Robert Gilbert. That is the name for my books and my songs. But I was born Robert Winterfeld. That is my real name."

"Well, we can't let you into the country under two different names."

My parents stood frozen in place and looked at the official without speaking.

"You'll have to choose one name," he explained.

"Gilbert is the name in which I get my royalties. My money comes with this name." Robert tried again. "My true name is Winterfeld, but I don't get money with the name Winterfeld."

"It doesn't matter to us which name you choose," the immigration officer repeated firmly, "But it has to be one name and you have to use it consistently."

My mother and father looked at each other. "You have to be recognized," she urged. "We need to get the money." They both nodded, hoping to bring to this country whatever connections with show business Robert could sustain.

"Gilbert," he declared. "Here in America, our name will be Gilbert." And so all our documents were adjusted and then stamped with permission to disembark and enter the United States. We were safe and I was no longer Marianne Winterfeld. In America, I would have a new life and a new name.

By then I knew that the name of Gilbert first came into our family when my grandfather was advised to replace his own name of Max Winterfeld with a French-sounding pen-name. Even my own given name was a sign of the general admiration for French culture. "You are named Marianne after the symbol of France," my mother often told me with pride. And now as we arrived in America, we once again adopted the smoother sounding pen-name. At the time, I accepted without question the financial reasons my parents gave for their choice. Later I wondered if in those ominous Hitler years some further unspoken reasons also echoed the earlier preference for a less Jewish-sounding last name.

By 1938 in Germany, Jews were prohibited from adopting Gentile-sounding surnames, and Nazi law further specified that all male Jews must add to their own names the given name of Israel, and all female Jews the given name of Sara. In America refugees like us were not the only ones changing names. Anti-Jewish writings and media campaigns funded by Henry Ford, and the radio tirades of Father Coughlin, fueled increasing anti-Semitism in the 1930s and many American Jews changed their names. Aside from actors and other public figures, the largest number were married prosperous men who believed their Jewish names would impede their success

We were met at the pier by two worried ladies muffled in dark shapeless coats and wearing hats with veils and feathers. They were Flora and Irma, my father's aunts (on his mother's side) who had come to America in the 1920s, years before Hitler came to power. Both looked like ancient birds to me, and they repeatedly cooed "*Gott sei dank*," throughout the greetings and hugs that followed our emergence from Customs inspection at the dock.

"We have an apartment for you right in the city," Flora, the plump one, announced when we reached the sidewalk.

"It's on 52nd Street," Irma, the stringy one, chirped. "We thought you would like to be near the nightclubs and theaters. It's small but it's the best we could afford."

"You can leave anytime," Flora said proudly, "We got it without a lease."

Not attached artistically or financially to Germany, my grandmother's two unmarried sisters and one brother had left during the country's hard times after the First World War and brought their skills across the ocean. They established themselves in New York City. The brother, Fiete, found work as an exterminator, a steady business in the city that teemed not only with human but every sort of insect and rodent life. The sisters, Flora and Irma, made ladies' hats, stylish enough to permit them to open a hat shop on Lexington Avenue. They fashioned the hats in the cluttered back room and sold them in the neat front sales space. The long hours of painstaking work left them stooped and weary, but earned them a modest living. As persecutions of Jews intensified in Germany and then spread across Europe to Poland, Austria, and France, the unexpected foresight of these two maiden ladies in becoming American citizens made them the first link in the chain of family members admitted under the United States immigration laws which gave preference to relatives of U.S. citizens.

Under the annual immigration quotas, citizens could sponsor one person or couple with dependent children per year. Sponsorship entailed signing an affidavit assuring the US Immigration Service that the new arrivals would have a place to live and employment so that they would not become a public charge in the foreseeable future.

The first relative Flora and Irma had sponsored was their older sister Rosa, my grandmother, who was ill at home on the day we arrived. Rosa had come in 1936 and also worked in the hat shop. Sponsorship for my father came next, since his anti-Nazi activities had put him most in danger of imprisonment. The brother, Fiete, was hoping to sponsor my Uncle Henry and his family, who were still waiting in Paris for permission to come to America.

Once our luggage was brought off the ship, we all crowded into in a large yellow taxi with our luggage strapped on the roof. Knowing my father's occupation, Flora and Irma had pooled their limited funds to rent a furnished apartment for us in the center of Manhattan's nightclub district. The taxi clattered down the cobbled street along the riverfront past trucks, stacks of crates and merchandise and other yellow taxis loading passengers and luggage. Then we turned into a narrow cross street of vans and warehouses that soon gave way to dingy brownstone stoops and doorways interspersed with occasional restaurants and bars. As we continued, the restaurants and bars, fronted by signs and sandwich boards, took up more and more of the streetscape. The curbs were littered with crumpled papers, discarded cigarette packs and broken glass. Crates and sacks of garbage obstructed the sidewalks.

"The streets are very dirty," my mother noted, "Don't they clean up the garbage?"

"That they don't do." Flora answered. "New York is very dirty everywhere you look. It's too bad."

"A little dirt doesn't hurt," my father said, "so long as one can live."

"Central Park is nice," Irma added, "you can take Marianne there to play."

The taxi pulled over to a curb in a block decorated with large pictures of nearly naked women and black men playing trumpets. As my father and mother lugged our suitcases, we all filed into a narrow doorway and climbed two long flights of stairs with metal strips on the steps. Flora took out a key, opened a door, and we entered directly into a small dark room. My parents set the suitcases inside and went back downstairs to drag up the trunk of my father's writings and manuscripts. Meanwhile, the aunts raised window shades and turned on lights. Once back upstairs, my father wiped his face and bald head with his handkerchief and we surveyed our first home in America. The room in which we stood was the kitchen. A painted table and four mismatched chairs were centered beneath a hanging light bulb. A green enamel stove on legs stood against one wall beside a double sink covered by a drain board that doubled as a countertop. One corner held an ice box, painted white, with a pan underneath for water from melting ice. Flora opened the ice box door. "Here is coffee, and eggs and some bread and butter and marmalade so you can make breakfast tomorrow. Tonight you'll come to us for dinner."

Another corner of the kitchen was hidden from view by a dingy green curtain. My mother pulled it aside. "*Um Gottes Willen*," she gasped. The curtain concealed a toilet.

"Don't worry, there is another toilet," Flora hastened to calm her.

I rushed to explore further. Separated from the kitchen by a half-wall, lurked a square room that held a dresser, a dark brown sofa and an easy chair covered with maroon upholstery stained to brown at the headrest. An inside door led to a bedroom with a single dusty window that faced a blackened brick wall across a narrow alley. That room was filled nearly to capacity by a double bed and another dresser with a clouded mirror. The apartment's only other inside door opened onto a closet.

My mother followed me, looking stunned, while the others waited uncomfortably.

"It's only temporary, of course. Till you get started. We had to find something quickly." Irma was getting flustered.

"But where is the bathroom?" My mother asked. It proved to be at the end of the outside hall, a cubicle containing a toilet that served the four apartments on the same floor. I flushed it by pulling on a long cord that hung from the water tank mounted high on the wall. Bathing and grooming, Flora explained, had to be managed inside the apartment which was known as a cold water flat. The multi-purpose kitchen's two adjoining sinks provided a shallow rectangle for washing hands and dishes, and a deep square tub for washing people and clothes. At wash times, water could be heated to boiling in kettles and pots on the stove and then added to cold water from the faucets. My parents stared silently at the two sinks.

"It was the best we could find so quickly," Irma explained.

"It's not far from our shop and you have all the night clubs here so you can meet the musicians."

Knocking her hat a bit askew, she tugged at a second dingy curtain (matching the one hiding the toilet) and demonstrated that it could be pulled across the half-wall for privacy during personal bathing. The arrangement was primitive, compact, practical and, in my childish view, completely satisfying. The prospect of being so enmeshed in the intimate routine of both my parents made me feel as snug as a nestling among twigs and bits of colored wool.

"This is so cozy," I enthused, "We can do everything together."

Everyone laughed, easing the tension for a moment, but my parents were less charmed than I was. This was not the life they had imagined in America. "But this is impossible; how can we live here?" my mother muttered, near tears.

"It depends on money," Flora snapped. "New York is expensive. As soon as you have money you can get a better place." Nobody, none of the family or friends who fled from Europe during those years had money. Everyone came with a carefully hoarded mite, hoping to make it last till some more could be earned.

"*Ja, meine lieben Tanten,* this is wonderful," my father chuckled, "and you have both been very good to us." With his soothing words and thanks in their ears, the aunts drew a little map that would lead us to their apartment over the hat shop and left us to settle in.

In the early evening, we went down the stairs again and walked, following the map, as the streetlights began to glow. Neon signs flashed in bright colors; the entrances to clubs and restaurants looked warm and inviting. Most were adorned by pictures of black musicians with glistening hair and women entertainers with oiled bodies embellished by tiny daubs of sequins and tassels. In the chilly spring air outdoors, people were more fully clothed. Men swaggered in long coats and wore their fedora hats pulled forward; women nuzzled fur pieces over their coats and anchored their delicate hats with gloved hands. The evening light conferred the glamour of a stage set. No one seemed worried about far-off ominous events. Men placed guiding hands gently at women's waists, and women smiled up at them. They all looked as though they were going to a party and we were walking among them. New York City sparkled around us, and our prospects suddenly seemed bright as a birthday cake with a hundred candles.

During the next weeks in our 52nd street apartment, my parents had no personal privacy and their sleep was disturbed by late night carousers who laughed and sang their way from one bar to another. I, on the other hand, slept soundly on the sofa in the tiny living room, secure in the nearness of both mother and father and pleased to drift off in the alternating red and white light of the flashing neon sign in front of my window. Aside from my initial delight at the idea of playing house with my parents in our cramped new apartment, I remember little of the weeks we spent there. Children live in a small frame. I mainly recall spending many hours with my grandmother and the aunts, playing with scraps of felt and feathers in the back room of the hat shop, only dimly aware that my parents were spending their waking hours scrambling to find a foothold in the city.

Though they were immensely relieved to have gotten away from the Nazis, starting over from scratch in mid-life was tough. The worst dangers were past but their new freedom meant learning to survive in an unfamiliar country. In Europe my parents had been articulate, well-known, and financially comfortable, with ties to a wide network of family and friends. They faced America with limited English, no status, few connections, and hardly any money. They were grateful and happy to be alive, but they had to find a way to live.

It fell to my mother to find day labor. Newly come to America, her stylish good looks and her talents for dancing and singing German songs were foreign, but the sewing skills she had learned in her youth could be marketed. With Flora and Irma's help, she found work with a small clothing manufacturing firm in New York's garment district.

She was placed at one of a row of sewing machines. The constant deafening drone of the machines forced all voices into shouts or shrieks. Elke was frightened of the male foreman who explained in a roar that her task was to set sleeves into blouses. The women who worked near her greeted her with rough humor, making fun of her tinted blonde hair, her European make-up and fastidious clothes. They called her "Duchess," probably because she didn't or couldn't respond to them. Outwardly composed, she was very nervous, especially at the speed expected of her. She began working as she had been taught as a girl in Berlin, pinning and basting each sleeve carefully into its armhole before sewing it by machine, then pinking the raw edges and pulling out the basting thread.

The foreman paused in his rounds and leaned over her to shout. "What the hell are you doing? What's taking so long?"

Elke showed him several basted sleeves.

He smacked his forehead. "You can't do that! You don't have time. Look at what's piling up next to you. And you're holding up the line."

She turned to look at the growing pile of completed bodices awaiting her sleeves, then looked at the woman on her right waiting impatiently to attach collars.

Turning back to her own machine, Elke concentrated on speed. No more basting, just two pins at first. By the next day she was able to do it freehand, holding and turning the garment as she sewed. She was still too slow; blouses still piled up beside her. Each time the foreman passed, he shook his head. She tried to hurry even more. In her haste, she cut a gash with her pinking shears into the center of a sleeve. She was terrified; not knowing what to do. The foreman was at the other end of the room. With shaking hands she grabbed a remnant of material from the scrap pile, made a small patch, and began to sew it furtively by hand over the gash in the sleeve. Just as she finished, the foreman was standing over her.

"What the hell is that?"

She tried to explain. "I pinked into the sleeve. I try to fix, you see?"

"Get your things," he snapped. "You're just too green. If you make a mistake, you should know enough to throw it out. Your fixing costs time and money we don't have. Sorry, but you're through." He scribbled on a pink slip and put it in her hand. "You can pick up your pay at the cashier."

In shock, Elke took off her work smock, picked up her purse, and walked past all the machines and the other women who watched without expression. She kept her head high as she walked to the cashier's window and presented the pink slip. Somehow she managed to sign some papers and collect the wages owed her. Then she walked out into the hallway and down the stairs. At the bottom, she leaned against a wall and sobbed until she was calm enough to face the bus ride back to 52nd street.

The next day, she answered a "Help Wanted" ad in the *New York Times* for a cosmetics sales clerk at Gimbel's department store. There, her knowledge of make-up and her cosmopolitan looks were an asset and she was hired. The long hours of unaccustomed standing were exhausting, but finding a steady job was a definite triumph. She now earned a small but regular weekly paycheck, enough to provide our daily bread.

In the meantime, my father was contacting everyone he knew who had come to New York from theaters or publishing houses in Germany and Austria. His friend and collaborator, Robert Stoltz, "the waltz king," had arrived the year before and welcomed him warmly. His former schoolmate Frederick "Fritz" Loewe had also set up residence, but could give no help. Those former colleagues and friends who had reached America were all struggling to establish themselves just as Robert was. Those who could, gave or lent him small sums of money and found him occasional one-night stints playing piano in cafes frequented by German exiles. But he found no market for his German libretti, songs and poetry that filled the trunk he had brought to America.

Poor as we were when we arrived in this country, no one ever suggested that my father might seek work for wages. As far as the family was concerned he was not unemployed. His work had earlier brought in a lot of money; now because of the international crisis, the same work brought in no money. The drop in income was painful but had no bearing on the importance of his occupation. Never did I hear any suggestion to the contrary. His writing and his music gave coherence to my parents' lives and, I think, to their idea of themselves, who they were and what they stood for. Without it they might have seen themselves solely as impoverished refugees whose single goal was basic survival. With it, they could align themselves with ideals of freedom of expression and creative energy in both art and politics. My mother's job could tide us over, but they believed that only my father's musical gifts, once he learned English and gained access to the Broadway theaters, could restore the family's prestige and fortune. Their hopes for the future were pinned on him.

For the present, it was time to find a more suitable apartment. To my regret, my parents felt they needed more private space, more quiet, and more distance from the boisterous night life of 52nd Street. They also needed a separate room that could house a piano for my father's composing, and a safe neighborhood with access to schooling for me. They soon discovered that Aunt Flora had been right; it was a matter of money. Rents in Manhattan's livable neighborhoods were far beyond their means. Friends mentioned Riverdale, high up at the edge of the Bronx but near the subway line to Manhattan, as a possible place to live. It seemed far from Broadway and show business but facing the reality of limited funds, my parents investigated classified ads for apartments in that area.

And while we were groping through the early days of our new life in America. that opportunity was denied to thousands of others. The elderly aunts because they were our relatives were able to become our lifeline. Many more who tried to escape but had no such family connections were denied entry. In 1939, the same year that my parents arrived with me, their seven-year old daughter, the United States Congress after extensive debate voted to refuse admission to twenty thousand German refugee children, mostly Jewish, whose parents were desperately trying to send them out of danger.

III

***

Melting

We arrived in Riverdale in April 1939. In those days Riverdale was a partly urban, partly still rural outskirt at the northern edge of New York City, an hour's ride by bus and subway to mid-town Manhattan and we didn't live there because it had green and pretty sections. We lived there because rent for our fourth floor walk-up apartment was cheap.

I met my first American friend, Erna Krueger, two days after we moved in. My parents were busy arranging the furniture they had gotten from the Salvation Army and sent me to play outside. Too timid to roam far once I had ventured down the three long flights of stairs, I went around to the back of the apartment building where several garages bordered a small courtyard. I had a little chamois bag of colored marbles and arranged them in rows along the cracks in the cement, imagining a school with the marbles as my pupils. Then a girl appeared around a corner and approached me. She wore green shorts, a white shirt and thick brown braids pinned in a circle around her head. When she spoke to me I stood up and carefully pronounced the phrase I'd been taught, "I don't speak English."

The girl smiled. She was taller than I was and sturdy. Her friendly snub-nosed face was decorated by fancy fringed eyes as blue as my best marble. "*Sprichts du Deutch?*" she asked.

A miracle. The first girl I met here in America, on the other side of the ocean, spoke to me in German. I was no longer a solitary child in the wilderness; I had a new friend to guide me. In German, Erna and I quickly exchanged names and ages. As befitting a protector, she was two years older than I. On July 9th, her next birthday, she told me, she would be ten. She asked when I had come to this country and then told me, "My parents came from Germany, too. It was before I was born but they still speak German at home."

So my first American friend was the child of immigrants.

Erna led me down the block to meet her parents who owned the neighborhood delicatessen. Both were white haired, old as grandparents and round as barrels in their stained white aprons. They were working behind the long display counter to serve waiting customers as we came in. Mr. Krueger was slicing long tubes of sausage meats, cheeses, and rye bread with a crust that crackled at each pass of the slicer. Mrs. Krueger was making sandwiches and packing them into individual waxed paper packets, each with a dill pickle. Erna presented me as her new friend from Germany but they were too busy to pay much attention. Mrs. Krueger just muttered, "Ja, Ja, Erna, take your friend in the back and give her a glass of milk."

We walked through delicious aromas, past the counter and a long wall of shelves stocked floor to ceiling with colorful packets and cans of food, into a back room that served as storage space, kitchen, and the family's sitting room. Erna led me through a screened door outside to a rear service yard for the row of four stores that fronted on Riverdale Avenue: the delicatessen, a drug store, a grocery store, and a beauty parlor (where some years later I got my first startling permanent wave).

"This is my yard," Erna said, waving her arm to indicate a square cement courtyard with a vacant lot on one side and an alley on the other. "All the kids come here when I let them. You can come, too." The invitation made me happy even though the prospect of facing "all the kids" was a little scary.

Several days after we moved in, my parents took me to the closest public school, P.S. 7, which was about two miles away from our house and meant walking down the long hill of Riverdale Avenue and several blocks further. School officials reviewed all our identity documents and my Austrian and Swiss school records. By 1939, Germany was accurately perceived as a hostile aggressor nation and because I was born there, the officials classified me on my new records as "Enemy Alien." I hardly understood the phrase but it marked me as different. Our status as German-Jewish refugees, a composite of aggressor and victim, was too complicated for me to understand but I didn't like the guarded look that came over people's faces when they learned our nationality. At last, however, I was registered and placed in the second grade. There I discovered that not only was my last name now Gilbert instead of Winterfeld, my first name, though spelled the same was now pronounced so differently that I felt no identification with it. I had always been called Mahr-yah-nne, long A's with the accent on the second syllable. The girl my new teacher called Mee-ree-yeen in a nasal Bronx whine seemed someone else. Frustrated at my lack of response, she tried pronouncing my name as "Marion," which at least had some resemblance to the familiar. For years after that I referred to myself as Marion.

On the next Monday Erna walked with me down Riverdale Avenue to our school, took me to my classroom, and then left to go to her own higher grade. I quickly saw that my clothes were wrong. None of the other little girls wore white aprons over their dresses or thick tan cotton stockings as I did. No children carried square leather briefcases like mine strapped to their backs to transport their books. When I got home that afternoon I stuffed all these items into the back of my closet and refused to leave the house with them on my person again. I was grown up by the time such things became fashionable and widely used. When I was a child, I just wanted to look like all the other children even though, on snowy days the then current fashion of wearing knee socks and open galoshes meant stinging thighs and icy ankles during my early morning walks to school.

Adapting my appearance was only one facet of my effort to blend in. As quickly as possible I set out to learn English and shed all traces of being foreign.

My parents applied for American citizenship, a process that would take five years. In the meantime, as resident aliens, they too felt it essential to gain command of the new language. They had only high school English, but with courage I didn't recognize at the time, they decided that we three should speak English at home. Since I was a child who learned languages easily, they designated me linguistic leader of the family. I was assigned to go forth each day to capture American phrases and bring them home to add to the family language supply.

At school, cascades of English washed over me, orderly and adult-controlled in the classroom, wild and shrieking in children's play at recess and at lunch. There I learned by total immersion. I must have made many mistakes at school as I groped my way toward fluency but the only moment that stands out was the time I misspelled the word "paper" on the blackboard in front of the class. I gave the word two middle p's and when I had to spell the letters out loud, some boys snickered. The "p-p" part seemed to have crossed the Atlantic without needing translation. I never made that mistake again.

Three months later when school closed at the end of June, I had shifted into the new language both in both speech and thinking. On the afternoon of July 13th, my eighth birthday, I waited in delicious suspense while my parents bustled behind the closed door of the kitchen. I heard dishes clink and paper rustle and finally the door opened, and my smiling parents beckoned me. There on the table, a cake glowed with lighted candles and beside it was a brightly wrapped rectangular package. I was so thrilled I didn't know what to do first; it was my first birthday celebration with both parents present. They helped me to blow out the candles and then stood arm in arm, smiling, as I opened the package to find my first real book in English, a gorgeous hard cover edition of *Heidi* by Johanna Spyri, the Swiss author. I had read and loved *Heidi* in German; it had been my favorite story. Now here it was in English and ever so beautiful with many full-color illustrations. "This is your birthday present because you have learned English so well," my father said. It was all I could do not to touch it while we feasted on the birthday cake.

In the next days I worked my way through the pages with pride and delight. No heavy boring dictionary for me; I knew the story and used the context to puzzle out the meanings of unfamiliar words. Reading *Heidi* in English was bliss in the act and in its aftermath. Reading, an essential part of my life that had seemed cut off was now restored to me, transformed and full of promise. I didn't have to remain a little German girl re-reading the two or three books I had carried with me from Switzerland; there was a public library near my school and, now that I could read English, I could take out four books at a time. I loved my new power. English was wonderful and America was full of books.

As far as I can remember, my enthusiasm for English was untempered by regret for the loss of German. In that, my reactions were quite different from those described by Eva Hoffman in *Lost in Translation* and probably accounted for by our different backgrounds and ages at immigration. She was thirteen when her family, fearing rising anti-Semitic violence, went from a closely knit community in Poland to unfamiliar exile in Canada. For her, the pain of being uprooted from supportive surroundings was added to the normal uncertainties of adolescence, and for years she learned every new English word she could, as though exploring an exotic new territory. It was a long time before she could relax into the new language as a natural habitat. In contrast, I was only eight years old, a child with a precarious sense of home, already transplanted several times to new places and

new languages. I was at the age when vocabulary expands naturally and so I grew into English naturally and with the pleasure
that accompanies growth and mastery. Rather than representing
dislocation, English for me meant gaining a home. No doubt adding to my pleasure was the fact that I was better at it than my
parents.

My father's relationship to English was more like Hoffman's.
He came to America as an adult and brought home words he had
read in newspapers or heard in conversation like samples snagged
from a rocky landscape, testing them for possible rhymes and
puns like a prospector hunting for gold. "Popocatapetl," he
shouted, having just read about Mexico in the *Times*. "What a
wonderful name! Popocatapetl. . . . Popocatapetl isn't just another stetl. Everyone will want to settle, down in Popocatapetl . . ."
And he was off, playing and rhyming with his new word treasure.
Soon after I did, both he and my mother also began reading
books in English. My father had little interest in Hemmingway's
stripped down style, but relished Faulkner's convoluted and
musical prose. He also loved the crime novels of Daschiel
Hammett because of the urban tough guy talk. "There's a couple
of mugs hanging around the corner that I don't much like," he
read aloud, then embellished further, "A couple of mugs . . . mug.
You're a mug, ya big lug, I'll throw ya in the jug." I thought him
much funnier than other fathers and a little odd.

In August of that year I was sent to summer camp for two
weeks. The expense was probably managed through some agreement between my parents and the camp owners or directors. Many
of my family's arrangements in those years involved barter or
someone's generosity rather than money which was in short supply. In the weeks before I was to leave, I watched with mingled
excitement and trepidation as my mother sewed name tapes into
two pairs of green shorts, a red tie, several white shirts, two pairs
of pajamas, a parka, underwear, socks, and a red beanie. On the
appointed day, other camp parents wealthy enough to own a car

picked me up for the two hour drive to Camp Hiawatha. I slept in a rustic cabin in the woods with seven other little girls and ate meals in a rough-hewn structure with beams and a roof but no walls. But though I had succeeded at school, I essentially flunked camp. Homesick and bewildered, I couldn't learn the sports, didn't know the songs, had not the slightest understanding of Indian lore, and was mystified by sunrise worship ceremonies and evening prayers.

The day began with everyone gathering at the central flag-pole. We sang "My country 'Tis of Thee" while a camp counselor assisted by one camper attached the American flag to the rigging and then pulled it to the top of the pole. Being selected as the assistant, which happened to me one day, was a terrifying honor. You had to make sure that no single corner of the flag touched the ground while everyone watched in suspense till the flag was finally on its way up. I wasn't sure what would happen if it ever did touch the ground, but clearly the consequences were sure to be dreadful. After the flag-raising, there were some pledges and prayers. Then we all shuffled around the pole in a wide circle, bobbing up and down and tapping our cupped hands to our mouths while chanting ho-ho-ho to welcome the day in what was assumed to be Indian fashion. At dusk, the flag was lowered again with more prayers and chanting and long moments of si-lence to conclude the ceremony.

The other campers, secure in their national identity, could enjoy assuming imagined Indian folkways, but it was too soon for an immigrant child still learning the mainstream culture. I didn't mind the unfamiliar rustic living, but the organized piety made me achingly uncomfortable. The counselors looked solemn, the little campers put their heads down during the prayers or stared at the sky in imitation of Indian reverence while I, spiritually unmoved, looked at them furtively and wondered what I should be feeling. Those two weeks at a woodland camp were my first exposure to public religious rites and may have sparked my life-long uneasiness at such occasions. And while I liked the camp-fires and toasted marshmallows, they were not enough to prevent my joy and relief when the vacation ended and I was at last taken back home. Ever afterwards I resisted any suggestion of summer camp. I was much happier being one of the kids in Erna's yard.

I soon learned that the stores around the corner from my house kept discarded and as yet unopened crates of merchandise in Erna's yard on the assumption that they jointly owned that space. But for the dozen or so children admitted to Erna's little troop, the cement yard behind the stores was her kingdom and served in turns, by her permission, as our reading room, softball court, skating rink, snack bar, and smugglers' cove. Etiquette demanded that crates or boxes left beside the stores' rear entrances was still considered store inventory. But once things reached the adjoining alley, they were garbage, and garbage was ours.

We never saw hungry or homeless people rooting for food in that alley, seldom saw any adults at all as we excitedly searched for treasure among trash cans and stacked crates and cartons. We never knew what we might find—shiny boxes, wooden orange crates that could be used as shelves or furniture, packs of paper, clean egg cartons, square wooden milk boxes, old magazines, even stray packets of greeting cards, a little dusty but still perfectly good. The only disappointments came on days when such booty was tainted by food garbage. Outer lettuce or cabbage leaves didn't cause much damage, but rotten fruit could spoil a whole stack of empty egg cartons. As we acquired goods, I became a connoisseur of garbage, a talent my parents didn't fully appreciate but which added to my anticipation of each new day in Riverdale.

While I was taken up with my return to my neighborhood friends, my parents were snatching up each day's *New York Times* to follow the crisis in Europe. After Hitler's invasion of Czechoslovakia, that nation ceased to exist. The British Prime Minister, Neville Chamberlain, was trying to negotiate a pact to prevent further German aggression, but Hitler was elated by the lack of effective intervention and continued his drive to expand Germany's *Lebensraum*. In September of 1939 his armies invaded Poland. This time England and France issued an ultimatum. Then Russia, Germany's ally at the time, also invaded Poland from the east, tearing that country apart. My parents and all their friends were deeply concerned at the combined might of Germany and Russia. They were enormously relieved when at last England and France took decisive action to stop Hitler and declared war.

Once we had set up our household in Riverdale, my mother, Elke, was gone for eleven hours a day during the work week, leaving the house to catch the seven o'clock morning bus to the subway and returning after six each evening. She worked in lower Manhattan, briefly as a cosmetics sales clerk and then as a seamstress for refugee clothing manufacturers. Her earnings paid the rent and bought us necessities and some credit from the local merchants to fill the gaps till my father's intermittent royalty checks arrived in the mail. Whenever a check came, my mother could pay the accounts run up at the drugstore and at Gristede's, the grocery store, and even buy some extras like fabric to make into curtains for the apartment and clothes for herself and for me. Her flair for fashion and skill as a seamstress helped us both to look well dressed even though money was scarce.

Once she made a summer dress for herself out of a print material that had a cornflower blue background covered with white daisies. When she had finished the dress itself, she used the left-over fabric and cut out individual daisies. Enchanted by her cleverness, I watched her as she embroidered the edges of each daisy with infinite care, and then sewed them around the dress' neckline and short sleeves. Cinderella at the ball could not have been more beautiful than my mother in her daisy dress.

Aside from the occasional royalty payments from earlier successes, my father earned no money but he wrote every day. There was no thought that he might do something else to help ease the lean times. He probably couldn't have done so anyway. A rumpled, good-humored man who could make rhymes before breakfast, he had few practical skills. He never repaired a lamp, made a shelf, or hung a curtain. In Riverdale, he did learn to peel potatoes and to boil water, and when my mother came home from work in the evenings, he could combine those two functions to help prepare our evening meal. He also came to excel at washing dishes after dinner, saying he enjoyed doing so because the sound of running water helped him to think about the songs he was working on. But his two real talents were words and music. During daytime hours, he used these talents to compose musicals and popular songs and to writing serious poetry. While in America, he continued writing poetry in German but also struggled to write song lyrics in English. In the late afternoons, he often took the bus and subway to Manhattan's theater district where he met with fellow émigrés in hopes of attracting Broadway producers.

People imagine that life with a composer must be a musical feast. In fact, during his working hours at home my father required silence. I could see him through the glass panes of his study door, wearing an old gray sweater, sitting at his desk or trying out a tune on the piano, not with the exuberance of his performances at parties, but with his face frowning in concentration, dark eyes squinting from smoke curling up from the slim oval filter-tipped Regent cigarette in his mouth. At intervals he put the cigarette down to make a notation on the score in front of him, and the ledge of the old upright piano from the Salvation Army acquired a row of burns like ridged black caterpillars where one forgotten Regent after another had expired.

I was not supposed to interrupt except in an emergency or sing or play the radio since that would disturb the music in my father's head. So, mostly I read or played in my room with dolls, or marbles, or clay that I formed into lumpy little figures with whom I populated imaginary villages. My villages were inspired by my Uncle Henry's book, *Timpetyll,* translated into English as *Town Without Grown-ups.* This was a story of a mountain village where the adults leave all the children behind and go off for a day-long trip. They lose their way in a forest and, unknowingly, wander across the border where they are arrested by guards and detained for a week. In their parents' absence, the children must run the town. They have to deliver the mail and the milk, run the trolley cars, outsmart the local bullies, and even perform emergency dental work. I loved *Timpetyll.* Not only had Uncle Henry dedicated the book to me and to his son, my cousin Thomas, on our own special dedication page, but the two central characters—children who led the action and performed most of the courageous feats—bore our names.

But I didn't want to read, play alone, or be quiet all the time. School filled my week days, but the stillness of weekend mornings when my parents slept late was long and boring. I woke early, waited for signs of life, ate my breakfast roll and glass of milk. Then when nothing stirred, I got dressed, put my house key on its cord around my neck, and headed for Erna's back yard, hoping to find her out early and ready to play. Mr. Krueger opened the delicatessen at eight o'clock and Erna and her mother arrived by nine, but I usually had to hang around and wait. Erna was not allowed to come out till she had finished her chores. The idea of "chores" seemed admirably American to me.

One Saturday morning, Erna had more chores than usual. After she had swept the front sidewalk and polished the glass in the display counters, she came to the back door and told me she had to slice potatoes. Accustomed to my father's five minutes of peeling potatoes for our dinners, I didn't expect that to take long. But Erna beckoned me into the cluttered back room and pointed to the stove which held a huge cauldron with more peeled potatoes than I had ever seen. Erna's father had boiled them; Erna's mother was just finishing stripping off the red paper-thin peel from a few remaining potatoes at the bottom of a white enamel tub the size of a baby's bathtub.

"Want to help?" Erna asked. I nodded. It was better than waiting outside alone.

"You have to make straight even slices," she explained, "right down to the very last little cap on the end." She demonstrated, holding a small round potato in her left hand and grasping the knife in her right hand, she drew it through the potato towards her thumb. Lovely uniform little circles plopped into the tub. I tried to copy her and dropped my first potato, then managed to hold on to the second, but my slices were ragged and lopsided.

"*Nein*, your hand is still too small, better maybe you use the board," Mrs. Krueger advised and stood me by the table at a wooden cutting board, where I could make careful downward slices that qualified as acceptable. My pace was slow and my fingers awkward but I was pleased to see my small stacks of slices added to the growing potato pile in the enamel tub.

Slicing cooked potatoes became part of my Saturday morning routine. With practice I learned the technique of slicing evenly toward my thumb and was able to do it while Erna and I planned our day. When we finished, Mr. Krueger banished us from the kitchen while he concocted his secret recipe for the dressing he alone would add to make the finest potato salad in the area, exceptional potato salad, potato salad so renowned that he had been offered enormous sums, in the hundreds of dollars, Erna told me, just to divulge the recipe.

Released from our contribution to the success of the business, Erna and I rushed to investigate the new trash in the alley and find places to stash our booty before the garbage truck arrived.

Erna was a tomboy; in dresses for school she looked awkward. After school hours, in her white shirts, shorts, and sneakers, with her braids pinned in a circle like a functional crown, her square shoulders and steady blue-eyed gaze, she looked just fine. She coached me in the basic athletic skills needed by neigh-

borhood kids; taught me how to roller skate, guided me past the
tremors of learning to ride a bike, and tutored me in the rules of
softball. I never became a star at any of these activities, but I
managed well enough to be included in impromptu softball games
in the back yard and cowboy and Indian raids in the adjacent
wooded lot.

By the end of my first year in Riverdale my German accent
was smoothed away and, with Erna's help, I could blend in pretty
well. But every now and then I still got tripped up by American
idioms. Once, Erna and I were hurrying through the potato-peel-
ing chore in the back room of the delicatessen because, when we
got them all done, we were expected to set the table with colored
paper plates and arrange a cake and candles hidden on a shelf
for a surprise birthday party for Mrs. Krueger. But when we finished the peeling, Erna went into the store to confer with her
father and came back, her face glum and angry. Mr. Krueger
appeared to add his famous potato salad dressing and sent us
outside as usual. Nothing else happened. No colored paper plates,
no cake, no candles. "But aren't we going to do the surprise
party?" I asked Erna.

"No we can't," Erna grumbled. "My father spilled the beans
and my mother said she doesn't have time now."

For a long time I couldn't understand why we couldn't just
have swept up the spilled beans and gone ahead with the party.

In May of 1940, fifteen months after our own arrival in the United
States and without prior notice, my Uncle Henry telephoned to announce that he, my Aunt Else and my cousin Thomas had just
docked in New York. They had managed to escape from France in
the nick of time. Whatever money they had scraped together from
Henry's books and assistance from the Hebrew Sheltering and Immigrant Aid Society had gone to expedite their exit visas. They arrived
in America with just enough pocket money to telephone my father.

"Henry, Henry, *das ist ja wunderbahr*, wonderful, wonderful." My mother and I hovered nearby as my father shouted into

the phone in joy and disbelief. He gave Henry directions to our apartment to relay to a taxi driver. I was sent to the delicatessen for cold cuts, bread, and some of Mr. Krueger's famed potato salad. Half an hour later, we all clustered at a front window waiting for the taxi to arrive at the street below. When it came, we watched them emerge, called their names in joyful frenzy and waved wildly till they looked up and waved back. Then my father ran down the flights of stairs to pay the driver.

Over the impromptu meal we heard their stories. Their experiences in France were quite different from ours. Whereas we had spent only two weeks in Paris before embarking for America in March 1939, Henry and Else had reached Paris a year earlier in 1938. At first, they had no plans to emigrate further, but then found themselves among the large numbers of Jewish refugees from the Third Reich who faced increasing hostility. Though not as dangerous as Germany and Austria had been, Jews in France were targets of anti-Semitic propaganda, government restrictions on foreigners and random police raids and document searches. After my parents and I had sailed, Henry and Else also decided to apply for entry to the United States. They had to wait a year for the second family visa to be approved. Then, when France declared war on Germany in September 1939, citizens of enemy nations residing in France became suspect even though, ironically, most of them were refugees who had fled from the Nazis. In early October of that year, 15,000 immigrants from the Third Reich, mostly non-Jewish and Jewish men, were arrested, my Uncle Henry among them. He was taken first to the Roland Garras tennis stadium where he and some thousand others were detained in open air for a week. Then he was sent to a camp at Nevers, about 150 kilometers south of Paris and was interned there for six months while Else and Thomas waited anxiously in Paris, pleading for his release and for early action on the visas to the United States.

Fortunately for Henry, large numbers of foreigners arrested at that time were released before May 1940. Those over age forty, those in poor health, and those with French wives were generally freed. My uncle who had developed stomach ulcers in the Nevers camp was released in April. He returned to Paris just in time for the approval of their visas. Without delay, they boarded the next ship and sailed for New York, fortunate to escape the fate of those who stayed behind. The German army invaded France in May and the French re-arrested and interned all male immigrants. Immigrant women and five thousand children were sent to separate camps. By the end of 1940, forty to fifty thousand people were interned in camps throughout France. Seventy percent of them were Jewish.

"What did you do in the concentration camp, Uncle Henry?" I wanted to know. He exchanged glances with my father while fussing with his pipe. Then he chuckled.

"I waited for food and tried to keep warm," he said. "And I played chess, little niece, we all played a lot of chess."

With help from my parents, the trusty aunts and Jewish relief agencies, my uncle and aunt settled in a small fifth floor walk-up apartment on Mosholu Parkway in the Bronx on the other side of the large and wondrous Van Cortland Park which lay between us. Their household was similar to ours in that both men wrote at home while the women went "downtown" to work for steady wages. Henry continued writing books for children while Else found work in a downtown factory that made toy stuffed animals. She proved to have a real flair for this work and began experimenting with design. At home, she designed a doll she named Trudi. Trudi's head had three faces. Only one face showed at a time because the doll wore a pink and blue hooded plush sleeper. A child could rotate the doll's head by turning a knob in the shape of a rosette on the hood, to reveal a smiling or sleeping or crying face. Else took a model of this design to a friend, Armin Rosenberg who was so enthusiastic about its potential that he sold the idea to backers and, with Else as chief designer, opened the "Three-in-One Doll' toy factory which survived for several years.

Unlike my parents, Henry and Else did not convert their

home language to English and continued to speak German to each other and to Thomas, who was sixteen when they arrived in America. Later, I was able to compare the results of these contrasting decisions. Within five years, both my parents spoke fluent, if accented, English whereas my aunt and uncle still groped their way through a forest of unfamiliar words and pronunciations. My cousin, though completely bilingual, to this day sounds like Henry Kissinger when he speaks English. On the other hand, he speaks, reads, and writes German with ease, whereas my own German has remained that of a second-grade child who can't spell.

Our neighborhood was perched between city and country. Riverdale Avenue, the wide main street, began at the edge of Kingsbridge, an urban section crammed with large five and six story walk-up apartment buildings, ranks of row houses, small retail stores, two movie theaters, my school P.S. 7, the IRT elevated subway station at 231st street and Broadway and a central bus stop. A mile-long hill separated Kingsbridge from Riverdale which began at the first bus stop at the crest of the hill just at our corner. Riverdale prided itself on being higher up than Kingsbridge, not only in elevation but in money and social class. The few large apartment buildings boasted elevators. Most dwellings were comfortable single family homes that increased in size and luxury as one neared the Hudson River. Impressive estates and mansions lay on the slopes above the river's banks, barely glimpsed through trees or secluded driveways. Narrow lanes laced through this wealthy section, allowing weekend hikers and roving children to ramble down to the New York Central Railroad tracks bordering the river. Anyone could easily clamber across the tracks for direct access to a dirt foot path along the water's rocky shore. Tranquil estates, trains rattling past in a rush of noise and air, boulders and reeds on the bank of the wide glistening river, the view of the New Jersey Palisades on the other side, my father and I often rambled through this whole fascinating landscape which was only a half hour's walk from our house.

The cluster of homes and stores nearest ours was separated geographically by the long hill from Kingsbridge, and economically from Riverdale's affluent single family homes. We didn't know the children who lived in large houses and were chauffeured to private schools like the Riverdale Country Day School or the Fieldstone School. In my rim neighborhood, nobody I knew during my elementary school years owned a car and almost everyone lived in a one or two bedroom apartment, the rooms crammed with bulky dressers or wardrobes that compensated for inadequate storage space. Typically one family member slept on a studio couch or hide-a-bed sofa in the living room. Sometimes that space was assigned to a resident aunt, uncle, or grandparent; most often it was used by the family's only child. But I was lucky; in my family, it was my parents who slept on the pull-out studio couch in the living room One bedroom served as my father's study while I had the other one as my own domain. My parents chose this arrangement because it allowed them to stay up late in the evenings without having to tiptoe around a sleeping child or having me awaken them at unwelcome early hours on weekend mornings.

With the crowded conditions of most apartments, children gathered and played outdoors. We roller skated and bicycled on side streets and we hung around wherever we could, on front stoops, in rear yards, wooded empty lots, and in and around the neighborhood stores. During my second year in Riverdale, when I was old enough to observe traffic lights, my father often sent me for cigarettes across the wide Riverdale Avenue and further up the hill to Shapiro's candy store, which became one of my favorite places. Harriet Shapiro, the daughter of the owner, was a girl my own age. She was a wistful pudgy child with stringy black hair tucked behind her ears, small coffee bean eyes, skin the color of porridge. Harriet didn't go to my school; she went to P.S. 39 because she lived further along the bus line toward Yonkers. I never saw her home, nor did she ever come to mine. Essentially, her whole family lived at their store which was open from seven in the morning to ten or eleven at night. A long delectable soda fountain and lunch counter dominated one wall. There "Mrs. S" served sandwiches, coffee and ice cream concoctions to customers perched on the row of rotating red leatherette padded stools on individual chrome pedestals. On the other wall, floor to ceiling racks displayed newspapers and all kinds of alluring magazines and comic books. Mr. Shapiro controlled browsing from his post at the front sales counter where he also sold many varieties of tobacco and cigarettes. Every Sunday morning, along with my father's elegant flat boxes of Regents cigarettes, I carried home my parent's ritual week-end pleasure, the four pound Sunday New York Times solidly black-and-white without the colorful comics I envied in other Sunday newspapers. When I arrived early, I often saw Harriet stuffing previously assembled sections of various Sunday papers into the just delivered news sections. One Sunday morning Harriet couldn't seem to manage without dropping inserts while a growing crowd of impatient customers fidgeted nearby. I offered to help. The task wasn't hard; it just meant inserting one bundle into the correct other bundle and I soon felt quite competent. Harriet was grateful and on following Sundays I made sure to get there early enough for the stuffing process which I found much more interesting than keeping quiet at home while waiting for my parents to wake up. My enjoyment must have been evident because one Sunday Harriet asked, as though inviting me to participate in a secret rite, "You want to come help assemble the first parts on Thursday? My father says it's O.K."

Feeling important I reported for work after school the following Thursday. This time, things were more complicated. First Mr. Shapiro spread out stacks of individual sections of the Sunday *Times* along the length of the store in front of the magazine racks. Under his watchful eye, Harriet and I walked along picking up sections in the proper order—the *Times* had Arts and Leisure, Travel, Classified Ads, the Book Review and the staid black-and-white Magazine, all folded into the Real Estate section. We had to make sure each packet was complete and then we stacked them in the back room until Sunday when each would be inserted in the front news sections, the News of the Week in Review, and the Business section. After the *Times*, Mr. Shapiro spread out, in turn, the inserts for the *Daily News*, the *New York Post*, the *Journal American* and the other papers that had comics and special advertising sections. For each newspaper, Harriet and I repeated our assembling, checking and stacking. When we were done, with all the newspapers assembled, our hands were black up to the elbows and our faces smudged from newsprint. We washed at a grimy little sink in the small rear bathroom and when we were reasonably clean, Mrs. S allowed us the special treat of swiveling round and round on counter stools while she made us each a chocolate egg cream as a reward.

To Harriet the work of stacking newspapers was a tedious chore. To me it was a combination of fun, relief from solitude and, not least, a boon to my self-esteem. Peeling potatoes for Erna's delicatessen and stacking newspapers for Harriet's candy store under the approving eyes of their parents made me feel competent and virtuous in ways that my own household tasks did not. At my house, I was responsible for setting the supper table and for the weekly task of cleaning the bathroom where, because I was still small, I had to get into the tub to scrub it. I straightened and dusted my own room in advance of my mother's weekly vacuuming. She also taught me to darn socks, making me do the darns over and over until they were perfectly woven circles without any bumps to hurt the wearer. But these tasks earned me no glory and could not be shared with friends. Erna's and Harriet's chores seemed important; they contributed to the family business and my help did that too. I admired the solid occupation of owning a shop, of having things that people came to buy. The position of my friends' parents in the neighborhood seemed enviable to me, more to be desired than my mother's far away work "downtown" or my father's daily writing. I took no part in those activities and they had no recognized status in my childhood social circle. My own life seemed weightless and ephemeral. The sense of a solid and satisfying reality came to me only through participating in other people's lives. I was eager to adopt ways which were practical and lacked fancy talk or ideas beyond my understanding, ways I thought of as American. Not only was I too young to recognize class differences, I also didn't notice how many of our neighbors were themselves recent immigrants.

Our apartment was on the top floor of a flat-roofed four story brick building with two apartments per floor. The apartment opposite ours went through a series of tenants but the rest of the building was stable. Directly beneath us lived the only Anglo-Saxon family, Mr. and Mrs. Winslow and their son, Norman, blond, gangly, four years older than I, and unapproachable. The Winslows hardly spoke to us; my own family clearly figured as an annoyance in their lives. Because we couldn't afford carpeting, they were afflicted with our foot traffic on bare wooden floors: me clomping in and out with the heavy Oxford shoes I had to wear, my mother clattering around in her gold high-heeled mules and, worst of all for the Winslows, my father's 1920s-style heavy foot on the piano pedals during my parents' musical evenings with friends. My only contacts with Norman Winslow were his hurtling past me down the hallway stairs on school days and his ringing our doorbell at 9 or 10 on a Saturday evening, an awkward messenger sent by his aggrieved parents, "My father says it's late; would you please stop the pounding." That was the usual signal for the little band of refugees to end their revels, sort out their musty coats and ready themselves for their bus and subway rides back to Manhattan.

Except for a dentist's office on the street floor, the rest of the building was stocked with relatives of its owners, Mr. and Mrs. Lombardo, who occupied the front second floor apartment. The Lombardos were alarmingly old to my eyes. Mrs. Lombardo never went outside, and Mr. Lombardo appeared only in those months when our rent payments were overdue. Then, on a Saturday morning he would clutch the iron railing and pull himself up the two flights of marble-topped stairs to our door and stand there panting and speechless. He didn't have to say anything. My mother, our designated negotiator, never invited him in. She greeted him in her filmy negligee, and reproached him with concern, "We expect money in the mail on Monday, but Mr. Lombardo, you don't have to climb up all these stairs. It is too tiring for you and you know we always pay our rent. You always get your money, don't you? As soon as the mail comes, we will bring it to you." Then she closed the apartment door and Mr. Lombardo lumbered down the stairs again, grumbling in Italian but willing to wait for the promised check in the mail.

The mail. Getting the mail was a near-religious experience. In those days, mail was delivered twice a day on weekdays and on Saturday mornings. Therefore every morning and afternoon presented an opening for divine intervention in the form of my father's rare royalty payments, notices of song or theater performances somewhere in Europe, and letters from family and friends left behind and living in danger in Germany, Austria or France, or scattered by Nazi persecutions to other far flung havens. Those who could had come to America, but my mother's two sisters and her mother remained in Berlin. My father's father was in Argentina with his second family. Other friends and relatives had reached England and Sweden. Those fragile envelopes of pale blue tissue paper with striped borders, addressed in foreign handwriting, brought news that either increased worries or temporarily eased them. Any one of us, entering or leaving the building, would check the row of mailboxes in the entrance hallway. If I found mail on my way out, I took it directly back upstairs. If not, before continuing on my way I went to the alley beside the house to call out "no mail" to my mother or father leaning out of our kitchen window.

Our lives involved many such vertical messages between the upper floors and the street. Our Italian neighbors didn't mind shouting for each other to throw keys down from their windows or to run errands. My mother, however, didn't approve of shouting in public. The solution was the Winterfeld tune, six musical notes—CDE CDC—whistled as piercingly as lung power would permit. Back in Europe, the Winterfeld men had used it to locate each other on crowded streets or in outdoor cafes. In New York, my parents continued using the whistled tune as a signal. I practiced pursing my lips and blowing many times before I got the notes to come out. On the day I first succeeded, I raced up the stairs to demonstrate, but my parents' laughter at my fierce puffed face made me laugh too, and then I couldn't whistle. "Wait, wait," I begged, forcing a serious expression and while my parents also tried to look serious, I blew the CDE, until we blasted the little tune apart with more laughing. But I had learned it and it served us well for years. When heard from the sidewalk beneath our apartment, the signal tune could attract one of us to the window to see what was wanted.

"There's mail, throw down the key."

"Gristede's doesn't have heavy cream, do you want light cream?"

"Can I have a nickel for an ice cream cone?"

IV

***

The War Begins

Throughout 1940 the news from Europe was bad. Hitler conquered Belgium, Holland and Luxembourg. Italy under Mussolini entered the war; the English suffered major defeats, and France surrendered to the Nazis. Everywhere, Jews were being rounded up, crammed into railroad trains, and transported to ghettos and concentration camps. During the summer, the British suffered enormous losses and evacuated 350,000 of their troops from Europe. People in the United States grew alarmed by the accumulating defeats and President Roosevelt announced the build-up of a peacetime army. He was greatly admired by my parents and their fellow German immigrants, especially for his efforts to help those trying to escape from the Nazis. The United States admitted 250,000 Jews, more than any other nation. Unbeknownst to my family at the time, Roosevelt also refused opportunities to rescue many more

Only my parents' gasps at news headlines and their anxious conversations with friends made me aware of their fears for those left behind. I hadn't yet heard the word genocide, but stories of Nazi persecutions were the repeated refrain of my childhood. By comparison, fairy tales of dragons, giants and wicked witches preying upon handsome princes and golden-haired princesses were far less frightening. For one thing, in those stories youth, virtue and beauty always won out in the end. And for another, their magic world of castles and deep forests was marvelously unlike any place I knew. But the visions of blond ice-men in uniforms with swastikas and polished boots bursting through the doors of terrified poorly clad people, seizing them at their dinner tables or routing them from their beds and herding them with their pitiful suitcases into ordinary streets, those images of helpless people who looked like my family and whose children looked like me, recurred in the depths of my consciousness. Probably because of that, I didn't want to pay attention to the turmoil in the far-off world that troubled the adults around me. I preferred the American foreground and our daily life that now seemed stable as though we always had and always would live in our four-room apartment in Riverdale.

And for diversion from dailyness, like most children I was enchanted by those vivid beings who inhabited the movies. As soon as I could find my way to and back from the two movie theaters in Kingsbridge just a few blocks past my school, I joined the weekly audience screaming with excitement at the Saturday Children's Matinee. My big decision each week was which of the two theaters' double-features to attend. My parents gave me a quarter—fifteen cents for the show and ten cents for candy—and it bought a feature film, a "B" picture, a newsreel, "Coming Attractions," one or two cartoons, and an installment of a serial short. Three or four hours of bliss at which I and the other children learned how to behave, what to wear, how to fight, walk, talk, flirt, kiss, light and inhale cigarettes, get into and out of cars, and imitate the hallmarks of adult behavior. We loved the movies, perhaps even more because some adults feared that they might be bad for us. My parents, for example, never minded how many books I read, but determined that one afternoon a week was the maximum amount of time allowed for movies. Twice a week was not only too expensive, but they feared that so much passive watching might weaken or corrupt my brain.

As we began our second year in New York, my father kept at his writing and composing, and made his hour-long afternoon trips to Manhattan trying to raise interest in his work among expatriate show people. My mother began night school courses in engineering drawing, hoping for better working conditions and pay. This kept her away from home for long hours and as summer neared she searched for affordable places in the country where she could send me for at least part of my long school vacation.

Our top-floor apartment beneath the flat tarred roof was oppressive during hot humid weather. Many sweltering days and nights seemed to pass without a single breeze. We didn't own an electric fan and air conditioning was limited to movie theaters which hung banners with painted blue icicles from their marquees. Occasional thunder storms brought relief but it wasn't long before temperatures climbed again. My father mopped his face with his ever-present white handkerchief; his short sleeved white shirts stuck damply to his chest. My mother looked limp and exhausted returning from her daily commutes on steam bath-like subways. Everyone took long cool showers or baths two or three times a day.

Toward the end of my school year, my mother told me that she had arranged for me to spend the month of July on a farm owned by acquaintances in Connecticut. After my unhappy experience with summer camp, I didn't want to go away. Beautiful fields away from home held no appeal; I just wanted to stay in the neighborhood, run shrieking under the water hose with Erna and our friends in her back yard, and have supper with my parents in the evenings.

"You don't have to worry about me, Mommy. Daddy's here all morning and I can take care of myself in the afternoons. I do already. Why do I have to go away?"

"But with night school I won't be here till late in the evenings. No, it's much better for you to have some fresh air and green trees around. You will see. You will like the farm, and the Goldenbergs are nice people. Their daughter, Trudy, is just a little older than you and will be a friend for you. You will have a good time. Much better than here. "

"But I have friends here. I don't want to go away. I want to stay here with you."

"I often tell you, Darling, we can't do everything together. You have your life and I have my life." I knew this refrain well; it meant the decision was final.

As it turned out, my mother was right. I did have a good time. Herman and Frieda Goldenberg and their two children, John and Trudy, were a family of German refugees. Unlike those who stayed in the city, they had decided to start a new life by making a down payment on a family farm in Plainfield, Connecticut. They expected their main income to come from raising chickens and selling eggs and, without prior rural experience, bravely began to farm with guidance from books and manuals. The modest sum my parents paid for my month's keep brought a little extra welcome cash into the house and I was old enough not to make much extra work.

Unlike my first summer's misery at camp, I adored the farm. I loved waking up in the mornings and going outside to play with the new kittens while Frieda, plump, gray-haired and enveloped in an apron, churned butter or made yogurt. Her husband Herman was bald and slow-moving. He and John, their lithe and dark-haired son, worked in the barn. Later in the mornings I loved going to the hen-house to walk along the narrow aisles between the roosting chickens, gathering the warm eggs and putting them oh so carefully in my basket and then into egg boxes. I loved the sunny meadows of black-eyed Susans and Queen Anne's Lace, humming with bees, crickets, and birds. Everything charmed me. The family labored at their designated tasks in the early mornings and late afternoons and gathered in the cool house to rest during the heat of midday. During those hushed hours, the daughter Trudy, four years older than I, let me watch her brush her cascade of glossy dark hair exactly a hundred times and look through her movie magazines. I was too young to be her real friend but she was kind to me and taught me to cherish Lana Turner, Hedy Lamar, Veronica Lake, Robert Taylor, Tyrone Power, Errol Flynn, and all those other flawless faces that glorified the eight by ten sepia pages.

Twice a week the bread truck stopped by the side of the road and tooted its horn, creating big excitement, and we rushed out to see the wares. Each time, I was allowed to pick a cupcake for myself. On Saturday evenings, the whole family piled into the pick-up truck and went into town for a movie followed by an ice cream soda at the drug store. On hot sunny afternoons we swam at a nearby pond with reeds along the sides, the bottom silky-slimy, and the water clean and cool. But there was no swimming when the hay was cut and had to be stored in the barn before some chance summer storm could ruin the crop. Then we all bundled hay for hot sweaty prickly hours, and the men with two extra paid day helpers loaded it into the pickup, making trip after trip between field and barn till it was all inside.

The only part of farm life they kept from me was an arranged visit by a stud bull to service one of the two cows. On that occasion I was firmly shut into the house with all the doors closed and Frieda made sure that I didn't look out of a window at the noisy goings-on. They didn't want to shield me from the general facts of procreation. Rather, they felt that the thunderous scale of this particular mating would overwhelm and frighten a child of my age. With that one exception, I felt part of everything the family did and when the chance came the following summer for me to spend another month on the farm, I was eager to return. For the first time, my mother's pronouncement that she had her separate life and I had mine seemed a benefit instead of a deprivation. If my separate life included a month at the farm, I was happy to claim it.

Those two summer vacations seemed my ideal of what family life should be with everyone not dispersed into different activities in different parts of a city like my own family, but close to-gether in one place. Their routine I saw as natural and beautiful. I would gladly have returned to the Goldenbergs' farm summer after summer, but country life was not as idyllic for them as I pictured it. By the third summer, despite the heavy labor which exhausted them, the farm had failed to provide a living. They were forced to give up their dream, sell the farm, and return to the city where Herman's brother-in-law found him a job as a Fuller Brush salesman.

My stays at the Connecticut farm inspired me with love for the New England landscape, especially the romanticized painted versions that appeared in the *Saturday Evening Post*. Each week, I cut one or two scenes from the latest issue and adorned my room with painted sunlit meadows, country roads shaded by gnarled trees and picturesque farmhouses with impossibly neat barns, all Scotch-taped next to each other in a border that encircled the room. I longed for the life I imagined in those perfect doll-sized worlds, so enclosed and so warm with belonging. Occasionally, my parents asked me to show my "art gallery" to their friends. They walked around my room and admired the pictures with careful courtesy to me. But their amused glances at each other let me know that nobody truly shared my passion for those visions of rural harmony.

By late afternoon, most children were summoned home to get cleaned up for six o'clock supper. My own supper time had to wait for my mother's return from the city. A forty-hour work week and more than an hour's commute each way on bus and subway didn't bring her home until six-thirty or seven. When both parents were away in the early evenings, the apartment seemed very still. I set the table in the kitchen for our dinner and listened to *Captain Midnight* and *Jack Armstrong, the All American Boy*, and sometimes *Mary Noble, Backstage Wife* on the radio. Then, tired of being by myself, I moped through the rooms, just waiting.

One evening, my radio programs were done; the kitchen clock showed quarter after seven, but still no-one came. My mother usually got home by seven and I began to worry. Everything felt so quiet and lonesome. I tried to read but couldn't concentrate. I looked out of the front windows, but couldn't see anything except the houses across our street. Then I went to the side window in my room. If I looked straight down I saw only the narrow wooded slope that led to the yard behind the stores where Erna and I played, but if I looked out at an angle over the flat-roofed stores, I could see down the block to the other side of Riverdale Avenue where the homecoming bus stopped. I carried a chair to the window and sat down, resting my arms on the sill. A bus pulled up, halted, and discharged passengers. I had to wait till it moved slowly onward up the hill before I could see several lone figures scattering in various directions and a cluster of people waiting to cross the avenue. At that distance, I couldn't tell if either of my parents were among the group. Men and women wore hats in those days and their clothing looked dark and shapeless in the twilight. When the traffic light changed, people began to cross and I saw that they were strangers. Disappointed, I waited for the next bus. As the daylight faded, I kept my room dark because I couldn't see outside if I turned on a lamp. The time passed slowly. The buses came only every ten minutes. To speed the intervals between buses I sang. The sky became a deeper blue. The street lamps came on, making puddles of gold. I waited and sang songs from *Your Hit Parade,* the weekly radio program I followed with keen interest, marking down their rankings each week as they appeared, rose in place, and then declined in popular favor. I sang my way through recent weeks' top ten hits like "All or Nothing at All," and "The Last Time I Saw Paris." I loved "When You Wish Upon a Star" from the wonderful movie *Pinocchio,* and the mournful "I'll Never Smile Again" which seemed especially appropriate as buses lumbered up the hill, paused, and went on their way without restoring my parents to me. I didn't worry about my father; his returns were unpredictable. But where was my mother? She had never been this late before. Had there been an accident? Was she killed? Was I going to be alone all night, maybe forever? Time dragged on. The sky was black. Fewer people got off the near-empty buses. At last, at eight-thirty a bus pulled away, leaving two women standing at the curb. I held my breath, waiting till they could cross. Then, as they started to walk, one of them materialized into the figure of my mother. Oh thank you, thank you, I breathed to the universe, and hurtled down the hall stairs and out into the street to meet her.

"Where were you? You're so late." I rushed toward her, half angry, half crying.

"Ja, it is very late, there was a tie-up on the subway. We sat between the stations near 125th street for an hour." As we entered the building, I saw that she looked pale and tired from her long day. My relief at her return kept me close by her all evening.

After that, I often resumed my evening post at the window, watching the buses and singing during the intervals. On evenings when my father was home, I waited there till I saw my mother emerge from the bus. Then I shouted, "She's here," and he set the water to boil under the pot of potatoes he had peeled earlier. My mother made a salad and prepared chops or re-heated leftovers from the week-end roast while I set the kitchen table with straw placemats and bright yellow dishes. The wooden table and three chairs with round seats and curved bentwood backs were from the Salvation Army and my mother had painted them deep blue. When the food was ready, we took our places and shared news of our day's doings. To my parents, our small kitchen must have seemed a cramped substitute for earlier grander quarters they had known, but I basked in its cheerful colors and our meals together.

Over time there were subway tie-ups and bus break-downs and occasional unexpected late work assignments that made my parents' scheduled homecomings uncertain pleasures. I didn't always worry, but there was always a note of suspense. And always, my spirits lifted when a figure in the distance walked into focus and became my mother or my father, signaling safety and an end to the long silent afternoon.

As Anthony Heilbut pointed out in *Exiles in Paradise*, food was a central concern for German-speaking exiles to America during the Second World War. At first when all of them were poor, they struggled simply to earn enough to provide for an adequate diet. But even as things got better, food remained a topic of conversation and a reminder of their dislocation. My parents were no exception. American food, however abundant, disappointed them; the fruit was beautiful but tasteless, excellent meat could be purchased but American cooking often spoiled it, and American commercial baked goods were appalling. The packaged spongy white bread that filled grocery shelves was a special abomination. Only delicatessen sliced rye was acceptable. As for cakes and pastries, my father described the muffins, "Danish" pastries, and cakes with lurid frosted roses found in most bakeries as "chemical warfare." Whenever there was money, the refugees splurged on fruit tortes and petits fours at Eclair where pastry resembled what they had been used to on the Continent. Though they came to enjoy American lunchtime sandwiches, they cooked their evening meal with recipes from their youth.

What did we eat? Breakfast and lunch were simple because the three of us seldom ate those meals together. For breakfast there were hard rolls with marmalade or honey, expanded on weekends to include soft boiled eggs. (Friend or scrambled eggs with bacon were considered a simple adequate dinner, but not a breakfast.)

Lunch consisted of cheese or cold cuts on rye or pumpernickel bread for my parents, tuna fish or egg salad sandwiches on white bread for me.

Dinner was our main meal and, unless there was company, we ate together at the kitchen table. We had: Wiener Schnitzel (never with egg on top), boiled new parsley potatoes, diced carrots. Seared, pan-fried steak, home-fried potatoes, bib lettuce salad with dressing made with oil, lemon, and a heaping tea-spoon of sugar; roast rump of veal with mashed potatoes and gravy, tiny canned peas and applesauce. Roast duck, goose or chicken (never fried) with oven-roasted potatoes. Brussels sprouts or Kohl Rabi cooked till mushy. Pot roast, potato dumplings and red cabbage. Rouladen (stuffed cabbage rolls) with potatoes (every dinner had potatoes). And for desserts: Palaschinken (a thin crepe made of eggs and flour, rolled up with fruit or jam), Royal chocolate pudding with whipped cream, seven layer cake from the local bakery, petits fours from Éclair.

I liked many of these dishes when I was a child, but gradually diverged from them as I grew up. In my own home I cook hardly any of them, and when I recently asked my grown daughters to list the foods they remembered from childhood, their lists included none of the dishes from Europe. Clearly a family's transition from one culture to another involves changes in the kitchen.

Matters of personal taste also figured. I avoided a number of dishes my parents relished: *"Czhechili" Goulash* (a type of pot roast with sauerkraut and heavy paprika that was too spicy and looked disgustingly orange to me), *"Hammelfleish und Bohnen"* (lamb stewed with bacon fat and green string beans; the bones and strings horrified me), any gravy that contained visible translucent pieces of onion; fresh ground horseradish in unsweetened whipped cream (a specialty of my mother's that made our guests clutch their heads with gasps of agonized delight but was for me a serious torture), real Jewish rye bread (I disliked the sour dough), smoked herring or smoked eel brought home in heavy waxed paper (greasy and smelly); honey (sticky sweet with a strange undertaste); coffee, ginger ale or seltzer.

I also ate some things that my parents never ate. Chocolate sandwiches (buttered bread with crumbled pieces of chocolate on top); mayonnaise or ketchup sandwiches (could be fixed quickly when no-one was home); Wonder bread (soft, bland, unassuming); brownies with nuts and chocolate icing from the bakery; Cocoa, Coca cola, milk.

Though we became accustomed to many American foods, some never appeared in our kitchen: peanut butter (I never tasted a peanut butter and jelly sandwich till I was grown up), boxed dry cereal, doughy pancakes or waffles, or vegetables that crunched when chewed (all our vegetables were subdued into a tasty overcooked mush).

We each relished some foods, tolerated some, and refused others, but even then I knew that choice itself was luxury. We started out poor in 1939 and though our income continued precarious, we soon had enough to live on. Sometimes, when royalty checks were scarce or absent, my mother had to run up credit at the local grocery store and we were late in paying the rent. But we always had food on the table and it wasn't poverty rations but good and varied fare that could accommodate both cultural preferences and individual quirks.

On a snowy morning when I was ten years old, I was walking toward school down the long Riverdale Avenue hill. I'd won the habitual cold-weather argument with my mother about heavy stockings and wore knee socks. The freezing air stung my bare thighs but I was happy to look like the other girls in my school. Usually on my morning walk, the avenue was filled with cars and buses but today there was no traffic. The whole world seemed misty and still in the steadily falling snow. The night blue sky was paling into gray, everything I could see was muffled and white except where the street lights transformed the snowflakes into falling sparkles. I began to make up a poem about the snow, its meter matching my pace, about snow falling all over the world and comforting people by making ugly things soft, white and beautiful.

When I got to my classroom, I lifted up the slanted cover of my desk, took out my notebook with its black and white marbleized cover, and wrote down the poem I had composed. Then I showed it to my teacher. She read it aloud to the class and everyone listened in respectful silence. I was embarrassed but deeply pleased. For those moments, I didn't mind being singled out. After her reading, the teacher suggested that the last two lines could be improved a bit and amended my version to include her own thoughts about the beauty of the silent snow covering the pain of "countless millions suffering so." The phrase impressed me and I entered the teacher's last two lines in my notebook.

That evening, I read the poem to my parents. They were both proud of my first poem in English and my father asked to see it in my notebook. After a few moments he asked why I had crossed out and re-written the last two lines. I explained that those lines were actually my teacher's contribution.

And then my father, composer, lyricist and poet, told me quite seriously, "She meant well, but she shouldn't have interfered with your poem. Her words are banal. Your ending was better."

My ending was better. Was that the moment I first wanted to be a writer? Or did it start earlier, when walking in the snow spurred me to make a poem?

In 1941, Jews throughout the Third Reich were required to wear a six pointed yellow Star of David sewn to the front of their outer clothing. This Nazi law drew from centuries-old anti-Semitic history. In 1215, the Catholic church, to curtail Jewish participation in normal life, borrowed from an even earlier Islamic ruling and required Jews to wear distinctive dress as a "badge of shame." Most often this was a sewn-on yellow circle, like a large coin, meant to stand for the Jewish love of gold. Many local jurisdictions also added a required yellow conical hat. Such rulings, both in medieval times and during the Nazi era, had profound consequences for Jews, imposing social isolation and making them visible targets for hostility and acts of aggression.

Like all children, I loved to hear my parents' stories of when they were young. The best time to get my mother to talk was when she was sewing. Then I'd pull a chair close to her and say, "Tell me about when you were a little girl," and she'd tell several stories that I liked to hear over and over again. Her memories began early, with herself at age two, wearing a large white sunbonnet, crawling under a fence out of her garden into a field, and being seen, a small moving white dot, by her mother from an upstairs window, and then being retrieved and spanked.

When she was four or five, she loved being swung in circles by her father. One day, he lost his grip on her and she slid into the edge of a door. The accident broke her nose, giving it its distinctive strong bridge.

Then, a little older, at age six or so, she was out with her sister Lotti. They watched two trolley cars pass each other in opposite directions and Elspeth then urged Lotti to stand on the narrow median strip and wait for the next trolleys. Both little girls were seized by a horrified lady passer-by who flung them to the side of the road. A dusty, bloody, howling few minutes ensure, but all were safe. Another spanking followed. My mother told this story without remorse; clearly enjoying her own mischief.

She told the story of herself at age ten, seeing the Kaiser in procession and resenting his privilege. "Why should *he* be in a golden carriage and not *me*?" she wondered at the time, and never found a satisfactory answer

When she was fourteen her father left for the sanitarium where he died two years later and the family was reduced to being dependent on the grandparents she hated. But even as a girl, she told me, she had a good eye for fashion. Limited by lack of money, she made do with her talent for sewing and her sense of the dramatic. One day, she told me, she wore an ordinary white blouse twisted to one side with the top button open on one bare shoulder. With this, she wore a hat to which she had affixed two large feathers, one on each side, like wings. She was walking along the street quite pleased with her appearance when some construction workers caught sight of her. One worker called to another with gruff amusement, " Get a load of that one—she's gonna fly off any minute now!"

This chance remark amused my mother ever after. These

same vignettes from her youth that charmed me as a child lived on in her memory. Out of a life so full and varied, it was the small personal incidents that remained vivid in her final years. Understandably, when I was a child her stories didn't focus on politics, but also not later on. The sweeping movements of history—revolutions, wars, global shifts of power—irrevocably changed her life and those of her family and friends, and formed the context that shaped her experiences. She was aware of this context, but when she spoke directly of her life, ideology was dim, far less important than small triumphs of emerging selfhood and the responses of other human beings, loved and hated, clung to or lost.

Sometimes, I was lucky enough to be present when my father entertained a group of friends with stories from the early days. His father had been conductor of a circus orchestra which filled Robert's childhood with a series of wonderful perils. "When Henry and I were boys, we spent a lot of time at the circus," he began as the group in our living room quieted in expectation of one of his tall tales. "One day we were playing marbles in the sand in the middle of one of the rings while my father was rehearsing the orchestra in a trumpet piece to announce the entrance of the circus horses. At the climax of the trumpet crescendo, tara tara tata, the big doors on one side of the arena opened to let the horses in. Henry and I were crouching in the sand absorbed in our game, completely oblivious to what was happening. My father had his back turned facing the orchestra. But two workmen saw us, rushed over and dragged us out of the ring. We were indignant at this treatment and kicked and struggled. Then suddenly a herd of forty circus horses thundered by us. What a surprise." Everyone laughed at the memory as I shuddered at his narrow escape from death.

"We used to wander around among the circus animals," my father continued. "Henry was especially fond of a giraffe which used to take an afternoon nap. Henry often hugged it around the neck while it was sleeping. But one day, the giraffe stood up, and there was my little brother dangling from its neck."

His listeners smiled at the image. "What happened then?" I was breathless to know.

"Well, he just slowly slipped down one side of the giraffe till his feet touched the ground. But he didn't hug that giraffe so much from then on."

Robert paused to light a cigarette, then continued with stories of the circus. Somehow, the two little boys climbed up onto an elephant. The trainer was leading the elephant peacefully around the ring of the circus with the boys in the howdah on top. But all at once the elephant caught sight of an open gate and decided to go for a stroll in the country. Off he went at a rapid clip, the boys clinging tightly to the jouncing howdah, with the keeper and all the other circus personnel running behind. "It was a merry chase," my father said, "till the elephant got tired and quit. He stood next to a tree and ate the leaves till the trainer and the others caught up. Everybody was huffing and puffing from all that running, even the elephant. Then they led him back to his pen and we got down."

The guests enjoyed his tall stories, sipped their coffee, and waited for more.

"Ja, those were great days," my father concluded. "I liked those years in the circus much better than all that came later. My father became rich and famous and we moved to the Wannsee villa. He gave dinners and partied with famous people, and I didn't want any of that. It all seemed snobbish and boring to me. Those stuffed shirts, they never seemed like real people. All they cared about was impressing each other with things they owned—houses, jewels, cars. I didn't want to grow up to be like them. At my bar mitzvah, my father gave me a smoking jacket that went with short pants—it was a remarkable outfit. He also gave me a diamond ring which I promptly lost the next day. I never in my life wore another piece of jewelry."

"But you wouldn't mind if Elke wore some diamonds, would you?" someone asked.

"Ah well, the lovely ladies deserve to sparkle," Robert conceded.

Through the refugee network throughout 1941 my parents kept receiving alarming reports about arrests and deportations of large numbers of Jews. The break in the alliance between Germany and Russia brought some encouragement but America still kept out of the war. Finally came the surprise attack on Pearl Harbor and Roosevelt's "day of infamy" speech. The United States declared war on the Axis powers of Germany, Italy and Japan. Russia's turn-about and the American entry into the war brought great relief to all those who had watched and suffered through Hitler's expansion. Though there would yet be years of struggle, battles lost and won, and many personal tragedies, the American entry on the side of the Allies brought a long awaited turning point in the European war. In the winter of 1941–42, Hitler's ill fated decision to invade Russia ended with German losses of more than a million men.

This was difficult news for the circle of refugees. The loss of so many young lives added to their horror and grief at the ruin Hitler had brought to the country of their birth. Their only hope was that Germany would soon be defeated and with Hitler's regime totally destroyed.

For most of her life, my mother was very proud of her body, at any rate she was proud of what she had made of it. After my birth, she'd had reductive surgery on her breasts because they did not suit her standards of how she should look. In her late thirties when she couldn't yet have needed it, she'd had a face lift because a Parisian friend, in training as a cosmetic surgeon, suggested it. All other parts of her body seemed acceptable. I think she would have liked more people to see her body, would have liked their compliments, and was always a bit annoyed that the days had passed when great ladies, like her idol, the French courtesan Ninon de L'Enclos, held audiences with friends and trades people while still in their boudoirs. To make up for this lack, she spent much of each day in a state of partial or complete undress.

On all days that she did not need to leave the house in the mornings, she wore a nearly transparent nightgown and/or negligee till noon, along with backless high-heeled golden slippers. Then she showered and settled down for her make-up ritual. After that, she put on transparent bra, panties and stockings and clattered about the house, still in the mules, deciding what to wear. To me, it seemed like hours till the last, the very last, step in her toilette which was donning her outer clothing. During these hours of semi-undress, she walked by open windows, called down to the postman, chatted with my father and me, dusted furniture, ate breakfast, read newspapers, sewed, and lived whatever each long morning held.

She often allowed me into the bathroom after she had showered. It was a time when I could chatter about my concerns while she, still naked, concentrated on her appearance and answered me with little absent-minded mm-hmms. I don't know whether she was as oblivious or unconcerned about her nakedness as she seemed or was aware of the impact of a parent's naked body on a child. In any case, she enjoyed it. I would sit on top of the closed toilet, watching her as she dried and talcolmed herself, showing herself off for me. The effect on me was probably not what she imagined. Though fascinated by that grown-up body, I felt somehow oppressed her physicality. A little Puritan, I longed for modesty and restraint. Instead she preened herself, and when she had finished combing the golden hair on her head, she combed her light brown pubic hair as well with quick flicks of the comb, "to fluff it up," she said, laughing at my solemn interest, but also as though giving grooming lessons. I think she wanted me to find her beautiful, to tell her so, perhaps to look forward with confidence to the time when I would be similarly "embellished." But to me her skin looked white and pulpy with faint freckles and greenish veins, not like the neat golden skin of girls my own age. She had translucent white scars along her ears, a faint brown line down the middle of her abdomen and a knotted white scar beneath each perfected breast, scars hardly visible to her from above but obvious from where I sat. I did not find her body beautiful, only overpowering, and I always felt relief when at last, at mid-day, she covered herself.

Though I didn't like my mother's naked body, I did like her early morning face. Pale and lightly freckled without make-up, it was a friendly kind of face with a natural wide smile and green eyes with golden flecks. But she adorned that face with even more care than the body. Once, watching her ritual, I told her, "I like your own face best, Mommy. You look so pretty without your makeup, why don't you just leave it off today." But she laughed and said, "Oh no, you wouldn't like that at all. I would just look pale and tired," and she set to work like an artist with her brushes and pencils, blending colors, powders and tinted creams.

"You must always put on your make-up in daylight," she instructed while staring at her face in the mirror. "A lamp will make you look prettier, but you can't see what you are doing. You need bright morning light to get the skin color right."

Foundation cream, two shades of rouge, eye shadow, mascara applied with tiny brushes to lashes which were then curled with a silver clamping tool, brown eyebrow pencil over the pale plucked eyebrows, blended shades of face powder and then a new mouth, first outlined ever so carefully with a dark red stick, then filled in with tints of red, white and rust colored lipstick, and then blotted with a meticulously kissed Kleenex. When complete—eyes green and tiger-gold, perfect red mouth, even white teeth, gleaming gold hair—it was bright armor fashioned for the world to conceal the simple gentler face beneath. The final layer of clothing went on quickly along with two gold bracelets, a snake ring, and a three-strand pearl choker. A last combing through

her hair, a wide smile into the mirror to check her teeth for lipstick and our conversation was over. After a quick inspection at
the full length mirror inside the hall closet door to check her
stocking seams, Elke was ready to appear in public.

V

***

Friends, Relations, Religion

Although I was allowed to have friends to visit, if we forgot
the need for quiet and bounded around the apartment or erupted
into giggling fits in the kitchen, my father would emerge from his
study bereft at the loss of some melody we had routed from his
brain. I found it easier to take my social life outside as did most
children who lived in apartments too small for company. But in
fifth grade I met Lillian Pennington who moved into a nearby
apartment building and was eager for visitors. Lillian and I were
put into the same class and walked to and from school along the
same route. She was a pretty hazel-eyed blonde with looks that
suggested the cornfields of Iowa more than any city, but her family had moved to Riverdale from a small sooty apartment in
Manhattan. Her parents still worked downtown which meant that
they were both away from home all day. One day as we were
walking home Lillian asked, "Wanna come over to my house?"

I hesitated. "I'd have to call my father in case he's home." I
knew he'd let me go but didn't want to worry him by not returning
from school at the usual time.

"OK," Lillian said, "we've got a phone," and it was settled.

Lillian lived on the tenth floor of an apartment building larger than most which had an elevator. The apartment was laid out in a more fashionable floor plan than ours; instead of walking through a series of box-like rooms for separate functions, one entered directly into a large combination living-dining area with a small open kitchen. Lillian led me down a short hallway that led to the bathroom and her parents' bedroom. We peered in but I couldn't see much beyond the glint of a mirror because the shades were drawn. The room remained darkened during her parents' absence at work and was clearly off-limits for us. Lillian had the run of the rest of the place. In that family, she was the one who slept on the living room sofa and each morning stuffed her bedding into the hall closet which also held her clothing.

I noticed a few magazines on a low table but unlike my own home, no books or bookshelves. Instead, multiple stacks of pamphlets covered the surface of the dining room table.

"What are all those?" I asked.

"Oh, those are my father's."

I walked closer to the pamphlets and saw Jesus Christ, with long hair and in full color, on more than half the pamphlets. Jesus, full length, carrying a lamb in his arms. Jesus, hands extended, blessing blonde curly-haired children who clustered about him. Jesus in three-quarter close-up, bathed in radiance, a portrait I'd seen before, with light brown wavy shoulder length hair and blue eyes. Other pamphlets had print covers with headlines, "Jesus heals our sins," "Come back, Jesus is waiting," "God loves you."

"Is your father a minister?" The pamphlets made me uneasy. Because we didn't go to church like other families, any mention of religion or church had begun to make me uneasy.

Yes, he is," Lillian said proudly, "and do you know what his name is? His name is The Reverend Arthur Daniel Diestersack Dingley Dingley Pennington." She grinned.

"That's a lot of names. Arthur Daniel . . ."

"Diestersack Dingley Dingley Pennington." We chanted it

together slowly, "Arthur Daniel Diestersack . . ." then faster and faster, "Dingley Dingley Pennington," jiggling up and down with the rhythm till we collapsed laughing on the sofa.

"What does he do with all those pamphlets?"

"He makes up little bunches of them and then he takes them all around to give to people. He used to give them out on the subway, but they made him stop so now he leaves them in people's mailboxes. Sometimes I help him."

"Couldn't he just give them to the people when they come to church?"

"Well, he doesn't have a church right now," Lillian explained.

I had never heard of a minister without a church, but I knew little about religion. Not having a church evidently didn't deter The Reverend Arthur Daniel Diestersack Dingley Dingley Pennington from his mission of calling sinners back to Jesus. "So does he work like a mailman, delivering these?"

"Oh no, he only distributes the pamphlets on weekends. He has to go to his job other days. He's a conductor on the subway. But that job is only for now," Lillian hastened to add, "because he has to make money to support us. Just till he gets a church."

I nodded as if I understood, though I was baffled at the idea of a minister, a man who must be frighteningly holy, working as a subway conductor. But Lillian was bored with the Jesus pamphlets. "Wanna play Monopoly?" she asked and rummaged in the closet for the game.

In time I met the Reverend Mr. Pennington who was a disappointment. He was a nondescript looking grown-up, not frighteningly holy at all, but pale and pudgy from his days underground, with a crease around the back of his short dark hair from his conductor's cap. I became more familiar with his pamphlets as Lillian and I helped to fold and stack them. Despite some unpleasant incidents when he was chased out of apartment building lobbies for stuffing mailboxes, Mr. Pennington continued trying to do the work of the Lord. I could see that it meant a lot to him, especially because of the lewdness and wickedness he saw sinners engage in almost every day right there on the subway trains, but the work of the Lord in these circumstances seemed kind of embarrassing to me. I didn't envy Lillian her father. I admired Sunday church-going families, but stuffing peculiar pamphlets about sinners into mailboxes on weekends didn't seem a good alternative.

As time went on, I could see that her father's evangelical fervor made Lillian uncomfortable. He couldn't seem to get a church of his own and by the time we began to care about the regard of *boys* we knew, Lillian's discomfort with her father's walkabout ministry increased. When his route led through the neighborhood where Billy Morgan lived, she rebelled. Her crush on Billy Morgan generated several fits of screaming at her father. But Mr. Pennington continued his solitary leafleting rounds wearily and doggedly, wearing a dark suit, white shirt and tie to look respectable, carrying his leaflets in a black leather briefcase and stuffing them into mailbox slots for miles around, despite his daughter's hysterical pleadings that he stay out of neighborhoods where she knew *anybody* because she could just about die when people asked her "was that your father I saw? . . ."

When I was little in Europe I didn't notice or care, but in Riverdale the absence of a religious affiliation began to disturb me. I certainly wasn't motivated by a spiritual quest; but rather by the feeling that being unaffiliated made us different from other families. While I soon realized that Mr. Pennington's zealotry was not the norm, I wished I could be part of the dominantly devout culture so glorified in movies and magazines. I was, however, ignorant of actual religious practices. During the 1930s my parents, like many other former secular communists, had been horrified and disillusioned by the brutalities of the Soviet regime, but they never thought that a return to religious faith was a cure for human cruelty. In fact, religion presented its own history of wars and persecutions. They therefore gave me no religious training and this lack made me feel ignorant and vulnerable in my neighborhood. But having a parent who was eccentric in re-

ligious matters was as disturbing to Lillian as having parents
without religion was for me. We both just wanted to be like the
other kids we knew.

By the end of 1941, Jews had suffered years of persecution,
arrests and deportations to concentration camps and more than
700,000 Jews had already been murdered by gunfire. But the
shootings were slow and troubling to the men who had to carry
them out. Under Richard Heydrich's direction, SS engineers had
been testing poison gas as a means for killing larger numbers. In
June of that year, the construction of great gas chambers had
begun at Auschwitz.

In January 1942, the SS High Command met at Wannsee,
the same elegant suburb where my grandfather had once owned
a villa where my father and uncle grew up. The Wannsee Confer-
ence, where Adolph Eichman kept minutes, determined the
strategy for eliminating the entire Jewish population. As Eichman
later stated, "The final solution of the Jewish problem was kill-
ings by poison gas." By June 1942, secret mass gassings at
Auschwitz began.

Decisions about Mischlings were postponed after debate
about whether the "final solution" should apply to first degree
half Jews as well as full Jews. The consensus reached was that
such half Jews should be sterilized to prevent further racial pol-
lution of the German people.

During pleasant afternoons when he didn't travel into Manhattan, my father often took a walk across the Henry Hudson
Parkway and into the green sections that bordered the Hudson
River. Sometimes he would invite me to go with him and I was
pleased to share his thoughts and conversation. One afternoon, I
asked him why we didn't go to church like other people. He
explained that most people who went to church believed in an
all powerful being who had created the world and looked after
everything and everyone in it. And they believed that after they

died, God would send their souls to a terrible place called Hell if they had been bad in life, or to a wonderful paradise called Heaven if they had been good. However, my father added kindly, neither he nor my mother believed any of that and therefore they didn't go to church.

"Why not?" I wanted to know.

"Well, Mausli, we've never seen any evidence of such a God or any truth to the stories people tell in the churches. But when you are grown up you can look into the whole matter and make up your own mind. And then if you decide you want to believe in God and you want to go to church, you can. Mutti and I won't object; we made our own decisions, too, when we grew up, and I don't think you'll ever see either of us in a church or a synagogue."

We walked for a while in silence as I absorbed this. We crossed the viaduct over the Parkway and continued along a tree-lined street of large individual homes.

"What do you think happens after you die?" I asked.

"A lot of people worry about that. Whether they will live on somehow or not. But I'm willing to be in doubt. A long long time ago in ancient Greece there was a famous old philosopher named Socrates and he loved the truth and he loved teaching people to seek the truth. For that he got in trouble with the rulers of the country—that often happens to people who insist on speaking the truth—and he was put in prison. They had a trial and they said that he had to die by drinking a poison called hemlock. And his friends came to visit him in prison and asked him, 'What do you think will happen to you when you've drunk the poison? After you are dead, will you sleep forever, or will you maybe awake on Olympus and live on up there? And Socrates thought for a while and said, 'I don't know. If it turns out that after I have drunk the poison I will be asleep-—well, I've always enjoyed sleeping. If it turns out the other way and I find myself on Olympus and can have conversations with my friends and even with the famous philosophers of the past, that would also be very nice. I don't know what will happen, I can only say either way is fine with me.'

I always remember that story," my father said, "and I agree with Socrates. Either way is fine with me, too."

It sounded fine to me as well while I held my father's strong square hand as the two of us walked on till we glimpsed the river glinting through the trees ahead of us. But later, back among my friends, issues of personal belief were less important to me than symbols of belonging. For me, my parents' direct answer of "atheist" to questions of religious affiliations was not adequate. 100% true blue Americans were not atheists. My young friends didn't know what the word meant and when it was explained, they couldn't grasp the concept. "You mean your parents don't believe in God? That's impossible; everyone believes in God." Their tones conveyed shocked disapproval. The word "agnostic" which I learned later, softened the impact but still left me outside the circle of safety. I had to be something. Too fearful to consider declaring myself Jewish, a persecuted outgroup whose practices I knew nothing about, I decided I should be Christian. But I was equally ignorant of the details of Christianity and knew the major holidays only in their secular enjoyments. We celebrated Christmas with a tree and presents. We colored Easter eggs and my mother hid baskets with chocolate bunnies. I went trick-or-treating in Halloween costume with the other neighborhood kids. But I learned that those kids also attended church in connection with such occasions. They displayed their new Easter outfits there while I had no place to go on Easter mornings, and some mentioned attending midnight mass on Christmas Eve.

A schoolmate of mine, Joan Corcoran, spoke in solemn tones of having "holy days of obligation." One morning, I pointed to a smudge on her forehead and suggested that she should go to the girls' lavatory and wash her face. She reproved me in the smarmy tones children reserved for religious matters, "that's for Ash Wednesday," whereupon I could only cringe with embarrassment. I couldn't say "Oh, I forgot," because real Christians probably didn't, and I couldn't bring myself to admit that I hadn't the faintest idea what Ash Wednesday was. I did know that Joan came from a large Catholic family, but I didn't want to be Catholic because that didn't seem too safe either. Irish and Italian Catholics were the butt of jokes and seen as somewhat less than equal. Some kids in my school, like Joan, and Mickey O'Hara, looked like everyone else but were segregated out each Wednesday afternoon when they had to get up from their anonymous classroom seats and leave the school for something termed "religious instruction." Other Catholic kids, like my downstairs neighbor, Gloria DiSanto, led segregated lives in separate church run schools. There they were overseen by nuns and uniformed in navy blue or plaid pleated skirts, a brand of difference I thought as obvious and as vulnerable as yarmulkes.

Protestant was clearly the thing to be. I tried claiming that affiliation, but learned that wasn't an adequate answer either because people didn't say they were Protestant, they said they were Lutheran, or Methodist, or Episcopalian. Since the distinctions among denominations were completely mysterious to me, the whole topic of religion was a quagmire.

Several times, Erna, Lillian or Joan Corcoran invited me to attend services at their churches. The families seated together dressed in their Sunday best, the respectful voices, the statues, crosses, candles and religious regalia at the enigmatic altar, the stained glass windows, the soaring ceilings, even the wooden pews that felt like silk as we slid across them to our places, all emanated a sanctity that, rather than welcoming me, made me feel ignorant, insignificant, and excluded. Once the services began, I anxiously copied the kneelings and risings, the singings and responses all around me, but what I felt was certainly not piety. It was more akin to the bewilderment I had felt during my first summer in the United States watching re-enactments of unfamiliar Indian ceremonies at Camp Hiawatha.

I felt no more comfortable with Jewish ritual. At home, Judaism came up only in terms of persecution as my parents and their friends worried over the fates of European Jews in hiding or in concentration camps. But one of my school friends, Ruth Weinstein, was the daughter of a Rabbi. She invited me to her house one Friday for a sleep-over, which meant I was there for the start of the Sabbath. Again, ceremonial lightings of candles, chantings in an unfamiliar language, and the solemn self-importance of a family at their devotions. I watched, outwardly respectful, inwardly uncomfortable. They explained each step in the evening's ritual to me and I nodded solemnly but none of it seemed appealing, only strange.

While I never actually lied about those aspects of my origins that were out of favor, as time went on I did try to keep them hidden from others. I longed for the sustaining feelings of community that most people derived from their churches or temples, but though they might have welcomed me as a sincere convert, I could not absorb their beliefs and was made uncomfortable by their rituals. I never got over that discomfort. Whenever there was a possibility that I might be accepted into a religious congregation, I wanted to flee, to get out. And once I was out again, I felt vulnerable and isolated, wishing again to be somewhere inside, included, enclosed.

Beyond the brutal and reductive Nazi category of *Mischling*, I came to feel myself to be a mixed being in a deeper sense, as though divided in my very essence. I was half Gentile, half Jewish, half German, half American; half this, half that, wholly nothing, belonging nowhere.

One morning in the autumn of 1942, my father was reading the *New York Times* while having his coffee. Without prior warning he came upon a headline on the obituary page, "Jean Gilbert, popular German composer, dies in Argentina." My grandfather was dead. I heard the shock in my father's voice as he told us and I waited for him to cry. But he didn't cry, he was just very quiet for a few days.

After the flight from Germany with his two sons in 1933,

Jean Gilbert, born Max Winterfeld, who had once reigned as "the king of Berlin's musical comedy," and "the Napoleon of the phonograph record," spent the last ten years of his life in restless exile. He stayed in Austria till 1936, but received no income from all the music he had composed in Germany. Conditions for Jews in Austria deteriorated so rapidly that he could not earn a living there either and accepted the position of orchestra conductor in Barcelona. Before long, Spain was engulfed in civil war and he had to flee once more. With his second wife Gerda Stehlik, a former chorus girl, and their three teen-aged daughters, he went first to Paris for a year and then to London where they lived close to poverty until 1939. By then he was sixty years old and in poor health. Loyal friends, concerned for his well-being, succeeded in securing a contract for him to be visiting conductor with the radio station *El Mundo* in Buenos Aires. During that time, when colleagues and friends left behind in Europe were being arrested and imprisoned, the Buenos Aires assignment was a lifeline. The family emigrated to Argentina, all except for Eva, the youngest daughter, who refused and at age fourteen remained alone in London. In Buenos Aires, Jean Gilbert was expected to be ready to perform whenever a substitute conductor was needed, but in fact he was rarely called upon. His health deteriorated until arthritis and a weakened heart made even occasional conducting a torment. One Saturday morning, his wife found him dead in his bed.

My father devoted hours each day to his writing and composing but he wasn't having any luck at getting recognized on Broadway. For a while there was talk of translating and reviving the big 1920s German hit musical *White Horse Inn* which included his songs but the times were not favorable. With the war raging, even pre-war German culture couldn't attract financing. He turned his attention to the big Broadway musicals for clues to success in the American theater. He studied the lyrics of Irving Berlin and Ira Gershwin, with special interest in Cole Porter whose wit paralleled his own. Like most of his colleagues, he was impressed by *Oklahoma* when it opened in 1943, revitalizing the American musical by using songs and dance numbers to advance the story line rather than as separate set pieces. Using the hit song "Oklahoma" as a model, he wrote a similar song for the state of Colorado:

> To your everlasting snow
> Colorado, Colorado, Colorado, Hi Ho
> To your mountains and canyons
> My silent companions, Hi Ho
> Oh beautiful Colorado. . . .

I thought it a wonderful song and often sang it along with my Hit Parade favorites, but it never caught on. Taking his inspiration from closer to home, he wrote a ballad "The Green Hudson Valley" which was actually published as a two page sheet music spread in the widely read *Good Housekeeping* Magazine.

> With the sunset I go.
> Where the nightingales rally
> And I linger where the lilacs grow
> In the green Hudson Valley.
>
> And the moon lingers too
> Over lovers that dally
> And I dream of how I strolled with you
> In the green Hudson Valley.
>
> The weeping willow tree
> Always whispers of you and me
> And the sound of a distant bell
> Repeats our fare-thee-well.
> But someday who knows when
> When the nightingales rally

We'll be walking hand in hand again
In the green Hudson Valley.

The song had a lovely lilting tune, but it wasn't recorded or sung on any radio station and moldered quietly in stacks of old magazines. No nightingales rallied along the Hudson River and Robert just couldn't crack the American market. But he kept experimenting with lyrics in English and traveling into Manhattan to seek backing for his songs. With a surer hand, he also kept writing poetry in German which he occasionally read aloud to friends who listened with serious attention and sometimes clapped at the close of such a reading.

"When I was young, I actually wanted to write more poetry," he told me one day when we were walking near the river, and I was humming the tune to "Green Hudson Valley."

"The songs were just pleasant games for me," he continued. "The real work was writing poems and articles about what was happening to ordinary working people in Germany and Russia. I wanted to write serious poetry and to be active in the underground against the Nazis. But friends who were leaders in the movement told me, 'We have many people who can be couriers and street demonstrators, but you are the only one who can write songs. The poems are good but the songs make money. We need the money; keep writing the songs.' So I had to do that. In those days my songs made lots of money; not like now."

"Well, I think your songs in English are even better," I said.

He smiled down at me, "Ja! It would be nice if a few more people thought so too."

I began to feel torn between my parents. I adored my genial rumpled father who took me for long walks, bought me brownies and, except for the hours he spent in his study, seemed to enjoy my company. But my love for him did not please my mother. She warned me, "He's a very charming man but you mustn't trust him. You can't depend on him." Her warnings made me feel hostile, not toward my father, but toward her. My dour silences roused her to repeat the stories I'd heard earlier about the pains she had suffered during my birth and how my father left her shortly after I was born.

"Your father told me one evening he was going out for a pack of cigarettes and he didn't come back. He went off and I didn't see him for five years." She implied that my presence had driven him away. I hated her for trying to poison my feelings for my father. I wouldn't believe that he didn't love me.

But my mother must have been feeling desperate. "Daddy is seeing other women now," she insisted. "Don't you see how late he comes home at night?"

I hadn't noticed. I'd been sleeping. But I started to wake up in the middle of the night and when I stumbled to the bathroom, I found my mother there, tense and often in tears.

"Don't cry, Mommy," I tried to soothe her. "He's probably working. Go to bed."

"Where would he be working so late? But you're right. I shouldn't wait up for him."

A strange nighttime mother-daughter alliance formed in which my mother told stories of my father's mistreatment and I provided comfort. She liked the alliance but it made me uneasy. I didn't want to take sides against my father; I loved him. I didn't want to be on my mother's side. I didn't want there to be sides at all. My father looked at me with affection, seemed to think I was OK as I was, and wasn't concerned about what I was doing every minute. When my mother looked at me, she always found something that worried her. Often it was my posture. "Stand up straight," she said a dozen times a day, and when she passed me in the kitchen or the hall, she rapped her knuckles on my shoulder blades with the repeated caution, "you're growing wings." In fact, any growing I was doing seemed to give her more worry than pleasure. When I was eleven, she arranged for surgery to have my flat feet fixed. After the operation I wore casts on my legs for three months and then had to relearn walking with the help of a physical therapist. The whole long process took about a year. My mother's intervention was probably justified because the reconstruction left me with new feet with beautiful arches strong enough for ballet lessons. Later, however, when I started growing breasts and she told me that if they got too big I could have them reduced by plastic surgery as she had done, the idea appalled me. I refused to discuss it, fearing that she might insist on that surgery also.

My cousin Thomas was eight years older than I and resembled no one in our family. Thomas was fat. No kinder adjective could describe him which was too bad because, though I didn't see him often, he was always kind to me. But he wasn't just stocky, plump, or heavy-set. At five feet eight inches and over two-hundred pounds, he was fat. When he walked, he waddled. He had sad brown eyes set close together behind glasses, and a crooked jumble of prominent lower teeth. He wore his black hair combed straight back and slicked down with goo so thick that it displayed the comb's teeth marks and so firm that not even a hurricane could lift a single strand out of its sealed place.

During Thomas' early childhood, his mother, my aunt Else, had stuffed him full while the rest of the family watched his increasing girth with dismay. Else's misguided love for her chubby toddler and its subsequent effects on his appearance sentenced Thomas to a shy and difficult boyhood and to a series of failed diets and health risks in his later years. In Austrian schools he had been reviled for being Jewish and bullied for being fat. In France, as a foreigner, he had been prohibited from attending school at all and had spent two isolated years. When he arrived in America at age sixteen, the taunts and teasing he endured about his weight in his first months at DeWitt Clinton High School were so painful that he dropped out. He spent the next two years riding trains.

He began with the New York City subway system, an intricate marvel of elevated and underground trains that one could ride all day in many directions for a single nickel. Thomas started out close to home, then rode further and further out into the five boroughs, a lonely displaced boy, fleeing from his loneliness and exaggerating his displacement by ceaseless traveling. When he was eighteen, my father helped him to register at Theodore Roosevelt Evening School. There he completed his remaining two years of high school in one year. Then in 1943, he was drafted into the Army, stationed at Fort Monmouth in New Jersey, and assigned to the Medical Corps. He used his weekend passes and some of his Army pay for train travel on a larger scale. He rode the Royal Blue to Philadelphia, the Liberty Bell Inter-Urban to Allentown, the National Limited to St. Louis, and the Pennsy to Washington D.C. The highlight of his Army travels as a medical technician was when he accompanied a contingent of German Prisoners of War being transported by train to internment at San Antonio, Texas.

Our different situations resulted in different adaptations. Thomas, who was not physically attractive as a boy, looked Jewish and had a strong German accent. I was lucky enough to be pretty, with less clearly identifiable appearance or speech. Our positions corresponded in some ways to those of African-Americans of mixed racial ancestry. Some looked unmistakably black; others could choose to hide their black origins and pass into the dominant white society. Some, like Thomas, had to cope with open bigotry and thwarted opportunity from childhood on; others like me could avoid those abuses, but only by concealing some essential part of their identity. I spent my first years in America just trying to blend in with the kids in my neighborhood. Thomas realized he couldn't do that and became a loner always on the move.

While Thomas was off on his travels, I had some lovely times with his parents, my aunt and uncle. My uncle Henry looked like a whittled down version of my father but, unlike him, was silent and somber with grown-ups. His gloom disappeared when he was with children and he loved to think up games and stories they found enthralling. With me, a favorite pastime was to take out the large photograph album of the estate at the shores of the lake of Wannsee where he and my father had grown up. We would sit together as he carefully turned the pages and guided me through the photographs. Hardly faded, the pictures gave views of an imposing square main house and several other buildings: a boat house at the edge of the lake, a separate garage for the family's three touring cars, and a school building for the four boys where a resident tutor taught academic subjects and a visiting music teacher gave weekly lessons in theory and piano. Throughout the album, various family members stood carefully posed before dark overstuffed interiors: my short, pigeon breasted bustle-bottomed grandmother standing beside a pillar, one plump arm holding a fan; her sons, Robert and Henry, standing stiffly side by side in black buttoned-up suits in front of a shawl-draped grand piano; my awesomely mustachioed grandfather wearing driving goggles and an arrogant grin, one foot on the running board of an open car shaped like a lozenge. For Henry those visions of lost splendor brought back vivid memories of his boyhood; for me they depicted people and a world as distant and unreal as flickering images from silent movies.

My aunt Else was sweet to me and I thought her beautiful, except for her spiky blue eyelashes and thick ankles. Her voice was high and soft and her shyness made her approachable since I fancied that it matched my own. Their apartment was always filled with stuffed dolls and animals that Else was working on and miniature railroads and towns that they assembled together. Since they let me play with everything that wasn't freshly pinned or glued, my visits there were as exciting as exploring a toy shop after hours.

In nice weather they took me along on their rides in the country and though I was too young to appreciate long drives through scenery, I did love being singled out for their attention and affection. I rode in the back seat of the open second-hand Buick convertible, sometimes looking out at the passing hills, sometimes lying down to ease my recurrent car-sickness while watching

Else's pale hair rippling out from under her kerchief, and Henry's nearly bald head getting sunburned. The best part of those outings for me were when we stopped by some roadside picnic area, spread a checkered red and white cloth, and munched the sandwiches and hard-boiled eggs Else had prepared. Afterwards, for a special treat we'd have soda or an ice cream cone at some village store.

The best treat Henry and Else gave me for several years was a New Year's Eve excursion tailor-made for a child's fancy. In the afternoon they drove me and my overnight bag to their house. Then, leaving the Buick safely parked, we rode the subway downtown to 42nd street and walked several blocks to Times Square which, as everyone knew from newspapers and the radio, was *the* most exciting and grown-up place to celebrate. We ate dinner at the Automat. Horn and Hardart's Automats were an early chain of fast-food restaurants designed for economical and speedy meals. Like today's MacDonald's, the uniform design of Automats was functional for adults while for children it was art, technology and delight rolled into one.

A windowed storefront exhibited the large interior with walls lined floor to ceiling with hundreds of gleaming chrome cubicles with their own small glass doors. Each was lighted from within and displayed an item of prepared food like a precious museum artifact. A plump sandwich of creamy yellow egg salad with crisp pale green lettuce peeking from between two perfect triangles of white bread; a poppy seed roll mounded high with pink ham and sunny American cheese, accompanied by a spear of pickle; a brown ceramic crock of baked beans topped with a rich brown baked crust; further down, a piece of pie, its gluey lemon filling topped fearsomely high with foamy white meringue; and in the next cubicle a divinely large wedge of three layered chocolate cake with thick chocolate swirls of chocolate icing on top and between each layer. The delights went on and on, up and down the walls, but before we could sample them, we had to prepare ourselves properly.

First we had to stake out a table and claim it as ours by putting our coats over the chair backs. Then Henry went to the cashier stationed near the front entrance and exchanged folding money for a supply of nickels. Only the correct amount of nickels could open a cubicle and permit its dish to be removed. Finally, we had to gather silverware, napkins and trays that we could slide along the long shelf in front of the wall of wonders. Then at last we could ponder each artful display and the sign behind each little glass door that announced how many nickels it would take to open it.

"Here, you have a whole dollar's worth of nickels to spend, " my uncle said as he poured the wealth into my cupped hands. "How many nickels is that?" he tested me and patted my head when I gave the correct answer.

I drifted along, sliding my tray, totally absorbed in considering choices while mentally adding up nickels, making sure to leave enough to buy a coca cola at the beverage counter. There were also steam tables where one could buy entire hot meals. but those were boring and didn't merit my attention. What should I get? Deciding was hard but thrilling. The crock of baked beans for five nickels was essential. So was the chocolate cake for four nickels. But what kind of sandwich? Ham on roll would be best if I could find one without cheese; I walked back and forth studying the sandwich exhibits and found exactly what I wanted and carried my filled tray back to the table, happy with my loot.

After our meal, we walked toward a first-run movie theater for our main event. The streets were choked with cars, trucks and yellow taxis, the sidewalks swarmed with people bundled up against the cold winter air. Henry took hold of my hand, and with Else beside him, pretended we were snaking through enemy lines and steered us through the crowds. We stopped at the end of a wide line of people waiting half a block before the movie theater for the next showing of the picture my aunt and uncle had chosen just for me. One year it was *Lassie Come Home* starring Roddy

McDowall, Elizabeth Taylor and a beautiful collie. I grew worried as we joined the end of the line. What if we didn't get in? The line hardly moved. What if, just before we got to the box office, they closed it saying all the seats had been sold and we were turned away?

"Don't worry, *kleine*, we will get in. The theater is large enough," my aunt tried to calm my fears, but I didn't relax until the line began to move and the lady behind the box office window accepted Henry's money and put three tickets into his hand. Then we joined the throng moving into the enormous theater, ornate as a palace with chandeliers, scarlet hangings, pilasters and painted cherubs. We found three seats together and, nestled in red plush, surrounded by music from the majestic organ, we waited for the movie to begin. At last the golden curtains parted and the story of courage and hardship and unfailing love between a boy and his dog drew me into its glorious Technicolor spell.

After the movie came a stage show with an orchestra, performers singing and tap dancing, and a line of sparkling chorus girls kicking their legs in rhythm as precise as an intricate machine.

We emerged from the theater's splendor into a kaleidoscope of neon lights, black night sky, and jostling laughing revelers eager for Times Square's midnight climax. We would celebrate midnight, too, but not there. Henry and Else judged the crowds too charged up and unpredictable for a child and arranged a cozier party just for us. We rode the nearly empty subway back to their apartment, and there they brought out all the New Year's trappings I could want. Shiny paper hats, streamers, tin noisemakers that twirled and screeched when spun, and small horns to blow. We turned on the radio and listened to descriptions of the elegant couples dancing at Guy Lombardo's ballroom and the roiling Times Square block party we had just left. I was bursting with excitement, as if midnight would bring a torrent of flowers and candy and jewels. At five minutes before twelve, Else closed the door to the hall to keep the heat in the other rooms, Henry opened the window in the living room and we all leaned out into the starry night. Here and there a faint horn, or a shout from the street below. And then the noises came closer together until at last, at one minute to midnight, while they both held on to me carefully, I was allowed to climb out onto the fire escape. In tune with joyful squawks from open windows up and down the blocks of five story apartment buildings, I spun my noisemaker, shouted "Happy New Year" into the night, and blew my little horn as loud and long as I had breath.

My father and his brother lived different lives, just as they had in Europe. Henry and Else kept very much to themselves, and only occasionally saw two or three long-time friends. Meanwhile, though Robert had left celebrity behind, he and Elke maintained a wide circle of friends and acquaintances among refugees like themselves. Since both my parents had work in downtown Manhattan, they enjoyed a steady stream of lunches, *Kafe Klatches* at Eclair, visits to museums with like-minded companions, and discussions of culture and politics over home-cooked dinners at various friends' apartments. In fact, my parents' social life was so active that my aunt and uncle believed that I was emotionally neglected. My exciting New Year's Eve outings came about because my parents always went to Hannah Arendt's New Year's Eve party in Manhattan and didn't return home till three or four a.m. Henry and Else, disapproving of the party whirl, had decided to come to my rescue. I certainly benefited from their kindness and loved the entertainments they arranged just for me. I also savored their subtle pity. I quite enjoyed being seen as a child who deserved more love and attention than I got at home, especially since I too thought my parents went out far too often. I hung on Else's stories of how in earlier years they had had watched my party-going parents and pitied the adorable little toddler left at home with only a maid for company. In fact they assured me that in Vienna my failure to eat enough was not the cause of my being sent to boarding school. Not at all, my aunt told me; I'd been sent away because a small child interfered with Robert and Elke's late night party whirl. Thus Henry and Else's kindness to me included a tinge of sanctimony that, I imagine, was also quite satisfying to them. While their attention definitely enhanced my value in my own eyes, they themselves could enjoy the complex pleasure of at once helping, criticizing and irritating my parents.

Our Times Square new year's ritual was repeated until I grew too old to thrill at such lovingly designed childish pleasures and too constricted to want to be seen as a child chaperoned by my relatives. I cringe now when I remember how I became ashamed of my aunt and uncle for their poor English and their shabby clothes, and for the way Henry would call out "Niece, come here!" when he wanted my attention, and shout a loud "Hah!" right in front of other people whenever he thought up a new game for us, like avoiding stepping on cracks in the sidewalk, or counting out loud all the women passing by who wore red shoes. Not only my growing older, but my growing gawky and perpetually embarrassed, prevented me from continuing to enjoy our outings. Like many adults in such circumstances, Henry and Else were baffled by the change from eager affectionate childhood to silent and sullen puberty. I was no longer fun to be with and, unlike my parents, they didn't have to be with me. Without any open rift between us, our New Year's celebrations ceased.

In 1943 rationing began We received coupon booklets with weekly allotments of points for scarce foods such as butter, coffee, cheese, flour, sugar and meats. Gasoline was also rationed but that didn't affect us because we didn't own a car. People collected old automobile tires and metal to recycle for the war effort; and aluminum wrapping paper or tin boxes for cigarettes disappeared. Billboards and magazine ads carried the slogan,

"Lucky Strike Green has gone to war," showing happy smokers holding white paper cigarette packs.

The war news was improving. Movie newsreels showed the Allies invading Africa and then Italy. In July, Mussolini was defeated, and in Asia, the Japanese withdrew from Guadalcanal. But dreadful news came to us along with the good. In the fall of that year the American Jewish Congress reported that over three million Jews had been killed by the Nazis.

The turmoil in the far-off world troubled the adults I knew, but we were so removed from those ominous events that I paid little attention. I couldn't face the large political struggles of the twentieth century; I just wanted to "pass" as an American girl. I never disclosed this desire to my parents which makes me think that I knew it to be cowardly, but I couldn't have articulated it even to myself. Gradually I became embarrassed to be seen with my parents in public. Though this was a typical facet of much pre-adolescent awkwardness, my reasons were different from those of my friends and had nothing to do with economic status.

Being poor was not an issue during that post-Depression era in my neighborhood where amusements were inexpensive. I read countless library books, exchanged comic books with the kids in Erna's backyard, had a gift subscription to *Calling All Girls* magazine, and went to children's Saturday movie matinees. A bathing suit, roller skates, and a bike were adequate athletic equipment in good weather; a sled and ice skates sufficed for winters. A nickel would take us almost anywhere by subway, bus, or trolley. Two cents more would buy a transfer that got us all the way to Orchard Beach. My best friends, Erna, Harriet, and Lillian, were the daughters of local shopkeepers and a subway conductor. But where they saw their families as dowdy, strict or old-fashioned, I knew that my mother was too elegant for our neighborhood; her hair was tinted a brazen blonde, her make-up and the clothes she sewed for herself smacked of *Vogue* rather than *Good Housekeeping*. My father's foreign accent was too obvious, his humor

too full of word play and puns. They declared themselves atheists, and they didn't look or sound like anyone else's parents.
They were not only unmistakably foreign, but intellectual as well.

One evening each week, my parents gathered for dinner with
fellow refugees. Many were long-time friends from political or
theatrical circles in Europe, like Bob Rindl, editor of a socialist
newspaper; Heinrich Blücher who spoke eloquently about phi-
losophy and art, and his wife, Hannah Arendt who spoke less
but was later to achieve international renown as a political philosopher; Otto Schwartzkopf, who had been active in the
resistance; Wolfgang Roth, the stage set designer, and his red-
haired wife Lee; Fritz Eichenberg, the illustrator; Armin
Rosenberg, the lyricist. Others were more recent friends who had
also fled the Nazis, Gunther Reiman, Walter and Claire Farkas,
Felix and Alice Ahlfeld. Most of them now lived in Manhattan in
small dingy apartments with second-hand furniture and crammed
book shelves. Like us, they were poor but all could scrape together enough money to make a dinner of Goulash and noodles
for friends, and someone would always splurge and bring *petits
fours* from Eclair, the Viennese bakery on Broadway. Usually, my
parents went by bus and subway into the city for these evenings
and came home on the last bus at midnight, but every few weeks
their friends reversed the process and made the long trip to
Riverdale. My mother would spend most of the day preparing
her Czechili Paprika Goulash and arranging the table. Then,
moments before the guests were due to arrive, she would dash
into the bathroom to take a shower and get dressed. She was
always late for her own dinner parties, scurrying naked through
the hall, gathering up clothes just at the time the guests were
scheduled to arrive, putting on her make-up in the bathroom as
the doorbell announced the first arrivals. I would answer the
door, greet people awkwardly and usher them into the living room,
then rush back and forth to my mother, bringing her last-minute
items she needed to complete her attire, and hissing "hurry up,

they're here." I was always more frantic about her delayed appearance than she was, or probably the guests who were used to her ways.

These evenings always began with talk of world news events. Large ominous newspaper accounts from Europe were made immediate by personal stories and rumors about those who had been left behind—one friend's brother had been sent to Theresienstadt, the showcase concentration camp where prominent Jews were interned. Someone's aunt and uncle had disappeared in the round-up of Jews in France. These calamities brought silent moments. Then there were heated discussions about politics in America, about Russia, and also about the war with Japan.

Mostly, I would back away from these adult discussions that raged all through dinner time. I was happy to have a sandwich in my room, especially since the Goulash was too spicy for me and the talk too serious and complex for a ten-year old child. It highlighted underlying truths I had known since infancy, that human beings killed each other for no crime or rational reason, that life could end violently for anyone who was Jewish at any time without warning, and that no one would come to help. I didn't want reminders of those ominous truths and, as much as possible, tried to avoid them. But I came out after dinner when the women helped to stack plates in the kitchen sink and my father went to his study and sat down at the piano. One by one all the guests drifted toward the music. Some sat on the sofa, some brought their chairs from the dinner table. Taking a break from their worries and fierce arguments, their faces relaxed into smiles and their bodies responded as they listened, bobbing heads, swaying shoulders, tapping feet in time to the familiar songs.

"Play 'Sigismund.' Play 'O Marie, Wie Kalt Ist Die Welt,' 'Das Giebt's Nur Einmal'". . . .

I claimed a spot in a corner where I could watch. Though I was too bashful to sing aloud, I knew all the songs. We were all waiting. At last, Elke, having refreshed her make-up, entered the room. Everyone cheered as if she were a movie star, someone shouted, "*Jetzt geht's los*" (now it starts), and Robert nodded and smiled at her and kept on playing as she took her place next to the piano. They began to sing his songs together. There was no prearranged sequence. Sometimes they began with "*Das Ist Die Liebe der Matrosen,*" (That's A Sailor's Love) or a medley of the songs from *White Horse Inn.* At special favorites, some of the guests would sing along; mostly they listened and hummed and watched the two performers. Robert played with vigor, squinting over the cigarette in his mouth, pumping the pedal in strong rhythm. Between songs, he mopped his head with his handkerchief and accepted a coffee or a small glass of Kirsch from a solicitous lady guest. The men's eyes were on Elke as she sang, strutted, and flirted her way through the repertoire. During those moments, she was in her glory, blonde hair shining, eyes sparkling. With her wide inviting smile, her insinuating shoulders and coaxing hands she brought all the glamour of cosmopolitan night life into that cramped room. Perhaps even more than the others, I was enthralled by them both, by the talent, beauty and unity that transformed them for the hour or so until the downstairs neighbors sent their son to ring our doorbell and ask for an end to the rollicking piano.

In that enclosed space, redolent of a time before my birth and of places I didn't remember, my parents were happy and powerful. Outside of that room, this country of America, which was becoming all I knew, diminished them, made them seem odd instead of beautiful, foolish instead of witty, patronized instead of admired. Outside of that room and others like it around the city, all those people appeared badly dressed, poor, and inescapably foreign. Formidably intellectual but clumsy at expressing their complex thoughts in English, haunted by past persecutions, fearful of future disasters for those they had left behind, German Jewish refugees, they could never fully assimilate and in time, as I became an adolescent ever more absorbed into American ways, I too saw them with cold uncomprehending eyes.

VI

***

Stirrings

It was with Lillian Pennington that I previewed adolescence. Erna Krueger, my earlier close friend and protector, exchanged her circle of braids for a shoulder-length pageboy, put away childish things like street skating and scouting good garbage in her alley, and moved on to high school. Our meetings now were brief and awkward. The gulf of two years which hadn't separated us as children could no longer be navigated as we grew older. Erna in her boisterous childhood had been captain of my ship, but she was not the kind of teen-ager I admired. Her shorts were replaced by serviceable navy blue skirts; she wore no make-up; she didn't seem to care about boys, and she never giggled. The fringed blue eyes still bloomed in her square face but Erna didn't blossom in her teens, she grew stodgy and seemed to be turning into a junior version of her elderly mother.

Lillian and I were the same age. Together we idled through the long summers of our twelfth and thirteenth birthdays, mine in July, hers in August, before our graduation from elementary school at the end of eighth grade. If we'd held onto our weekly allowance, we went to the movies for three or four hours of double feature diversion from the shimmering heat that softened tar in driveways. When money or time were scarce, a cool shower or bath could bring twenty minutes of bliss and a following hour's respite from the high heat. Lillian and I spent a lot of time in her bathtub. We talked, giggled, splashed and, as our bodies developed, we spent some interludes soaping each other with sudsy washcloths, paying particular attention to our smooth newly developing breasts. Such moments of sexual froth were unacknowledged. Our talk focused on boys in our class. Most were not worth our attention; two or three were total horrors, and a few were desirable. To pursue our idols, Billy Morgan and Cliff Solomon, we marched purposefully to their neighborhoods, then loitered and strolled in seeming oblivion past their houses, erupting into fits of giggling and shoving as soon as we were out of sight. School dances featured awkward boys on one side of the gym and whispering girls on the other. More prolonged encounters took place at the Miramar Pool which we reached by a short subway ride once a week. There, in one-piece bathing suits chosen with agonizing care, we sunned ourselves on towels, shrieked at all the glistening boys who splashed us, and gained some skill at teasing chatter. These exchanges were rehearsed beforehand and replayed afterwards with more shrieking and giggling. My mother blamed my new smart-alec behavior on Lillian. "You're like a different person with her, not like yourself at all. She's not a good influence on you." Her displeasure bothered me but made me cling to Lillian all the more. I felt that with her I *was* like myself, the self that was emerging out of childhood.

In October, Joan Corcoran, our classmate who lived in Kingsbridge invited both of us to our first boy-girl Halloween party. The invitation threatened to cause Lillian some problems with the Reverend Arthur Daniel Diestersack Dingley Dingley Pennington who, for religious reasons, had forbidden her to attend any parties where there might be dancing. We assured him that this party was in an apartment with no room for dancing; only for the traditional Halloween games of bobbing for apples and Pin the Tail on the Donkey. Not included in descriptions given to Mr. Pennington or any other parent was our knowledge that the main business of real boy-girl parties was kissing games. Raising the ante of our anxiety was the fact that this was to be a costume party. The sheets with cut out holes for eyes, or colored cardboard face masks that we had worn for trick or treating as mere children wouldn't do and our weekly allowances wouldn't cover an expense like a costume. Lillian had the further problem that her father saw parties, even without dancing or kissing games, as occasions for sin. Eager as we were for such an occasion, we were not about to arouse his evangelical zeal by waving any red flags such as costumes. Since she had the freedom of her apartment during daytime, Lillian was able to smuggle a curvy black dress of her mother's out of a closet and into my house. With a conical hat made out of black oaktag pinned to her blond hair and a black fringed shawl borrowed from my mother, she made an attractive young Halloween witch.

My own need for a costume inspired my mother to help with her creative sewing. She decided that she could alter a white pleated skirt of hers to fit me and add a white blouse to copy the traditional costume of Greek dancers. We went to the Five and Ten Cent store and bought packets of rick-rack and narrow ribbons in yellow and red to be sewn onto the white garments. My mother also bought some stiffened fabric and clusters of artificial red, yellow, and white flowers to make into a headdress modeled on those worn by said dancers. She was a stickler for authenticity. The skirt and blouse turned out fine, adorned with the colorful rick rack borders. I had pleasing visions of myself wafting to the party in white, trailing colored ribbons, with a dainty circlet of flowers adorning my curled (nightly with rag strips) hair. Then my mother announced that I had to wear white knee socks. This didn't fit with my image of Greek sylphs wafting about in dainty slippers and I objected.

"Oh, it wouldn't look right without the socks," my mother insisted. "They wear white socks and black shoes with poufs on them."

"Poufs? You mean pompoms?"

"Ja. Pompoms on their shoes, when they dance."

Pompoms. Babies wore pompoms. I saw that open rebellion wouldn't work and subsided. It was a long walk down Riverdale Avenue to Joan's house in Kingsbridge. The socks and pompoms could be removed on the way.

A greater obstacle loomed. My mother began stitching colored flowers onto a piece of buckram the size of a wide-brimmed straw hat without a crown.

"I just want one little circle of flowers," I cautioned.

"Oh no, that wouldn't fit at all. They wear high crowns all made of flowers. Of course, they make them out of fresh flowers, but we can't do that. They wouldn't stay fresh for your party, " She looked regretful

"Mom, I don't want a big headdress. I just want a little circle."

"That wouldn't look like anything. No, it wouldn't be a costume at all. No one would know you are a Greek dancer. This will be beautiful, you will see." She sewed on determined.

"No one will know anyway," I wailed. I knew my peers; it was all they could do to memorize principal crops and capital cities of distant places. National costumes were beyond their frame of reference.

"But you will know. You can tell them this is what dancers wear in Greece and then they will learn something."

My misery didn't lighten at this prospect. I didn't want to go to the party to teach anyone about Greek culture. I didn't want to be authentic. I only wanted to be pretty enough to be selected for an airmail letter in the game of Post Office.

"Now don't be silly," my mother said in the face of my dismay. "And don't worry, you will see how beautiful this will be."

She worked and worked on that loathsome headdress. In her first attempt, the buckram buckled under the weight of its flowers. I hoped for a reprieve. But she returned to the store for more stiffening and applied a second layer of fabric. It held up.

"Marianne, come here and try this again." She placed the

creation on my head and anchored it by means of an elastic that went under my chin. A further indignity of childhood. The headdress was magnificent as she had intended and worse than I had feared, a veritable tower of red, yellow, and white flowers." Under it, I didn't feel like a sylph or even like a dancer; I felt like one of the statues holding up the Parthenon.

"There, isn't that beautiful?" My mother moved me to the mirror and admired her handiwork. "You look wonderful. Just like the costumes the Greek men wear."

"Men? They're men?" My voice rose in horror.

"Certainly, it's the men that dance. You see the pictures. They dance together in a circle. They don't let the women dance in Greece."

I couldn't believe it. Not only was the costume embarrassing, it wasn't even a traditional costume for women. My mother had made me a costume for a man. I would rather be dead than walk through the street and into the party's front door wearing that ridiculous tower on my head. Speechless, I tried to keep the rising tears from spilling out of my eyes.

"Now listen, Darling. I spent many hours making you this costume. It looks beautiful. I don't know why you make such a sour face, but it isn't fair to me. You should be happy."

She had indeed worked very hard. I knew that, but I hadn't asked her to do all that work on that stupid hat. I'd told her right away I didn't want it and wouldn't like it, but she went ahead anyway and now I was supposed to be grateful for it. Miserably, I squeezed out "thank you, Mom, it is beautiful," gave her a stiff hug and escaped to my room where I raged on in secret.

On the afternoon of the party, Lillian came to my house where we dressed in our costumes and then put on our coats. My mother affixed the headdress to my hair with bobby pins, beamed at her handiwork, told me to be home by nine o'clock and kissed me good-by. Lillian and I walked regally down the stairs and along the street. At the corner I looked back. Sure enough, my mother was at the window. I waved a last goodbye, then we turned the corner and skittered to a doorway where she could no longer see us. There, I carefully removed the bobby pins, lifted the elastic from under my chin, and tore off the offending tower of flowers which never again touched my head. A few blocks further on, I removed the knee socks, pulled the pompoms from my shoes and stuffed them into the pockets of my coat. I carried the head-dress nonchalantly by its elastic and once we got to the party, deposited it with my coat on Joan's bed under all the other coats piled there.

The party was a kaleidoscope of giggling shrieking girls and boys expressing their nervousness by bouts of shoving each other into the furniture. We began with the kid games of bobbing for apples and Pin the Tail on the Donkey. We skirmished at the table set with an orange crepe-paper table cloth, gorged on cream soda, ice cream and cupcakes with orange and black icing and threw orange and white candy corn at each other. Then came the expected moment. Joan held up an empty soda bottle and, with increased shrieking, giggling and shoving, we arranged ourselves into a circle on the living room floor while she spun the bottle in the middle. The game began tamely with awkward pecks on flushed cheeks and hasty near-miss on-the-lips kisses exchanged in full view. The spinner and the chosen one lunged awkwardly at each other across the circle and a chorus of shrieks and groans accompanied each kiss that landed. When this grew tame, the post office heated up, kiss deliveries were made in a more pri-vate setting, and I received my first airmail special delivery letter in the cluttered darkness of Joan Corcoran's hall closet. During all these festivities, my flowered headdress lay squashed and forgotten under coats piled in the bedroom. At the party's end, flushed and bedraggled, I retrieved it and swung it by the hated elastic as Lillian and I walked back up the hill toward home, giddy from our moments in the closet. To my great relief, no-one had asked me what my costume was supposed to be or forced me to utter a single syllable about Greek culture.

In 1944, Thomas Dewey, the aggressive New York governor whose ill-advised mustache reminded refugees of Hitler's, ran for president against their hero, Franklin Roosevelt. The war was entering a crucial phase and the American people, warned against changing horses in mid-stream, elected the ailing Roosevelt for an unprecedented fourth term.

Every summer, my mother continued to find places for me to spend some weeks in the country. She paid a modest weekly sum for me to board with accommodating friends or relatives with country homes as she had for my two summers at the Mildenbergs' Connecticut farm. One summer I went on weeks-long automobile jaunts with my aunt and uncle through New England; another summer I spent two weeks in Larchmont with a lawyer's family who made me a fledgling waitress at their dinner parties. Each summer's destination varied until my mother found the ideal place when I was twelve.

Through the network of expatriates that radiated outward from the city, my parents had come to meet several painters and theater people who spent weekends or vacations at the village of Woodstock in the Catskills. A three-hour trip by bus or car from Manhattan allowed for Friday evening departures and early Monday morning returns. There were enough other ex-Europeans who offered sleeping space in cottages or converted farmhouses amid the lovely mountain scenery. My parents spent several such weekends in and near Woodstock and on one of them they arranged for my first summer stay.

For three summers, I boarded with the Schuylers, a couple whose way of life I accepted without ever questioning what enabled them to sustain it. (Many years later I learned that Carl owned some apartment houses in New York that provided a steady income.) Carl was a painter, Edith took care of everything else. He was art; she was practical matters, social work, and crafts. He, the solitary observer of hillsides, weath-

ered barns, mild sway-back horses; she, the organizer of exhibits, artists' cooperatives, town fairs, even meetings of the
Grange. They lived in a pleasant old farmhouse which they
had modernized with indoor plumbing and electricity, then
filled with a profusion of Mexican rugs, Indian batik wall-
hangings, ceramics and drawings from artist friends, books,
painting supplies, and baskets of colored raffia or wools. Sunlight streamed in through large French windows and glistened
on polished pine floors. The only somber colors were on Carl's
paintings which hung in every room. In his pictures the barns
were always dingy red or faded moss-green, the horses muddy
brown, and the sky a washed-out gray that had seeped into
Carl's vision from his rainy youth in Holland.

Carl was sturdily built, fair, almost handsome, but he was not
a healthy man. When not tanned from summer days painting
outdoors, his skin was sallow, and his breathing often painfully
asthmatic. His voice had an oddly penetrating timbre that could
be heard throughout the house, particularly when the asthma
made him peevish. He moved methodically, lacking Edith's quick-
ness of abundant energy.

In contrast, Edith was never still; her Swiss upbringing and
her own rough good cheer kept her in vigorous motion. She had
a thousand skills and interests and spoke in rapid little bursts.
She was always in the grip of some new enthusiasm which absorbed her for months until a newer interest took hold that might
bring in more spending money. Since she made no claims to
serious art, it didn't really matter that she skipped from plaiting
raffia baskets to raising Angora rabbits, to making enameled jewelry, to attending pottery classes, to baking good bread, to nursing
sick neighbors. Trained as a nurse, she explained that she liked
to keep her hand in and her license current. She was thirteen
years older than Carl, divorced with two sons, but despite their
surface differences, something in their characters meshed. Edith's
need to take care of people and Carl's need for care blended
well. Her perpetual motion and cheer balanced his lethargy, and

his steadiness provided a dependable fulcrum for her scattered activities.

When I was their boarder, Edith tried to take me on as one of her projects. I don't think I was a very rewarding one as I spent most of my hours reading. I went along with her for the ride to town any time there was a chance to borrow books from the Public Library, but I resisted her other attempts to enliven my days. I read in a hammock strung on the long verandah of the Schuylers' house, or in a lawn chair shaded from the mid-day sun among the trees and the hum of meadow insects, quite content when nothing was asked of me.

While Edith respected books and reading, she didn't believe that a twelve-year old girl could thrive on so passive a pastime. I was happy with *Sue Barton, Student Nurse* and her progress toward higher titles. I ventured toward adult reading with *A Tree Grows in Brooklyn* (my first glimpse into the literary erotic), and I was spellbound through many re-readings of *Jane Eyre*. I also embarked on a long sequence of historical novels which I read for many more years. Edith kept trying to rout me out. She repeatedly suggested adventures which, shy as I was, made me very nervous. I refused, with tense politeness, classes in beginning ceramics, jewelry-making, sketching, modern dance, and basic guitar. At last Edith realized that I did not want lessons of any kind. She then coaxed me to accompany her on her own errands across the countryside, to sell eggs or buy vegetables, to deliver a cake to a friend, to purchase raffia, to find an outlet for angora wool. I went willingly if she'd let me loose near the library and she consented, though that was at odds with her purposes. She kept trying to liven me up. I can still hear her chirpy voice proposing one entertainment after another, her feathery hair in an agitated cloud, her strong freckled arms and hands always lifting, cutting, plaiting, washing, baking, planting, pounding the raw material of the world into goodly shape. But regrettably the silent bookish child I was proved unresponsive clay for her. It wasn't lack of interest that prevented me from accepting the opportunities she placed before me. I dreaded the role of novice at any of the arts or crafts in Woodstock because it might reveal to the world how little I could actually *do*.

Sometimes, in rainy weather, Carl painted portraits or still lifes in his studio, most grayer than his landscapes. I sat for him one summer, but it was not a success. I wore a cotton dress of a soft yellow print with tiny red flowers. I grew to hate that dress, the rainy-day sittings and, most of all, the painting itself. In it, the dress looked a mustard tan, my body an undefined mass, my face a sad smudge. Something went wrong early in the portrait's composition and couldn't be righted. It never quite got finished but mercifully at summer's end the sittings did stop. The canvas remained leaning against a wall in the studio and in time, to my relief, other landscapes or portraits were stacked in front of it. For a girl who had watched Dana Andrews fall in love with Gene Tierney's portrait in *Laura*, the whole thing was deeply embarrassing. Since I had little understanding of the struggles between an artist and his medium, I took it personally and felt a failure as a muse.

Carl wasn't granted the talent or passion that makes great art, yet year after year he kept on painting. His pictures filled the walls of the house, the studio, and even the barn. Edith, ever practical, arranged for occasional exhibitions and once in a while a painting sold. She also had photographs of his sketches of horses and cats made up into greeting cards which sold quite well in the artists' cooperative. Over years, it all did finally mount up to an "oevre" of sorts, though not an enviable one. Still, even if the harvest isn't memorable, one should get some credit for working steadfastly in the vineyards.

Woodstock wasn't all quiet landscape painters, though. Abstract art, expressionism, and the bold contemporary art movements reached there also. Several times I accompanied Carl and Edith to openings at local galleries. We saw the work of their friend, Sidney Geist, a young sculptor who was creating witty abstract figures, and one evening we attended a one-man show of sculptures by another friend, Avram Stahl. In contrast to Carl's pallor and short breath, Avram was brawny and strong, with wiry gray-black hair and a broken-nosed boxer's face. His sculptures looked like him, rough stone in chunky massive shapes. I didn't understand the sculptures but the grown-ups around me spoke of their power to express a turbulent inner life.

I was more intrigued by Avram Stahl's young wife. Edith told me she was just twenty-two, only ten years older than I, and had been married twice before. Avram was in his forties; his face was battered and lined, his voice full of whiskey, tobacco and hard living. I could have pictured many marriages for him. But his wife looked so young with her dark shiny hair in a pony-tail, her pale face unadorned with make-up. I watched her as she moved about the gallery on her husband's arm. In no way did she look to me like the alluring heroines in the romantic novels I was reading. I had thought that worldly experience such as three marriages would leave visible traces on a woman's appearance, perhaps a kind of erotic weariness. Evidently it did not; the young woman before me was greeting people and laughing like an eager child.

For several years I enjoyed summer weeks with the Schuylers in Woodstock, but I never minded returning home to the pleasures of my own neighborhood among my friends.

Around this time I gave up my scotch taped art gallery of Saturday Evening Post landscapes. Despite my love for the pictures I had cut out, I realized that grown-ups indulged them as a childish fancy and did not respect them. I was eager to move out of childhood and felt I had to wean my affections away from tiny scenes of blossoming trees, split rail fences and neat New England farmhouses. We had now lived in Riverdale for five years and our apartment was due for repainting. Ready or not, I had to remove my taped pictures. One day, I took them all down and put them into a large Manila envelope for safe keeping. All that remained on the walls was a sprinkling of torn corners preserved under bits of yellowed scotch tape. These too were then carefully peeled off and the entire apartment was freshly painted. For my thirteenth birthday, my mother redecorated my room with a tan rug, a new lamp, and a shiny pink satin quilt. On the walls were three properly framed Impressionist prints: a wooden bridge by Van Gogh, a sun-dappled cove by Monet, and a still-life of some outlined pears and apples by Cezanne. The room looked splendidly grown-up and feminine to me and so, with my mother's guidance, my taste was passing from kitsch to the realm of art. I felt proud at the passing and liked the new pictures, but I had a different relationship to them. The kitschy little magazine scenes had beguiled me into stories and playlets, as had my childhood dolls and clay villages. I came to enjoy the Impressionist landscapes, but I didn't inhabit them. I'm not sure if this change marked a natural passage from childhood play to adult aesthetic appreciation but I had really loved the kitsch and I suspect I left it behind mainly to appear more grown up.

My other tastes were also changing. I gave up children's Saturday matinees in favor of Sunday afternoon movie showings and my interests switched from children's films to costume dramas with beautiful heroines in long-ago or far-off places. I loved pirate epics with Maureen O'Hara and Paul Henreid, safaris in the African jungles, and South Sea island romances with Dorothy Lamour in a sarong. My parents gave me a portable "Victrola" for Christmas and I began listening to Beethoven's symphonies. On Saturdays I listened to the Texaco sponsored weekly radio broadcasts of the Metropolitan Opera. My special favorite was *Carmen*, the story of the beautiful outcast gypsy and her power over men. For my birthday, my parents gave me the full record album with Rise Stevens as Carmen, and I played it over and over, following rich music with the libretto, learning the arias, and thrilling to the inevitable coupling of "L'Amour" with La Mort." Because of my newfound interest in classical music and because

I had always liked to sing, my parents hoped that their musical talents might surface in me. Sometimes my mother harmonized with me, filling our small kitchen with a rich beauty surprisingly different from the sound of my single voice. Two women's voices blending in song still bring me intimations of heaven. But my actual musical studies were far from heavenly.

When I was in sixth grade, my mother's night school course had enabled her to find a better paying job doing engineering drawing for the Leitz Camera Company. She went to work each day with a little case of delicate tools and brought home incredibly detailed drawings of camera parts which I admired immensely. Her hours were shorter, her work more meticulous but less tiring and the increase in her salary made our finances more comfortable. Hoping that I might have a musical future, she decided to spend some of her newly earned extra income on piano lessons for me with an elderly refugee lady, Frau Meierbehr.

Frau Meierbehr, who supported herself by giving music lessons in her home, was one of a string of refugees employed to enhance my development. Dr. Renée Begun, the French physician and my mother's longtime friend who looked like an owl with her huge glasses tended my childhood illnesses. Dr. Frieda Sturm, the dowdy opthalmologist prescribed eyeglasses for my nearsightedness and smelled of the peanuts she munched as she brought her flashlight and her chewing face unpleasantly close to mine. Dr. Julian Wolff, the sleek orthopedic surgeon who gazed at my mother with hooded eyes, had operated on my feet to correct my arches, and Dr. Gross, the dentist, fixed our teeth in exchange for her smiles. Since my visits to them usually involved some discomfort, I wished them all a hundred miles away from me, but I wished Frau Meierbehr, my piano teacher, onto another planet entirely. Square in her shapeless black dress, her granite hair in a bun, she beat time with a ruler which she also used to hold under my hands so that I would curve them properly over the keys. I was supposed to practice after school in the afternoons when my father was not at our piano but I didn't want to repeat boring finger exercises, or play stupid little Bela Bartok tunes for beginners. I just wanted to sing popular songs. and spend time with my friends. At age twelve, my gloom at the lessons alternated with my resistance to practice at home. I avoided playing or "forgot" whenever I could. Over the next year, my mother and I had many arguments about my missed practice sessions, and Frau Meierbehr and I endured weekly mutual torment without a scintilla of talent emerging. At the winter recital, I labored grimly through a two minute version of Mozart's Minute Waltz after which she finally gave up and informed my parents that, though I had a nice singing voice, I was unsuited to the piano. Further lessons were called off to everyone's relief. Seizing one skimpy strand of hope, however, my mother made one last attempt to steer me toward a musical future.

In 1944, my last year at P.S. 7, she decided that the regional high school would give me only a mediocre education and looked around for a better one. Friends first recommended the Dalton School in Manhattan as particularly suited to encouraging creative talent. By 1944 we lived in modest comfort, but there was no extra money for tuition payments. Private schooling was out of the question without a scholarship. Arrangements were made for me to be tested and interviewed at the Dalton School to see if I might qualify for a scholarship. I didn't make it.

Next on my mother's list was the High School of Music and Art, a public high school that selected talented young people and provided them a superior education in the arts without tuition. Though I had convincingly demonstrated my lack of interest or talent for the piano, my parents still had faith in my pleasing singing voice. Frau Meierbehr was induced to coach me for a voice audition at the High School of Music and Art. She and my mother agreed that since I'd had no formal voice training, I should prepare something from a light operetta repertoire, something that might at least display musical promise. Frau Meierbehr selected "In the Garden of My Heart," a late-Victorian song complete with sentiment and delicate trills at strategic intervals.

We struggled over this song for weeks—breathing, phrasing, stance, facial expression, voice quality—until I had the performance memorized.

On the day of the audition, I took the subway to the high school and went to a designated classroom where I joined several other girls who were also voice candidates. Each of us clutched sheet music, waiting for our turn to be called to the auditorium where we were to hand the music to an accompanist at the piano and then perform our rehearsed selections. One by one, girls' names were called by a teacher. who escorted them out of sight. Finally only one other girl and myself were left. I was extremely nervous. My companion on the other hand tossed her curly dark hair and began to practice scales in a confident somewhat nasal operatic soprano. I was impressed and even more nervous.

"You have a beautiful voice," I said politely when she came to a pause.

"Yes. Thank you. I'm singing 'Caro Nome.'" My name is Jessica, what's yours? What are you performing?"

I told her. She began another round of scales.

"I wish I had some tea with honey," she said. "Honey is good for the throat. It loosens up the vocal chords. My voice teacher always gives me tea with honey to drink before I sing."

My voice teacher never gave me anything to drink. To my general nervousness, I added worry about the state of my vocal chords, but was far too shy to try them out. In fact, I was so pierced by shyness in my thirteenth year that I dreaded performance of any sort and was certainly a poor candidate for a singing career. Then I head my name called and followed the teacher down a long hall to an auditorium. We entered onto the stage and, as told, I handed my music to the woman seated at the grand piano. Looking down at a small audience of six or seven people scattered around the orchestra, I proceeded carefully through "The Garden of My Heart," registering the sentiments I'd rehearsed and inserting the trills in the proper places. When I was finished, a man in the audience said, "Thank you very much. We will notify you in the next two weeks." The lady at the piano handed back my music with a perfunctory smile and I left the building and took the return subway home. I never learned whether Jessica's aria earned her a place at the school, but two weeks later we received a letter informing me that mine had not. After this misguided swan song, Frau Meierbehr at last faded from my life. My parents regretfully but accurately concluded that I was just not going to make it in music. I felt guilty at having fallen short and disappointed them, but relieved to have the subject dropped for good. None of my musical activities had felt right, not the piano lessons, not the singing practice, and least of all the performances.

Fortunately, my mother didn't give up on my future. Though I wasn't as creatively or musically gifted as she had hoped, she had faith that I was at least intelligent. With agreement from my grade school teachers, she arranged to have me take the entrance test for Hunter College High School for girls, the training school for Hunter College's education majors. Hunter High admitted bright students from all five boroughs of the city on the basis of their school records and their scores on an entrance examination. This time, my third time at bat, I redeemed myself and didn't strike out. I was notified that I would be admitted to Hunter's Freshman Class number C-1 the following September. The tests were over and a good high school education was assured. I didn't really want to leave my familiar neighborhood, but the regional high school would have made that necessary anyway. All in all, I was pleased and relieved to have scored well for at least one recommended school.

Due to the complex network of civilian and police surveillance, those Germans who opposed Hitler were afraid to do so openly. But there were periodic attempts at resistance. A group of about a hundred Communist sympathizers who called themselves the *Rote Capelle* (Red Band) infiltrated important civilian and military agencies and conveyed information to Moscow. Their activities were discovered in 1942 and most of their leaders were executed.

In Munich, the city of Hitler's early rise, university students led by a brother and sister, Hans and Sophie Scholl, formed a resistance network called the White Rose. They distributed letters and leaflets to other universities urging opposition to the Nazis. An informant reported them to the Gestapo in 1943 and the Scholls, along with their mentor Professor Kurt Huber, we arrested, tortured, and publicly executed. Given such brutal consequences, it was not surprising that most resistance was secret or poorly organized. Even when desperate military officers formed a large-scale conspiracy to plant a bomb to assassinate Hitler in 1944, their plan failed. Hitler suffered only minor wounds and subsequently hundreds of those even distantly connected to the conspirators were hanged.

VII

***

Disaffection

I think I knew that it was my mother I had to depend on for survival. She was conscientious in raising me. She took care of me when I was sick, made and bought my clothes, taught me table manners, household skills, personal grooming and social rules. She also spent time introducing me to cultural life, wanting to equip me to enter the world of her interests. Periodically, she took me to museums and to concerts. These excursions were informative but I doubt that they were enjoyable for either of us. Elke adhered to the belief that children were small empty cups waiting to be filled with knowledge from capacious adult vessels. Therefore she saw it as her responsibility to school me in her likes and dislikes at each occasion. She possessed little formal background in history or theory of art and music but was convinced that what she liked was good and what she didn't was not. She didn't explain anything; her critiques were either rhapsodic or disdainful. At concerts she either would sway with pleasure and grip my hand at passages I was supposed to admire; or grumble and groan at performances she felt below her standards. At museums, she marched me through the rooms, from painting to painting, breathing "marvelous," or "such a genius," in front of works by the Impressionists whom I liked; or the Cubists and abstract artists whom I didn't understand. Her enthusiasm and aversions were vocal; while I squirmed in embarrassment, she was more than pleased to enlighten bystanders as well as me, a trait that years later caused Hannah Arendt to dub her friend Elke a "public educator."

Elke also took me shopping at the big downtown department stores like Macy's, Gimbel's, Altman's and Saks Fifth Avenue where she never hesitated to take out of my hands any items that had caught my eye and to substitute others she judged as better with a firm, "Now *this* is nice." Clearly, what I had chosen wasn't.

Our expeditions into Manhattan were forays into the wilderness for me. Companionable commutes were not my mother's strong suit. She liked to demonstrate her agility in moving through downtown crowds. On congested sidewalks she watched for openings and where she saw a sliver of space she would dart between people, nose in the air, coat billowing behind her, and flit rapidly onward. She never adjusted her pace or her sudden dartings to accommodate a companion. Once she had passed through, of course, the spaces were gone, the configuration of people shifted. As a child or awkward adolescent, I spent many Saturday mornings stepping on feet, bumping into one pedestrian after another, striving to keep sight of my mother's blonde head receding before me. She never looked back. Whatever our destination, she got there first and waited till I arrived, triumphant at her own speed, baffled at my slowness. She dashed into subway trains, and onto buses or elevators with the same unpredictable bursts of speed. For years I schemed that I would remind her of my presence by becoming absent, by missing that last breathless lunge after her onto a train before the doors closed. I pictured her dismay at having lost her precious child. But since I seldom knew how to get to or back from wherever we were going, the temptation to lag behind was overruled by the fear of being lost somewhere in the dark heart of New York City's transportation system.

Because she paid attention to me, and my father, kindly as he was, took little notice of my daily care, my mother felt that I should love her more than him. But her attention made me wary. She seemed to survey me with bated breath and an assessing anxious gaze that scanned my appearance for some inadequacy. I felt impaled under that gaze like a moth on a pin. Our relationship was intense but stormy. As a young child, I had adored her and accepted her decisions and judgments even when they were difficult for me. As I grew older, we still had some moments of closeness but I wanted less to be like her than to be like my friends. But when in new-found rebelliousness I tried to resist her decrees, my range of expression was limited. I could express disagreement with her in only two ways, either by sullenness and slamming doors or by fits of screaming at her. No more skilled at moderation than I, she responded by screaming back at me or by delivering a loud stinging slap to my face, after which she retreated into a martyred silence that could last for days. When I couldn't stand it any longer, I was expected to apologize for having driven her to such a loss of control.

In contrast to these episodes, my father's involvement with me was mostly limited to pats on the head and frequent homecoming gifts of brownies. But the brownies were delicious and his neglect, if that's what it was, was wonderfully benign. He took no trouble for me but I loved him, partly because he always made me feel just fine about myself. Regrettably, he didn't have the same effect on my mother. Weekly offerings from the bakery were not adequate sustenance for her. All her life, she was in love with my father, but it was not a happy love. Rather, it was a ferocious competition. Smitten early in her twenties, she stayed focused on him as her central reference point. She was beautiful, unschooled and fiercely possessive. He was genial, witty, sexually amoral and, apparently, extremely appealing to women. To me, he did not look the part. I saw him in his study wearing an old gray sweater, baggy pants, and slippers, balding, a bit overweight, chain-smoking the Regents cigarettes that he extinguished quickly or forgot when inspiration made him scribble intently. He littered his study with long slim cigarette butts that he later retrieved when he had depleted his supply. Between bursts of writing at his desk or trying out tunes on the big black upright piano, he sat on the couch and stroked Sandy, our Siamese cat, who snoozed on his chest. I loved my father but could not picture him as a romantic figure. Yet three or four afternoons a week, he went into the city to meet, not only with fellow writers and composers, but also with various women who found him attractive. He in turn found them all delightful and delightfully generous. To him they were all part of life's bounty and he never seemed to take any of them seriously.

My mother, alas, took them very seriously. His affairs with other women were a mortal insult to her pride and a deep injury to her sense of herself as special and irreplaceable. She did not react to his behavior in simple sadness; she took it as a declaration of war. She would show him. She would beat him at his own game. And so, early on, she set out to captivate a series of men. Where with my father it was play, with my mother it was earnest combat. Her men were trophies she needed to display in order to demonstrate her worth, often to me as her pained resentful audience. While my father never spoke to me about his "other life," my mother needed to chalk up her victories. She was ever claiming this or that man was in love with her and took their admiration where she found it—poets, sculptors, plumbers, dentists, co-workers, shop keepers, philosophers—they were surely not all her lovers, but if they declared themselves in any way drawn to her, they *counted*. She never said anything about loving any of them in return, only dwelt on what they felt for her, describing first one and then another as "terribly in love with me." Perhaps they were. The little parade of her suitors that marched down the years helped to hold high the flag of her beauty and her value.

Unfortunately for her, my father wasn't disturbed. He found

it quite reasonable for other men to find her as delightful as he did. Her intensity amused him like that of a child in a passion, and his indulgence baffled and infuriated her since it seemed to denigrate the importance of her conquests. It also suggested, of course, that he didn't really care, which bothered her most of all.

As for me, shy and desperate through one or another adolescent crush, pleased and captivated by my rumpled, gentle, bookish father, buffeted and dismayed by my fierce shining mother, I didn't know what to make of it all.

My father never spoke to me of matters of love or passion. My mother had theories. Because she needed to talk about her men, because she could not help talking about my father's women in our bathroom vigils during his late night absences, she had to devise a theoretical framework to give me, as child and reluctant confidante, a sense of stability and security. So we had the theory about what was "important" about a marriage. What was important was a basic affinity and commitment that could transcend, overcome, and outlast relationships with others. Her model for this theoretical long view was the traditional European marriage of the aristocracy or the gentry, where the man had a series of mistresses and the wife had lovers and this arrangement was mutually understood and tolerated with good humor so long as appearances were kept up and everybody was home in time for dinner. In this model, also, the people seemed to have little trouble making the right choices and their amusements never conflicted with their obligations. They were always attentive to family occasions, sick children, and genuine emotional needs. It was a fine picture, blending traditional marriage based on property and genealogy with modern marriage based on romantic love.

The trouble with this attractive theory was that it didn't explain a number of problems that seemed to afflict the people I saw as I was growing up. My mother, proponent of the theory, couldn't sleep and wept in the bathroom on nights when my father didn't get home till very late. Clearly the theory didn't seem to work all that well in practice. I was much more drawn to what

I believed to be the American version of marriage: total, undi-
vided, life-long, monogamous love between two people who never
wanted anyone else but each other. I didn't know if it worked
better than the European model but I found it far more appealing
and less confusing to look forward to.

On April 12, 1945, radio programs were interrupted by the
announcement that Franklin Roosevelt had died of a cerebral
hemorrhage in Warm Springs, Georgia. The single radio we owned
was in my room because my parents hardly ever listened to it,
but for the next days they and various friends gathered around it
waiting for news bulletins that described the national mourning.
We heard descriptions of thousands who waited all along the
tracks and wept as the train passed that carried the dead
president's body back to Washington. Roosevelt had been the
only American president we had known and he was gone. It was
as if the nation's patriarch had died. As people mourned his loss,
they feared for the future. His successor, Harry Truman, was a
relatively unknown Midwestern politician who looked and spoke
like what he had been, a small-town haberdasher. At gatherings
in our apartment people wondered how could such a man take
Roosevelt's place in the world and carry the war to a successful
conclusion?

As it turned out, Truman rose to the challenge. Month by
month he made the necessary decisions and grew in stature as
the pace of events accelerated. In April, the Allies took Vienna,
the Russians stormed Berlin and, amidst the ruins he had created, Adolph Hitler committed suicide. Despite the war's imminent
end, the slaughter of Jews continued. Then on May 7, 1945,
Germany signed an unconditional surrender. Afterwards, we began to hear reports that as American soldiers liberated the
concentration camps, they were horrified to find only few survi-
vors of Hitler's "final solution," like emaciated ghosts among
heaps of the discarded dead.

At the end of eighth grade in June 1945 when I was almost fourteen, I was designated salutatorian for our graduation ceremonies. This honor was bestowed on me because I had earned the second highest grade average of the graduating class, just a fraction of a point lower than that of the valedictorian, a boy named Craig Morris. I was to deliver a short speech of greetings to the audience and some brief thoughts about graduating. I worked hard writing my speech under the guidance of my homeroom teacher who made sure I included hopes for a bright future and expressions of gratitude to school and teachers. Then I memorized it and practiced it in a loud voice many times in front of our hall mirror at home. The prospect of standing up in front of everybody, as always, sent nervous prickles along my arms, but this time fears mingled with thrills like the swoops of an inner roller coaster.

To prepare for my appearance, my mother took me to the beauty parlor next to Erna's delicatessen for my first permanent. A beautician in a white coat first cut the long limp strands of my brown hair and then wound what was left around dozens of small rollers. A huge metal bonnet descended over my head and my nuggets of hair were electrically crimped. Afterwards, the rollers were removed, the hair was washed, wound around larger rollers, dried under a different bonnet, and finally carefully combed. The result was startling. Instead of long straight hair I now had fat brown poufs. The beauty parlor ladies told me I looked lovely and grown-up. While they cooed with pride over my head, I stared miserably at my beswirled reflection in the mirror. At home I tried to wash the perm out under the shower, but it dried into a frizzy brown cloud that looked as though I'd been struck by lightning and barely survived to tell the tale. I had to be re-washed and re-curled. Like it or not, I was coifed for graduation. On the big day, the assembly hall was filled with our teachers, parents and relatives. Piano chords sounded the opening strains of "Oh Beautiful for Spacious Skies . . ." and our graduating class, girls in white dresses, boys in dark suits, filed in slowly, carefully in step with the music, all of us trying, without turning our heads, to locate our families in the sea of faces turned toward us as we passed and took our places in the front rows. A city official welcomed everyone and led us in the Pledge of Allegiance. Then a minister intoned a benediction. The school principal gave a short welcome. And then my name was called. I walked up the curved side steps to the stage and took my place at the podium where the principal commended my grade point average. I clutched a few index cards with back-up notes but I didn't need them. In my biggest voice, I recited my memorized speech right through to the end without a mistake. When I was done, everyone clapped. The sudden rushing sound flooded over me like a torrent of praise and I loved it. The principal shook my hand, presented me with a bouquet of red roses tied with a red ribbon in honor of my achievement. and led me to a seat on the stage. For the rest of the proceedings, as one after another honoree joined me on stage, I sat in the row of chairs facing the audience, holding my roses, with snatches of my own speech reverberating in my brain. I was so flushed with glory that no-one else's words got through my happy haze until it came time to hand out diplomas. Then, the names were called one by one, and each boy or girl, in alphabetical turn, rose, came up to the podium, received a diploma, shook hands with the principal and several school dignitaries and walked back down the stairs off stage to continuing applause. We who had been seated on the stage joined the procession in our alphabetical turn, until all the graduates were again seated in the front rows of the auditorium. After a few parting words from the dignitaries, the piano thumped "Land of Hope and Glory" and we marched up the center aisle through the double doors to the entrance lobby where we clustered buzzing and shrieking with excitement while waiting for our parents. In a few moments, my parents emerged and I wove through the crowd to reach them, eager for the approval I expected.

"Did you like my speech?"

"Ja, it was fine." said my father, mopping his brow with a white handkerchief.

"God, it is so hot. Ja, very good, Mausli, very good, but they should have some fans in here," and he planted a kiss cool with sweat on my forehead.

A bit deflated, I turned to my mother. "Yes, very nice," she agreed, "But Darling . . ." I stiffened; she only called me Darling when she was displeased. "Darling, when you hold roses, you mustn't point the stems at the audience. We saw only the red bow and the stems while you were sitting there. You must hold them so people can see the flowers, not the stems."

All my fine high fallutin' phrases evaporated, forgotten by me and everyone else. I cringed at the picture of myself my mother presented, at the thought that what people would remember was my awkward display of a bundle of stems. Beyond my immediate shock, I paid for my imagined glory with many moments of retrospective embarrassment. And behind the experience lurked the larger lesson that in any performance, what members of the audience will focus on is seldom what you intend and hardly ever what you anticipate.

My little speech had been filled with the expected platitudes. Perhaps if it had been more genuine, more original, my parents might have responded with more enthusiasm, as they had to my childhood poem about snow. But my father was usually somewhat distracted by his own pursuits, and my mother's reality always centered on appearances. At any rate, their reaction confirmed my tendency to shrink from any public performance, whether athletic, artistic or verbal. Rather than exhibit myself in action, I preferred activities like writing or reading where I could work in private and display the results afterwards. Even then, I seldom showed my writing or discussed my reading with my parents, fearing the after-burn of their responses.

My uncle Henry and Aunt Else liked long distances between themselves and most other people. My uncle was the one who created and maintained their seclusion. In their younger years in Germany, Else's wheat-blonde hair, sweet smile and quiet ways had inspired a series of suitors who hoped to carry her off. In response, Henry, dark, somber and possessive, gradually constructed a tower of isolation around them both. This was partly forced on them by the dangers and discrimination they had lived through before escaping to the United States. After their arrival here, the language barrier and the power of habit conspired with Henry's acquired mistrust to keep Else apart from other people. After the Three-in-One Doll Company was sold, Else went to work as a designer for Ideal Toy Company on Long Island. Henry drove her by car from the Bronx every morning and picked her up every afternoon. She enjoyed her job and the camaraderie with other workers at Ideal, but never expanded those contacts into after-hours friendships. As for Henry, he spent the hours between his round-trips to Long Island writing his books for children. He wrote in German, but found a translator and an American publisher who put out modest runs of his books. Henry knew what appealed to children and created stories and games with child-like zest. On the wall over his writing desk he tacked photographs and letters sent him by various little fans as well pictures of pretty children from magazines. He lost interest as they grew older, around the time they entered puberty and lost interest in his books. Every few years there would be a new crop of pictures to inspire his writing. For the little girls he especially admired, he wrote *Star Girl* and *Pimi Ponytail*. He also enjoyed the antics of boys and, beginning with *Detectives In Togas*, embarked on a series of books about boy detectives in ancient Rome which sold well for many years.

On week-ends my aunt and uncle took long drives into the country and as their income from Else's toy designs and Henry's books provided them with a bit more money, they ventured further afield, sometimes staying overnight in small towns in upstate New York or one of the New England states. There were no brutal persecutions of Jews such as they had known in Europe, but certainly there was anti-Semitism. Many hotels and country clubs openly excluded Jews and often, when my uncle and his son

Thomas, who were both dark and Semitic-looking, entered country inns and hotels, proprietors declared no vacancies despite empty parking lots and verandahs. Henry and Thomas were neither stupid nor inexperienced. They soon deputized my blonde, blue-eyed aunt as the family scout to enter a place first and register for rooms. Then, when her husband and son emerged from their car, it was too late; they had a place to stay. My cousin told me of their strategy with relish at having outsmarted the Goyim and I laughed at his description of the disgruntled innkeepers, but it reinforced feelings that being Jewish, even in America, meant one was different and not wanted.

For several summers they traveled throughout the New England states, exploring ever farther north until they reached Roque Bluffs, a village on the Maine coast about sixty miles south of Canada. There they found a small house sheltered by tall pines and tucked into the rise of a hill that overlooked the ocean. An adjoining rustic cabin and a rowboat came with the house. Henry and Else stood on the front porch, breathed in the fragrance of pine, looked out across a bay dotted with several islands and found their New World Eden. To add to their delight, it was for rent at a price so reasonable they could afford to stay for a month.

In Roque Bluffs, Henry and Else enjoyed the splendid seacoast scenery and also the unpretentious welcome they received from their Maine neighbors. Being separated by distance from the city's bustle and by time from newspapers that brought news of the larger world, Henry and Else cherished their isolated summer haven. They and their two cats returned every summer for twenty years, and sooner or later had visits from all the relatives who agreed that the place was beautiful and unspoiled, but still considered it too far away. In those days, the drive from New York City up U.S. Highway One took sixteen hours and everyone thought my aunt and uncle were crazy to travel so far.

In July of 1945 I rode up to Roque Bluffs with them, slept in a small room under the steep roof, went with them on outings to explore the woods, picked berries and mushrooms, plunged shrieking into and out of the frigid ocean, walked along the beach, went claming, picked up shells and driftwood, helped row the boat over to Choppy Island, climbed over huge coastal rocks, fitted myself to the rhythms of high tide and low tide, read huge historical novels for hours each afternoon and evening, and basked in the uncomplicated joys of a beach vacation.

Today my uncle's special fondness for little girls might be suspect. Like Lewis Carroll, there may have been a dark side to his nature, but I never experienced the slightest reason for uneasiness with him in my childhood, nor did I ever see any avoidance in other children. On the contrary, boys and girls often came to the door of the house in Maine to ask if Henry could come out to play, as if he were a child like themselves. When he wasn't writing, he greeted them with shouts of "Hah! today we have a big adventure!" and they would follow him about shrieking with glee at the games he dreamed up. Years later, my own children were among them.

When I got home from my weeks in Maine that summer of 1945 after the war's end in Europe, my mother showed me one of the tissue-thin airmail letters that were always important in my home. The letter from her sister Lotti had been underway for many weeks. It brought the sad news of her husband Toni's death just two months before the war's end. Uncle Toni was Anton Mueller, who had once been a career soldier in the Austrian army. His military career had ended at the time Hitler invaded Austria when Toni resigned his commission and secretly joined the resistance movement. He was killed in one of the last Allied bombing raids on Berlin. The bombs hit the subway station where Toni was waiting for a train on his way to a resistance meeting.

A few weeks later another letter arrived from aunt Lotti with even more dreadful news. In it, Lotti enclosed a photograph of their only son, Karl Heinz, nicknamed Heini, in uniform. She wrote that he had been killed that spring a few weeks before the war ended. My mother's sympathy for her sister was made more painful by her feeling so far away and unable to help. She showed me the photograph. My cousin Heini though in a soldier's uniform looked like the boys in my grade at school.

"He was just four years older than you," my mother grieved, "poor Lottchen, it's so terrible." She rummaged in a drawer and found an earlier photograph of Lotti with Heini taken when he was about eight or nine years old.

"That's when they came to Paris when I was there with you," my mother said, "He played with you in the Tuileries Gardens when you were small." I didn't remember anything about Paris. The photo showed a boy with short pale hair and a small pointed chin. He was smiling up at Lotti who looked pleasant and round-ish; she wore a dark peaked hat with a veil and a flowered dress.

That picture had been taken when all of the Jewish side of my family had already fled Germany. My mother's family, she told me, hated the Nazis but not being Jewish they were not in immediate danger. Germany was their home and they waited for people to come to their senses and defeat Hitler in elections. Then the war came and they were trapped.

Heini celebrated his seventeenth birthday in 1944. He had expected to finish high school before seeing military service, but Germany's severe defeats had created a shortage of men in the armed forces. Heini, along with other boys earlier considered to young, was ordered to report for immediate induction. His parents were terrified at the prospect of sending their young son to face possible death or wounding on some unknown battlefield. Heini himself, who knew that his father worked with the resistance, hated the thought of having to fight on Hitler's side. For several days after the order came, Lotti tried to think of a way to hide Heini somewhere for the remainder of a war that everyone knew would be lost before long. Perhaps they could smuggle him out into the country, or perhaps he could even be kept hidden in the cellar of their house. But they also faced a greater fear in the climate of suspicion and treachery that had turned neighbors and acquaintances, even family members, into spies against each other. Everywhere, people were urged to report any slight infractions of official regulations and were subject to arrest if they did not do so. Should word of Heini's apparent disappearance reach the authorities and should he then be discovered in hiding, he would promptly be shot, as had several other boys in similar circumstances. The risk of a decision either way was nearly paralyzing. In the end, Lotti and Toni gambled that the war would end swiftly and gave Heini up to the army. Like many others among the boy soldiers he died at the front.

I looked at the two photographs and hugged my mother. I felt sorry mostly keenly for her distress. For my cousin, it was a distant sort of sadness. It was terrible for anyone to be killed at such a young age. But though Lotti and Heini were vividly real for my mother, by then they were far-off names from my early childhood, not real people I myself could remember or expected to see again. Still, I could imagine how terrible it was for my aunt Lotti to lose both her husband and her son within weeks of each other. It reinforced the stark contrast between our safe life in America and the sorrows of my mother's family who had stayed behind in Germany.

On August 6, 1945, the summer after I graduated from eighth grade at P.S.7, the United States dropped atom bombs on Hiroshima and Nagasaki. Everyone was stunned by the magnitude of destruction and deaths numbering in the hundreds of thousands. A week later, Japan surrendered. Despite official explanations about averting the loss of American lives, nothing could make my parents or their friends believe that Truman's decision to use the bomb was necessary or morally justifiable.

Final casualty figures at the war's end showed that American losses were 405,399. Though grave, these figures did not compare to those of other countries. World-wide the number of deaths totaled 54,800,000. After this enormous cost in human lives, the Second World War was over.

Almost immediately, it seemed we had new enemies to worry about. In New York, our circle of refugee friends began to hear of people fleeing to the western sectors of Germany before the Russian troops could reach them. Most Germans welcomed the Americans, French and English with hope for a lessening of the sufferings during the last years of the Hitler regime. But they were terrified of the Russians. As it turned out, they had reason to fear because the Soviet Army's advance through Germany was a brutal progress of rapes, beatings, and murders. My mother, worried though she was about her mother and sister Lotti in Berlin, was grateful that at least they were in the American sector of the city. Her youngest sister Irma, with her little daughter Barbara, had been evacuated to Czechoslovakia during the war years. After the war ended, they were relocated by the Allies to the French sector in Bavaria.

In the fall, I entered Hunter College High School. I was one of a thousand girls selected by exam from the five boroughs of the City. Each day we gathered from all directions, a shrieking, giggling, galloping horde of adolescents. I commuted by bus and two subways to get to the formidable gray stone building at 68th Street and Lexington Avenue, a ride that took a bit more than an hour. For most of the ride I found a seat and got used to doing my homework en route. Unlike subway riders of today, I never even came close to fearing for my life, but as I had earlier learned from the Reverend Pennington's warnings, subway trains were a favorite locale for smutty sexuality. When a train was very crowded men would surreptitiously grope and fondle girls' breasts or buttocks. When the cars were nearly empty they would expose themselves; sometimes sitting directly across the way; sometimes standing nearby with coat open to display their wares; sometimes masturbating in the alcoves at either end of the car. I learned to direct my eyes either heavenward or down at my book, and I grew adept at jabbing sharp elbows and textbook corners to ward off furtive hands. At school the other girls told each other with shrill hilarity about these encounters, but alone they were always a shock. I didn't know then that such men seldom posed a real danger and their feverish eyes and their busy hands were at once frightening and compelling. They signaled a shameful urgency nothing like the whoops, wolf whistles and inexpert kisses I received from the boys I knew or the series of "crushes" on various boys and movie stars my friend Lillian and I skittered through during our first year at separate high schools.

Lillian and I were still together most Saturdays and Sundays, spending hours at each other's houses trying out hair-styles, new lipstick shades and swear words, sharing giggling fits and deep secrets, meandering through neighborhoods where special boys lived, sipping ice cream sodas, or burning our mouths on the new delights of Italian "pies" at the pizzeria near the movie theater. In most ways, except for my long school hours and the girls I befriended there, my life continued in my own neighborhood much as it had before. My first date was with a boy from the neighborhood. We took the subway to the Museum of Natural History, wandered dumbly through exhibits of Indian culture and dinosaur bones, had lunch in the museum cafeteria, and went next door to the Planetarium where we looked up at the electric stars in rigid silence till his arm crept around the top of the seat to rest on my shoulder and stayed there till the lights came on as though neither arm nor shoulder belonged to either of us.

I ended my first high school year with several new girl friends, few athletic skills, an adequate though not impressive academic showing, and no clear interests. Though I would have liked to have done better, I wasn't motivated to work harder at my studies. The academic stars of the school seemed smug and unattractive girls and I didn't want to emulate them. My own new friends were a perky blonde from Long Island who, together with her equally blonde sister, was sometimes a fashion model for teen magazines, and an attractive brunette of Greek descent who wanted to become a dancer. I confided to my diary that good grades did not matter as much to me as having good friends.

During that year, the newspapers were filled with stories from the Nuremberg Trials which lasted from November 1945 to October 1946. Herman Goering and other remaining leaders of the Third Reich were tried for war crimes by an Allied military tribunal. At the trial were shown previously secret documentary films of the death camps from the meticulous German archives. As these pictures subsequently appeared in newspapers and movie newsreels, the weekly dinners of my parents circle of friends and fellow refugees became occasions for mourning. They had long known of Hitler's campaign to rid Europe of Jews through enslavement, starvation, and ultimately through mass murder. They had known about the death camps and the millions dead. But now, week after week brought searing images, those of emaciated figures in black and white striped garments behind barbed wire, their eyes huge and stupefied beyond comprehensible suffering, were interspersed with nightmarish views of mounds of discarded skeletal corpses. The émigrés were heartbroken. Even those who had known could not absorb the enormity of the horror. The shocks of disclosure spread beyond the refugee community and eddied across the country, renewing Americans' hatred of Nazi Germany as a wartime enemy by adding revulsion at the massacre of its own people.

When I saw the dreadful fate that had overtaken the Jews, my pain at being half Jewish was complicated by the fact that I was also German. I knew nothing about Germany except its miseries under the Nazis. I knew only two kinds of Germans, the circle of mostly Jewish German refugees which included my relatives, and the Nazi demons portrayed in Hollywood fictional films during the war and now emerging in real life horrifying newsreels . I was not alone in having difficulties with being German, even the Germans I knew personally were uncomfortable. Hitler's Third Reich, all it did and all it stood for, left a deep scar in the German psyche. This didn't stem only from the war because Germany itself suffered and lost so much in that fateful struggle to gain *Lebensraum*. But the systematic persecution and extermination of helpless peoples—Jews, homosexuals, gypsies, mentally retarded and physically handicapped persons—that dreadful campaign of mass murder made it impossible to take pride in being German. To be German in the shadow of the Holocaust was to be tainted with the stigma of having released and glorified the most dark and terrible side of human nature. And probably because of that taint, even those German traits which might have once been considered virtues, and which I had myself—studiousness, neatness, efficiency, obedience, productivity—were either parodied or suspected of being too easily perverted to the efficient service of evil. Thus I felt tainted by both aspects of the ancestry that defined me and while I knew that my uncle Toni and my cousin Heini had been good people who hated Hitler and never wanted to harm anyone, it was hard to reveal that I'd had a cousin who was a German soldier.

When my background came up in conversation, I admitted to having been born in Germany but always made sure to add some remark that wouldn't pin me too tightly to a specific German background. "I was born in Berlin," I would say, "but my family left Germany when I was an infant so I don't remember anything about it. We lived in several places in Europe before coming to the United States." This was true, but also served my preference for associating myself with the roseate haze of being "European" rather than with the Prussian "Achtung" character forever typecast as German.

Like most teen-agers I wanted to separate myself from my parents, and like many children of immigrants during that era of assimilation, I wanted also to obscure ties that might identify me with their origins. The separation I wished for began the summer I turned fifteen and went again to Woodstock.

VIII

***

Woodstock

Most people now think of Woodstock as the make-love-not-war symbol of an era—thousands of longhaired young people in colorful tatters crammed together on muddy slopes for days of music, marijuana, and sex. Films have projected a flickering memorial of those multitudes, their exuberant untidy bodies, their dazed passive eyes. The real town of Woodstock, as is now known, is miles from the hillsides of pop legend and distinct from its public image. Those young people came from other places, wove their brief communal spell, and left again, separate particles of "alienated" youth. Like an enormous flock of birds, they alighted, chattered, and were gone. The place itself did not assimilate or keep them, yet the name of that little town in the Catskills has become fastened to a global memory, apart from anything wished for or achieved by those who live there.

But that famous Woodstock was not mine. When I lived there, it was still just a real place. What people thought of it was grounded in the landscape and its inhabitants, the patterns of their daily lives and friendships, the weather and the work they created there. In the 1940s, my Woodstock was a peaceful outpost of farmers, craftsmen and, most notably, artists. The area had attracted artists from its early days, singly and in colonies. Men and women of all ages painted the soft Catskill hills, the valleys with their orchards and tidy wheat fields, the rocky winding streams, and the groves of tall green-black pines. They especially loved to paint the barns, faded red or brown weathered wood barns that leaned in sunlight and nostalgia into a thousand painted landscapes. Over the years Woodstock accepted strangers with tolerance and little fuss. Something about the landscape seemed hospitable; differences could be tucked into the folds of the hills, hidden around the curvings of the streams. That older smaller place has grown larger and more commercially savvy, but the country of my youth still persists there.

The country of my youth. Though I stayed longer than the brief tide of the later generation, I also came there from another place and left again. At the time it was a three-hour bus ride from the city. In terms of history, though, my journey was much longer than that, beginning when my parents left Berlin with me shortly after I was born. I had no memories of Europe as such, only of vague domestic settings, and an atmosphere of fear as we moved from place to place. But even though we settled and I grew up in Riverdale, it wasn't till Woodstock that I had some sense of what it might mean to think of a landscape beyond any immediate dwelling as home. I didn't think of Woodstock as home either, until the summer I turned fifteen.

Edith Schuyler's schemes for my improvement culminated during that summer. She persuaded my mother that, instead of boarding again with them, I might be of some help as a companion to a Dutch woman friend, Berthe van Dorn, who was living alone in a big house at one edge of the village. The situation was what was then described as "Bohemian." Love, hate, jealousy, passion, rage and despair had somehow been tamed into unorthodox but workable domestic arrangements. I was in fact brought into the aftermath of a classic love triangle, though I didn't recognize it as such. For a fifteen year old girl, the principals of a love story can't be middle aged. Like most young people, I believed that feelings must wear out along with the body, grow flabby or thin and threadbare until at last a mantle of serenity provides a decent covering. Much later, I came to know that that's not at all what happens. Instead of a quieting, there's a blazing upward. Everything that's been thwarted or evaded rises up and insists on its time.

The outlines of the story I entered were that Piet and Berthe Van Dorn, after years of traveling, had decided to come to America when the war broke out. They settled in Woodstock to raise their son, Nicky, through his high school years. As the war spread, they took in a younger cousin of Berthe's who had managed to escape from Holland. Annie was not pretty but she was glad to help by taking hold of any tasks in house and garden that required more vigor than Berthe could muster. In time, the husband Piet and the young cousin Annie fell in love. Their unforeseen liaison, as such things will, complicated and permanently changed the patterns of their family life. Piet and Annie bought and went to live in a ramshackle farm just outside of town. Berthe stayed in the main house with Nicky, who had just graduated from high school.

By the time I came on the scene a year later, what had been high drama and intense emotion had ebbed to aftermath problems in managing daily life. Nicky, born in the United States, had been drafted into the Army which left Berthe by herself in the big house. Throughout her personal disaster she had clung for love and reassurance to her son. His absence in the Army had removed her main emotional support. She lost interest in eating and grew increasingly frail, so much so that Piet and Annie were spending two or three days and nights each week back at the house so that she wouldn't be so entirely alone. This temporary solution was awkward. Their attempts to patch up the tatters of Berthe's life may have actually increased her pain, but it was a confused time and no one knew quite what was best to do. As the summer approached, Berthe's loneliness and depression worried her friends. With this in mind, Edith suggested that I might bring some companionship and also perform various small errands and chores for her. I don't know if anybody bothered much about questions of compatibility between a fifty-five year-old discarded wife in poor health and a fifteen year-old high school girl—perhaps Edith thought my quiet habits would suit her—at any rate it was arranged and when the time came, my parents borrowed a car and deposited me at Berthe's house at the beginning of July. She welcomed me shyly with tea and cookies, showed me to a small room at the top of the stairs where I would sleep, and seemed pleased to have me there.

While I boarded with Berthe, Piet and Annie still came two or three times a week to look after her needs, but they stayed overnight only on Fridays so that Piet could drive to Kingston and bring Nicky back to the big house. Nicky was then a nineteen year-old soldier who took the Friday night train home from his Army post at Fort Dix every possible week-end he could get leave.

I have to wonder, with all my longing to become a true blue indistinguishable American, why my first love and the family I adopted should have been Dutch immigrants. My parents' foreignness embarrassed me in our Riverdale neighborhood. But the Van Dorns were also obviously foreign. They spoke with a Dutch accent and at home their English was laced with Dutch words and phrases. They even pronounced my name as "Maryahn" a shortened version of my name in German. But while my parents' interests and activities made them seem out of place in our Riverdale neighborhood, the Van Dorns and their friends were surrounded by like-minded people in a community that honored the arts and paid little heed to national origins. In most towns in mainstream America, I too might have felt out of place but Woodstock with the Van Dorns gave me my first sense of a home town.

I still remember everything about the big house that came to seem like home. Once through the wooden garden gate, one was in the heart of summertime. The garden wall enclosed a secluded courtyard, half shaded under the leafy grape arbor over a study log table and benches. The large grape leaves made a sunny green canopy that descended into a curtain between the terrace and a small meadow that led to a cottage and a shed behind the house. Further up the slope were stands of spruce trees and hillside fields. Beside the terrace two huge old lilac bushes flowered each spring, and in summer bright yellow and orange nasturtium flared like paint splotches at the corners of the house. Once in a while somebody dug something up, Annie put in a few bulbs of tulips or daffodils, or cut away some dead branches, but I can't recall any sustained gardening. Everything seemed sturdy, comfortably gnarled and accustomed to the seasonal round of blossoming flowers, green maple tree wings that children pasted across their noses, bunches of blue-black grapes for jam, and acorns that bounced onto the slates in the fall. All that burgeoning seemed to continue with little human assistance or anxiety. But maybe I was still too young and, as with many other aspects of adult life, too heedless to recognize the constant and hidden care involved.

Our days centered around the large kitchen, dim when I first stepped in after the bright outdoor sunlight, but soon shapes would begin to emerge from the shadows. Often Berthe would be bending over the massive black cast-iron stove, her face a little flushed, lifting the black round lids with a pronged tool and moving the tea kettle closer to the hottest part of the fire. The heavy round oak table seemed the center of family life. Nicky's father, Piet, his eyes squinting from the smoke that curled up from the ever-present cigarette in his mouth, would sit there and prod with a screw driver at some small out-of-order appliance.

I can still picture all the rooms in that house, each holding images of my life there. The pleasant book-filled living room stayed quiet, seldom used except as a retreat from the kitchen's bustle. On rainy afternoons, Nicky and I would put records on the old victrola and read or, more likely, pretend to read as we sat by each other on the sofa. Rain slanting on the window panes, Vermeer's "head of a young girl," on the wall with dusky blues and yellows of her turban glowing over her pearl-like face in the dim light, Lalo's Spanish Symphony sobbing all around us—all blended with the lure of smooth young skin beneath our clothing. That cool and somnolent room, quietly away from the center, was always a second choice, a bad weather substitute for some livelier place, but its stillness survives in my memory. Only when one has lived in a house, not just visited there, can one reassemble it so completely in one's mind

Upstairs was a small bedroom with a wide casement window that overlooked the terrace. A dresser, a little antique desk and chair, and a large four-poster bed beside the window was all the furniture the room could hold. It also held me, becoming my room. Sitting up in bed there, on summer mornings I could look down to see if the day had begun, with the top half of the Dutch door to the kitchen open, the cats on the steps drinking their morning milk. I could then hear the faint noises of breakfast in the making, or see Annie outside flicking a cloth across the table under the arbor, or Piet looking across the fields estimating the day's weather.

I can't know if the sad shock of Piet's betrayal had made Berthe old, but I suspect she must have seemed so before that. She was almost six feet tall and gaunt. Her hair was white and she fastened its thin waves in a loose knot at the nape of her neck with hairpins that were always slipping out. She moved tentatively as if unsure of her purpose. It was said she had a weak heart; certainly she needed to rest a great deal and clearly she could not manage on her own. Both her frailty and her temperament prevented her from openly expressing her fury at her situation and from moving toward greater independence. Something girlish persisted even through all the signs of age, a shyness and a faint appealing charm. I could picture her as a willowy young girl with thick pale hair and deep blue eyes, but the demure grace that must have once attracted suitors had not served her well. The best she could do to lighten her depression was to long for her son and to mutter occasional spiteful comments against Annie, the vigorous younger cousin, the "snake in the grass" who had replaced her, and who was now so often back in the house as Piet's consort. Berthe found the situation humiliating, but their returns brought practical help with cleaning, marketing and the constant upkeep needed by a large old house. They also brought, intermittently, the protection that human voices—even hated ones—oppose to the void.

So long as Nicky had lived there with her, lifting her spirits had been his responsibility. In his absence, to a lesser extent, it became mine. To my surprise, my presence really did help. If nothing else, I provided a buffer between Berthe and the couple that Piet and Annie now were, and also some lessening of her excessive need of Nicky during his weekends home. He was exceptionally tall at six-foot-four, slim, blond, and blue-eyed and probably resembled his mother in the days of her youth. As I got to know Nicky, I could see that he loved Berthe and was angry at his father on her behalf. On his own behalf, too, for being delegated to take care of her. It was not easy for him to manage the love and anger at both of them, the mother who clung to him, the father he still needed. Mostly he also adjusted by blaming Annie. But Annie seemed impervious, organizing the housework and meals and striding through her days with good humor. If she suffered from her anomalous position and from the dislike of those she worked to help, she didn't show it.

After the strangeness of my first few days with Berthe eased, I found that I didn't actually have to do much for her. A little conversation and a little affection seemed to suffice. My presence alone must have lessened some of the anxiety of her solitude. I had never before known an adult who, by comparison, made me feel capable. She seemed so unsure of her place in the world, so unsuited to typical American ways, and so shy with people she didn't know, that her fears made me brave and I would venture out for both of us. I bought her personal items at the drug store, got her library books, and picked up her mail at the Post Office. I coaxed her to tell stories of her youth in Holland and once in a while I could make her laugh by telling her she had navy-blue eyes. Our days were simple. We both liked the early mornings and breakfasted together, then busied ourselves with whatever light housekeeping we needed. Annie and Piet did the heavier work when they came. In the afternoons, while Berthe rested, I went swimming in the creek across the fields or rode my bike into town. Sometimes we had tea when I returned with news of gallery openings or the week's movie or summer stock play. Later I'd help with setting the table for dinner and with washing up. In the evenings we read. Berthe read different books than I. She particularly loved Virginia Woolf's *Orlando* which to me looked long and dull. Unlike Edith, she made no efforts to broaden my outlook or my talents and seemed to enjoy my company. In return, I became very fond of her.

Berthe and I created a ritual each Wednesday afternoon, as a special treat to mark the mid-point of the five weekdays between Nicky's Sunday departure and his Friday night return. We walked slowly, to suit her pace, to the ice cream parlor in town for a treat, lemon sherbet for her, a chocolate sundae for me. Then we bought *Life* magazine and walked home again. A simple outing but a pleasing and sufficient focal point to the day.

Over the course of that first summer, despite the difference in our ages and our prospects, we became good companions. But docile as Berthe was in her ruined sweetness, it was hard not to leave her. Energy had to rush outward, away from that plaintive grief, away from those eyes that often seemed puzzled at gaiety or happiness. No matter how strongly conscience and affection kept me near her, or love and obligation brought Nicky back nearly every weekend, life and activity kept moving away from the big house in town out to the farm with Piet and Annie.

Piet was not as tall as his son, only about five feet ten or so. His body had settled into a sturdy paunchiness and his trousers always bagged a little. His hair must once have been blond like

Nicky's, but was by then a dun beige color. Fine and sparse, it wafted lightly around his face which had the furrows and lines of late middle age, undistinguished really, without Berthe's or Nicky's fine bone structure. His mouth was always pursed around a cigarette, smoke wafting upward, drawing his eyes into a faint squint, turning his head a little to one side. The eyes were pale as water in a bowl, but shrewd and lively. His arms and hands were strong, the veins prominent, the skin tan and toughened almost like hide. Nothing was young or smooth; he was worn, grooved, seasoned. He had passed beyond physical good looks, yet was an attractive man still. I liked his looks, and especially his manner, the mixture of homespun sturdiness and worldly experience with a hint of spice and adventure. When he was young, he told me, he had run away from his stolid Dutch parents and shipped out as a cabin boy on a freighter. I was thrilled to imagine a time when boys actually could do such things. At age sixteen he had first come to America, but kept on traveling. He had worked at many trades and been many times around the world. With little formal education, he had nonetheless honed his knowledge of the customs and arts of the places he'd seen. He liked building and restoring houses, having skillful hands and a good eye for pleasing lines. For me, in the circle of his family, he was the one who provided the zest, the impetus toward discoveries, plans and activities that enlarged and connected the days to each other in patterns beyond the steady round of meals, marketing, and upkeep.

At first, I was shy and quiet when Piet and Annie and their two excitable Dachshunds came clattering through the house. But as I stayed there longer and Berthe seemed a bit stronger, Piet and I became friendly and easy with each other. In time he referred to me as "la petite" and I became a kind of pet. We both liked the sparkle of the early morning and liked to watch the sun go down across the fields. Often we would stand on the porch of the farm together and gaze outward at the light changing over the hillside.

The first time that Nicky ever looked at me past the point of simple courtesy, so that I could feel his gaze after we had finished speaking, was one day late that July. Nicky was home for the weekend and we were still stiffly polite with each other. I thought his mother might like some time alone with him, so I created an outing for myself. Since we were all expected at the farm for dinner, I decided to bicycle on ahead and stop off to visit Alicia, a girl I had befriended during previous summers with the Schuylers. My plan seemed to concern Nicky and he offered to give me a lift to Alicia's house. I declined and as I pushed off along the road I sensed, with a little hum of exhilaration, that he was looking after me.

As Nicky must have suspected, the ride was longer than I had thought, hillier, and hotter. Alicia was not home, not even expected till August, so I had to keep going, my city legs unaccustomed to the long rising hills and the abrupt blind curves. I grew thirsty, tired, and impatient to be done with it. My impulse was turning into a grueling afternoon. Rounding a turn on the gravelly shoulder of the road, I lost control of the bike and skittered across the gravel. I slithered along a few feet as I fell, scraping my knee and one elbow. Bruised and tearful like any hot sweaty child, I used water from the stream beside the road to daub at my wounds and then slowly limped and rode the remaining two miles to the farm. I was glad no one had witnessed my fall or my exasperated tears. By the time I got there, I was composed enough not to reveal my mishap and in the evening, when Nicky sat beside me at dinner, I said I had had a fine ride. My accident left its mark, though. Bits of tar and gravel that were never properly cleaned out left several faint but permanent gray streaks on my left forearm.

The next weekend Nicky asked me if I would like to ride along with him to Kingston to pick up some lumber and paint for his father. I needed no promise of a library book to sweeten that outing. Two-by-fours and gallon paint cans and a bumpy old pick-up truck, the run-down streets of Kingston, the plaid work shirts piled high in Montgomery Ward's, all these were the trappings of a magic afternoon for me, made vivid by Nicky's glinting blond hair, his clear blue eyes, his appealing accent, his being so tall by my side and paying attention to me.

Little by little we spent more hours together on the weekends. I could see he liked having me around, but he confessed to being bothered that I was only fifteen. That seemed very young to a soldier of nineteen and it struck at his dignity. He worried that people would think he was "robbing the cradle." It was better when we were just by ourselves. Then, our feelings could blossom without concern for appearances. Soon the weekends became reason for living through the weekdays. By August, he told me that he thought about me more and more, and had come to feel that the main reason he came home was to see me. Around that time we began kissing, and somewhat later we sought out secluded places where he could take down the straps of my bathing suit and in breathy excitement we struggled against going "all the way."

I still have a photograph from that summer. Nicky and I are standing beneath an apple tree at the farm. I am leaning back against a wooden picnic table, my face turned upward to look at the tall blond young soldier who is smiling down at me. The date penciled on the back of the photograph indicates that I am fifteen. I look a bit plump. Nicky hunches his shoulders shyly before the camera. We look happy but unsure, not quite grown up, our eyes hold to each other for safety.

During that first summer, every Friday night I slept fitfully in my little room at the top of the stairs. I kept waking to look up at the dense sky, trying to estimate the hour, waiting for Piet's soft tap on my door at 3 a.m. Knowing I couldn't sleep long, I slept little and badly, got dressed too early, pulled the pink sponge curlers out of my hair, and waited for the knock on the door. Then while the others slept, we padded quickly down the stairs and put on our shoes at the front door while shushing the two scurrying Dachshunds whose toenails made cascades of excited clicks on the bare floor. We let ourselves out into the mild huge night and moved quietly across the grass. The sudden start of the car's engine seemed to roar through the silence and Piet and I were off to Kingston to meet the 3:30 a.m. train that brought Nicky home on his weekend pass. We rode quietly each week, my damp newly washed hair smelling of flowery shampoo, the pinpoint of Piet's lighted cigarette tracing small orange arcs back and forth as he turned the steering wheel, the headlights cutting a bright tunnel through the blackness. At the station we paced slowly up and down the platform among the baggage carts till the huge single headlight of the train cut everything into silhouettes and brought us the tall slim silhouette we awaited.

Nicky was always eager to get home. He loathed the army where he was subjected to frequent teasing for his height, his Dutch accent and his innocence of American male humor. Fortunately the war had been over for some time and new recruits were not needed to guard New Jersey at all times, so he got leave almost every weekend.

That summer I first went along to meet the train for a lark in the middle of the night. Then to keep Piet company on the dark ride. Then weeks later, because Nicky and I couldn't wait any longer to see each other. On the ride home, I rode in the back seat, quiet and shy while the men in the front exchanged their laconic bits of news. We were all happy to be there, acting as though the important meeting was between father and son, while I think each of us knew otherwise.

But what did we know? With little hesitation, we each probably would have said that the reunion of the two young lovers was keenest need, deepest pleasure. I was sure of that then. Yet now I remember more vividly the silent dream-like rides out with Piet than I do the happy return trips with the three of us.

I thought of Nicky then as much older than myself, belonging to the world of shining near-adults in their late teens and early twenties. Beside them I saw myself as still unformed, awkward and untried. I felt full of intricate and interesting thoughts and responses, but I had no skills to display them. I could only look in awe at those marvelous young people, envying their worldliness, and nervous and pleased when, as Nicky's friend, they allowed me to be with them. I continued for some time awed by teen-agers several years older than myself. Full adults didn't scare me, only those more nearly adult than I was. Wanting to be old enough for Nicky, I skipped over what would have been a natural next stage in my adolescence and moved directly from spin-the-bottle party games with my grade school cohorts into the heady world of high school graduates and college students on the verge of maturity. They were starting careers, forming passionate attachments, and assuming distinctive personalities. I was desperate to keep up and would have denied fiercely that it was too much for me.

While I was taken up with Nicky and the Van Dorn family, my father brought out a book of his poems. *Meine Reime Deine Reime* (My Rhymes, Your Rhymes) was published in 1946 by Peter Thomas Fisher in New York. The volume contained one hundred and ten of Robert's poems in German, most written between 1933 and 1945, the twelve year period of his exile from Berlin. During these years, he had read aloud various poems to friends and refugee groups in Manhattan. A fellow refugee, Fritz Eichenberg, provided ten illustrations for the collection that captured the gruff humor and bleak irony of the Berlin dialect that Robert used to ridicule and attack the storm troopers and apparatchiks of the Third Reich. But the satire and parody of the illustrations of the poems only partly convey the anger and the underlying sadness of the collection as a whole in which Robert grieved for the sufferings of innocent people and the destruction of everything that had once been honorable or admirable about Germany.

Because the Fatherland's awakened,
Many have to go to sleep
Because long knives' night has come
Corpses are piled deep . . .

No one has to knock to enter
Take an ax to any door
Now the nation has erupted
Like an ulcerated sore.

To mark the volume's publication, my parents gave a dinner party for their long time friends. This evening was different from their usual dinner parties since it ended not with Robert's music but with his poetry. He read aloud, varying sharp satire with regret.

Oh how I'd like once more to visit Werder
At tree blossom time
When Johannesbeer wine
Races in a sweet-sour shock through the body
And on the way back home
Races out again.

Oh how I'd like once more to be in Wannsee
At the free pool
To watch the frolicking
My sweetheart gets a bunch of lilacs
And I get a kiss
And Bratwurst with a beer. . . .

Robert expressed a special grief for the obliteration of the old Berlin, a lusty, disheveled, creative, tolerant city of good food, pretty girls, loyal friends, and lively arts.

That you'll no longer be there
That maybe you

Will be a heap of broken stone
That snakes slide through
Berlin, Berlin, from Spandau to Neuköln,
Just to imagine it, makes me gasp for air.

The small audience in our living room responded actively, nodding with emotion at the feelings expressed, and repeating favorite phrases to each other with evident relish. *"Molle bleibt Molle"* (a beer's still a beer); *"Mutta, schmeiss mahl 'ne Bombe runter,"* (Hey Ma, throw down a bomb).

Robert was clearly gratified by their enthusiasm. "Ja, I always wanted to be known as a poet. That would have pleased me more than fame as a song writer. But then . . ." he added ruefully, "poetry doesn't pay. And I needed money. I had too many people to support to live on poetry alone."

Elke erupted. "*I* never asked you to make money. You can't blame me for that; you're the one who wanted all that high life."

Robert chuckled to avoid a scene. "No, no, Elkelein, I didn't mean you. I meant all those people in the Party, and then my mother, and so on." He turned to another poem and the awkward moment passed.

To me, at fifteen, the poems were less appealing than his songs. The Berlin dialect was unfamiliar; I didn't understand the political satire, and the mixture of wit and grief was too complex for me. I couldn't respond to the homesickness revealed by my father and his friends for their past in a country that had become so brutal. Most of all, I was too taken up with my new attachments in Woodstock to pay much attention to the book.

During the year *Meine Reime, Deine Reime* was published and for some time after, people in Berlin suffered more than they had in wartime. Many of the weak and the elderly succumbed during harsh winters of inadequate clothing, sparse food, and untreated illness. My mother worried about her sister Lotti and their mother in Berlin, but took some comfort from the knowledge that in the American sector her CARE packages could reach them. Communication systems were in ruins and many family members couldn't make contact or even find each other. It wasn't till a year after the war that my grandmother Hedwig learned that her favorite sister, Jenni, who before the war had lived with her in a retirement home, had died of starvation after their forced eviction and separation.

The sufferings were not limited to the city of Berlin. Millions of persons throughout Europe had been displaced from their homes and needed resettlement. Most Jews still remained in the Nazi concentration camps and, except for no longer being gassed or worked to death, they were hardly better treated than they had been under the Nazis. Thousands died from hunger and illness even after the war. President Truman (who was actually a stronger advocate for racial and religious tolerance than Roosevelt had been) initiated America's humanitarian intervention that led to major improvements in nourishment and treatment for those in camps awaiting resettlement.

Liberated Jews were not the only ones to be relocated. A growing stream of people fled to the west from central and eastern Europe before the Russian occupation could reach them. Among them were my mother's youngest sister Irma and her four year old daughter, my cousin Barbara, who had been evacuated to Czechoslovakia during the war. By January 1946 there were four million refugees from the east in Germany and more kept coming. Arriving with nothing, they were quartered in small towns and villages where their numbers soon exhausted food supplies, clothing and other provisions. The strain on scarce resources inevitably led to resentment and hostile incidents.

But at the time, in Woodstock, I knew little about world events and was totally absorbed in my own growing up. It was Nicky who taught me what we called the facts of life during that summer and autumn. Before his kisses and exploring hands on my body, my knowledge had been that of an intelligent child. My mother had given me the required facts about what men and women do but my questions about why anyone would *want* to do that embarrassed us both and we didn't pursue the subject. From movies and novels I learned that sex was supposed to be blissful. From my biology class in high school I learned the molecular details of gestation and the development of the zygote into an embryo. From seeing the troublesome effects of sexual passion on ordinary lives I had a wary notion of its power. But I had no knowledge about how it actually worked, either theoretical or personal. The interludes of kissing and touching that Nicky initiated were exciting, but I felt no need to go further whereas he seemed to have difficulties. His rapid breathing and tense body made me realize that whatever was happening to him was somehow different and more intense. At each "petting" session we agreed that we had to stop before we went too far, but then he had to struggle to regain his composure. Those moments affected me so that his feelings and his breathing seem to become my own, but the empathy was emotional not physical. We were both still so shy that many weeks went by before Nicky at last put my hand over the hard bulge in his pants and said, "Feel how hard I am. We've got to stop, I can't stand it." I was moved by his distress, but more than anything, I was puzzled. I knew the penis was inserted into the vagina, and I knew that a climax would result which was intensely pleasurable. I knew that sperm were released which could cause pregnancy, but I didn't know that all these processes were one and the same. I didn't know that thwarting climax was uncomfortable, even painful. And I'd never even heard of erection.

"Why does it get so hard," I finally asked Nicky. "Does it hurt?"

"No, it feels good except when it goes on too long. It gets hard so that it can go inside a woman," he explained.

I didn't see the necessity. "Why can't it just go in as it is?"

Nicky searched for an analogy to help my understanding. Finally he came up with one. "Well, you can't push a worm through a piece of paper."

Though his image was vivid, I was mystified. Not only hadn't

I known that the penis gets hard, I hadn't known it was most often soft. I'd imagined it somewhat like a finger with its own permanently available rigor. Secretly, steadily through that summer, I continued to learn about the male body in relation to mine.

Like most young people in rural settings, we knew how to fit our natural vitality into the countryside. We knew the best places to swim, to fish, to pick berries or wild mushrooms, and we sought out hidden pine groves, smooth patches of forest floor, and little-used barns to shelter our loving. In good weather, we spent our afternoons at a secluded swimming place where the stream deepened to form a natural pool. Not many people came there because it had no access by car or bicycle. One had to walk through dense woods on one side of the stream or cross several fields on the other. Once in a while, we'd find one or two other people there, but mostly we had it to ourselves. We came there through the fields which rose one after another behind the Van Dorns' house. The walk to the stream without stopping took about twenty minutes but, most often, we stopped. Narrow groves of spruce trees served as natural boundaries between the fields and contained sheltered areas of meadow grass and wildflowers. We actually spent more of our so-called swimming time there than at the stream. We had an old picnic blanket, sometimes even a picnic lunch, and we would lie together, encircled by spruce saplings, in sun-dappled shade not deep enough to harbor mosquitoes but sufficient to shield us from glare and from observation. A pretty forest bower for young lovers, it served us well.

One summer's night, we were part of a group of young people who sang and cavorted on a harvest hayride organized by the Batholomews, friends of the Van Dorns. Afterwards, we climbed up into the hayloft of their barn and looked at the stars through its open side. Nicky and I lay side by side, trying to reach the smooth skin beneath the rough country clothes we wore. Buttons were opened silently, one at a time. Nicky's hand was on my stomach, then my breast. Then he withdrew his hand, shifted his weight, worked the buttons on his Army chinos, and guided my hand downward till my fingers for the first time encircled his bare penis. It felt shockingly huge. Again, I'd imagined it to be about the size of a man's middle finger. The reality alarmed me. This long thick shaft would someday enter me. I couldn't picture it doing so without tearing me apart. Alarm quenched my ardor on the instant, though I tried to give no sign. Meanwhile, after the long built-up excitement, my hand moving tentatively along the shaft toward the tip of his penis brought Nicky over the edge. He quickly turned away from me in the darkness and I could feel his body's soft convulsions. In a while, he turned slowly toward me again and, both quiet now for different reasons, we watched the moon beginning to rise over the open hayloft window.

When I returned home to Riverdale toward the end of that summer, I felt as though I had landed on an alien planet. Instead of green trees and meadows with wildflowers, pleasant country houses and barns beneath the blue-purple curve of Overlook Mountain, there were drab brick apartment buildings, stores, and black tarred pavements softening in the city's heat. Instead of Nicky's warm blue-eyed gaze, there were yawps and whistles from rowdy adolescent boys when I walked into Shapiro's candy store one morning. I wore a T-shirt that I'd worn the previous summer without exciting notice, but it was now tight across my bosom and caused a riotous reception and much teasing. Thereafter I discarded the shirt and avoided the boys. When Lillian phoned to ask if I wanted to go walking with her past boys' homes as we had done before, I said I was too busy. Even being with Lillian alone had become uncomfortable. She wasn't interested in my descriptions of Woodstock or of Nicky, and I was bored by her stories of football games and dances in the gym. We had less and less of mutual interest to share and were both relieved when Labor Day came and we could return to our separate high schools and by now separate lives.

By that first autumn, my status as Nicky's girl was accepted by the Van Dorns. I didn't have to be specially invited to return to Woodstock each weekend. I was expected; it was routine. I boarded the Greyhound bus at 42nd Street each Friday afternoon after school, ate a hamburger for dinner at the Red Apple rest stop midway and arrived at Woodstock in the early evening. Piet met me at the bus stop, Berthe had a cold supper waiting and Annie brought sponge cake which we all shared at the large round kitchen table as we talked about our week's doings. Then an early bedtime in preparation for the nighttime ride with Piet for the Kingston train that brought Nicky. We had all day Saturday and most of Sunday together each weekend. On Sunday evening, we each went back, I on my bus to New York, Nicky on the train to New Jersey

My father had little to say about my changed routine since it seemed to be what I wanted, but my mother worried. "You shouldn't be with only one boy so soon. You should go out with different boys, get to meet different people. You are too young to be so tied down, you're just starting to grow up."

She didn't know anything, I thought. She didn't know how stupid and immature those different boys were or how wonderful Nicky was.

"Nicky and I are happy together; we don't want to be with other people. I love him."

"You *think* you love him. I know you think so, but you don't know what love is yet. This is puppy love. It's the first time you feel like this and you think it will always last. But it passes. You will see. Next year you won't feel the same way, and he is older than you, maybe he won't feel the same either. You should have nice times together but leave each other free. You still have time and many things to learn."

"You don't understand anything!" I flounced tearfully into my room and slammed the door. I was offended by the words "puppy love" and I didn't know how to convince her that our love was true and lasting. The only way was to prove it over time.

More than ever, I was determined to stay close to Nicky and to keep going to Woodstock as often as I could.

Later that autumn, inevitably and not so terrifying after all, came the first time Nicky and I went "all the way." One night that November, I stopped by his room to say good night and in a burst of affection and high spirits he swooped me up and carried me down the hall back to my own room. I though it wonderfully clever, more clever than he had actually intended. I whispered that Berthe who slept downstairs would hear only one person's footsteps to mark my return to bed, and with that encouragement he stayed with me in my four poster bed. Just before dawn, he tiptoed back to his own room. It was a nice first time. After all our petting and skirmishes, I was glad to have accomplished it. I knew it couldn't be announced but I wished that somehow I could be recognized as having moved beyond childhood and beyond adolescent gropings. I knew everything now; I understood all the secrets.

Such innocent smugness amuses me now. But I know that in keeping with my idea of romance, I wanted to see it all as simple and natural, that two young people, Nicky and I, ripened into love-making in instinctive trust of our senses. Maybe so, in some part. The love-making was certainly simple, seemingly natural and from then on frequent as suited our youthful energies. And they are pretty pictures that I recall—no city alleyways, no movie balcony furtive sex or automobile back-seat couplings. My young courting scenes were framed by a natural landscape.

But what was already in my head then was far from simple, anything but natural. My imagination was already crammed with so many fancy notions, so much baloney. I had learned my conception of physical love, like an apt pupil, from movies, from Gothic novels, from columns in magazines aimed at ignorant young women. From novels and films I learned that sex was supposed to be magnificent, simultaneous climax included, and that it was the main avenue to success and power for women. From magazines I learned that sex was a business of technique and simulation. From operas I learned that it could also be danger-ous. My heroines, the *femmes fatales*, the interesting women, had sexual magnetism that could generate ruinous passions in men. Actually, they themselves all died of it, taking with them their lovers' broken hearts. Then there was my mother who cried in the bathroom on the nights my father came home too late, who brightened her hair and reddened her lips to flirt with the mail-man the next morning. I dreamed of marriage, a home, an effortless fidelity, babies, the whole American dream for girls of my time. Yet I could also see that survival depended on being in control of one's feelings. Only in that way could a woman avoid destruction or abandonment such as Berthe had suffered. My confused fantasies blended the folk tales of our era with the ac-tual domestic patterns I witnessed and my own unknown interior life. I think that what for Nicky was truly natural, was for me already filled with anxiety and artifice. I didn't realize it and wouldn't have been able to even come near thinking about it then. It would have been to admit some deep failure to acknowl-edge that I had no experience of genuine orgasm, only ideas of what the trappings should be. And therefore actual intercourse which was a natural release and fulfillment for Nicky was for me essentially a performance. I was not able to face that fact until years later when I could begin to distinguish what I actually felt from what I thought I should pretend to feel. Then I realized that the moments I remembered, those that haunted me, had nothing to do with power or success or sexual artifice, but with something quite differed, a rush of feeling, unbidden and unplanned.

IX

***

Nicky

Though I accepted the menage-a-trois arrangement of Piet, Berthe and Annie without much thought, it was only possible because they suppressed their jealousies. When jealousy came to me, I could barely contain it. The Van Dorns had a small circle of good friends which included the Schuylers, my earlier hosts in Woodstock, and another couple, the Bartholomews, who were artists. Bart was a painter, his wife Sylvia was a potter. They lived and worked in a large rambling house in the nearby village of Bearsville. Delft blue and white tiles framed the fireplace and the old floor boards were bleached to an ashy gray by the fine pottery clay worn into every groove. Bart's paintings and sketches were everywhere, charcoal nude studies of Sylvia that I regarded with antipathy, oil portraits of young girls budding like delectable flowers, still-lifes of fruits or vegetables heaped up and scattered on rough tables, a bunch of black-eyed Susans like yellow stars against a dark wooden wall, colors deep and glowing, chiaroscuro effects of light and dark, brilliance against shadow. Once there was a mock argument; Bart's soft clipped British voice protested that Sylvia had stolen an onion and a tomato from an arrangement he was painting. She insisted with raucous laughter that he was mistaken and anyhow, he had filched the vegetables she'd bought for their dinner stew.

Bart attracted people and there was always a small group of summer art students staying into the fall, following him about, setting up easels near his house, walking the lanes with sketchbooks. He was kind to them, but elusive. Perhaps to get away or perhaps only, as he said, to exercise the horses, he would ride every afternoon. Sylvia rode only occasionally. They owned two golden Palomino horses, striking to see. Astride the golden horse, Bart made me think of King Arthur. I liked him but because Sylvia was most often with him, I spent a good deal of energy avoiding them both. If I knew they were expected, I would urge Nicky into outings that would take us elsewhere. They were family friends, but I detested Sylvia, and feared her. She had intimidated me from the arrogant rush of her first entrance. I disliked the rough voice and her piercing laughter, her cold agate eyes and the magnificent unruly mane of white hair that stormed about her sallow gypsy face. Above all, I was repelled by her aggressive sexuality which, in my young prudery, I thought unsuitable for an old person of forty. She, in turn, looked past me and never spoke directly to me, as if to her I was invisible.

I hated her because, after Nicky and I had been lovers for a few months, he told me that Sylvia had seduced him when he was sixteen. At first I found the idea incomprehensible, then nearly unbearable. I kept after him, asking him questions, how? where? how could he? for how long? He told me that the affair had lasted for two years, during which they had repeated sexual encounters right in the midst of the so-called friendship of the two families and no one suspected. He said he'd been ashamed of it and felt no love for her, but couldn't resist his own body's urgings. Finally, after he went into the Army, he managed to end the liaison by determined avoidance.

The knowledge tortured me. Though it had evidently ended before I ever met Nicky, I couldn't bear to picture them together. From then on I hated Sylvia, hated having to see her. Just seeing her red shawl tossed on a sofa aroused hard red hatred in me. Even worse was that everyone seemed to remain friends as though none if it had ever happened. Nobody knew except Nicky and Sylvia and now me, but it secretly poisoned for me all contacts between the two families. The poison also seeped into my love for Nicky which had seemed simple and sunny and now darkened into complex swings of unruly feelings. I was not his first love as I had thought. He had succumbed to Sylvia; he could succumb to others. I became full of doubts and suspicions, feared his gaze at any pretty woman, and hissed accusations. We quarreled, stormed off in opposite directions, returned, cried, made love again and again, trying to exorcise the demon of my jealousy that threatened to overpower our former happiness.

That winter Nicky was discharged from the Army. He was twenty years old, had served for two years, and was eligible to enter college under the GI Bill. Because he had always enjoyed working with his father to restore and re-design houses, he applied to Columbia University to study architecture. Plans were made for him to start with two classes for the spring semester and then to matriculate to full-time study the following fall. This fit in well with the Van Dorns' yearly schedule. Just after Christmas, their whole entourage shifted to Greenwich Village, and opened the Woodstock house only for occasional weekends. The farm in the isolated countryside remained shuttered, pipes drained, snows unswept from the porches until the following spring assured frostless nights. Their basic living arrangements were transported and duplicated in the Village. Piet and Annie had a three room walk-up flat on Jones Street; Berthe had a studio apartment on Bleeker Street, and during our first winter Nicky had his own tiny flat in a cluster of similar warrens over a warehouse on Christopher Street. Blessedly for me, the Bartholomews remained in Woodstock during winters. With distance between them and us, my jealous fits about Nicky faded and we regained our emotional equilibrium while establishing a new routine in the city.

The space and beauty of the countryside were missing, but for me the winters in the Village were an extension of my sense of Woodstock. City street life went on all year with colorful and oddly dressed people who were, or pretended to be, artists and "Bohemians." Zestful peasant types with eager eyes, abundant hair, and boisterous voices mingled easily with the haunted solitary visionaries who drifted through the streets and cafés. Every corner seemed to have its Italian market glowing with greens, golds, and shiny purples of apples, melons, and eggplants. Clusters of cheeses, garlic, and salami hung from the ceiling in a tangle of cords and netting. It was a delicious world steeped in aromas of coffee, garlic, and spices—a world that had not yet reached mainstream America which was still enamored of frozen vegetables and efficient supermarkets. Each Greenwich Village street also boasted a store-front art gallery or pottery studio, brightly lit and impressively bare of all but the tools and icons of art. Such galleries were in conscious contrast to the antique stores with their welter of flocked velvets, old brass, tarnished silver objects and grimy crystal vases behind dusty display windows. Countless bars and cafés punctuated the stoops and entryways of apartment and row-houses that had been subdivided into cold-water flats or rooms-to-let.

Here, before the Village became fashionable and expensive, art co-existed with poverty. In all but the worst weather, people walked outside, gathered in the cafés, or sat hunched on the benches in Washington Square. Painters leaned their canvases against the iron railing fence of the park. College students loitered with books. That lively scene has since been duplicated in hundreds of cities and incorporated into the commercial world of town planning and artful restoration. But in the 1940s the Village was a special place, regarded with some suspicion but left much to its own devices. Only a few tourists from uptown were drawn by curiosity to see its tolerant and colorful deviance, and incidentally, its art. The atmosphere was energizing in a part of the city I had not known before and seemed like Woodstock urbanized and intensified.

Though I didn't spend nights in the Village, I went there on weekends and after school on most days. Nicky only rarely visited me in Riverdale. I didn't want him to, there was no privacy in my family apartment, and no street life to escape to. The seclusion we had known in Woodstock seemed possible only in his surroundings, near his family and not my own. In Nicky's small room we could spend afternoons, a short while for lovemaking in bed, huddled together under the heavy blankets that the chilly room needed, then in whatever time was left, we made and sipped tea and tried to do some homework. In the late afternoons, I'd either start my hour-long subway ride home, or walk with Nicky over to Jones street for a family dinner. That winter and spring I was a perfunctory student at Hunter High School, and an unresponsive daughter at home. The Village held my essential attention and Nicky and I were full of plans for the future. He would be an architect, and I would be a writer. Our only worries were occasional pregnancy scares when my period was late. During one very long wait, we began to talk solemnly about having to get married, and ended by grinning at each other because the idea didn't seem half-bad. But I remained irregular, unpregnant, and unmarried. For the most part, the life we led at that time suited us and I was as happy as my teen-aged inconsistencies allowed.

I avoided most occasions when my parents and I might be seen as a family unit in public, but one Sunday in 1947, they invited me to the movies. They were eager to see Billy Wilder's film, *A Foreign Affair*, starring Marlene Dietrich as a glamorous German spy who used her wiles to enthrall American soldiers during the occupation of Berlin. It was a crisp autumn afternoon and we walked to the movie theater instead of riding the bus. I walked between them down the woodsy Riverdale Avenue hill, but as we reached the more populous area near the theater, I lagged behind. I pretended interest in shop windows near me, or focused my gaze at shops across the street, slowing my pace until I was half a block behind the middle-aged foreign couple walking arm-in-arm up ahead, the man's dark hat and long dark overcoat muffling his solid figure in contrast to the blonde woman's display of shapely legs under an electric blue cape. Now and then, one of them turned to look back, puzzled at my odd behavior, but I continued to loiter, catching up with them only when we reached the ticket booth. They especially wanted to see this film, not to enjoy Marlene or the repartée, but because they'd heard that it included the first film views of war-damaged Berlin. They dreaded but needed to see for themselves what had happened to their city and probably wanted me to see it also. As the film rolled, they looked past the action and characters in the foreground and gasped at the setting, street after street of bombed out-buildings and pathetic clusters of people grubbing for shelter amid mountains of rubble. Transfixed, my parents watched the patchwork of destruction which had once been the lively home of their youth. And though the rain of bombs had been delivered by the Allies, they always assigned the blame where it belonged. The ruin of their Berlin, and Germany as a whole, was the agonizing but necessary price for finally stopping Hitler.

We walked back up the hill toward home silently. Under cover of darkness I walked between my parents again, holding their hands in sympathy for their grief and shock at having seen what they had only heard tell of before. In the next weeks, as my parents and their friends shared their distress and worried about friends and relatives left in that ruined city, I could listen with fellow-feeling. But their loss was not my loss. I had no memories of the city of my birth and felt no connection with it. Though still father, mother and child, we were no longer natives of the same country.

The following summer, Berthe, Nicky, and I lived again in the big house in Woodstock while Piet and Annie moved back

out to the farm. Nicky expected to return to Columbia University
in the fall. In the meantime, he had agreed to help his father
during the summer with the farm's needed renovations.

The place had been badly run down when Piet bought it. A
porch half hanging off, broken windows, a muddy farmyard littered with heaps of rusted auto parts and old plows. Piet and
Annie, in their need to make a home, were rebuilding, sanding,
painting, changing walls or doorways, finding old furniture at
auctions and refinishing the pieces. The farm was always in a
state of becoming, of designs and projects in progress. A be-
mused suggestion would be followed by long hours of talk. "What
if we move the doorway of the living room?" "How would it be if
you could see the hillside from a window over the kitchen table?"
And then Piet and Nicky would stare long at a wall or a corner,
make sketches and figures on scraps of paper, and tap all around
to find beams and bearing walls. It was exhilarating, gave the
sense of something always in the air, in the imagination, about to
come into being or sometimes to prove unworkable. Practicality
wasn't everything though, the look of things mattered. Annie might
say to Bart who'd stop by, "We'll need one of your paintings right
here, opposite the fireplace. Maybe the one with the apples, those
dark red ones, so we could look at the colors in the evening." Or
she'd urge Edith Schuyler, "I hope you'll weave a nice shawl we
could put by that rocking chair; the room gets chilly in the evenings." Everyone was drawn in to creating the new setting.

The farm also meant living in a mess, with nails and boards
all around, and falling plaster, paint cans, curls of wood, and
shreds of discarded wallpaper. It meant being careful where one
stepped and what one leaned against. It meant not feeling easy
unless one had helped to work at it for at least an hour or two.

One sunny day Piet looked out at the landscape and said, "It
would be nice to have a pond over there. Wouldn't be hard; we
could dam the brook."

"We could even stock a few fish," Nicky agreed.

They walked out for a closer look and then spread out papers on the kitchen table and sketched the design for a scenic little pond to be tucked into the curve of the hill behind the farmhouse. Nicky and I were recruited for the digging needed to widen and deepen the edges of the brook in the agreed upon site. For days, the two of us stood knee-deep in water, wearing bathing suits and wet sneakers in order to brace a foot on the spade as we dug. Then we lugged huge clumps of muddy grasses out of the water to dry out and be scattered in the fields. On those hot summer days it was wonderfully sludgy slithery work, muddy and black, yet cool watery clean all at the same time. Finally we dragged and piled up rocks to build a small dam to hold back the water at one end. Then we watched day by day. In a few weeks of gradually deepening water, it was there, a real pond. We had adjusted nature into a modest beauty that in time on cooler mornings even held the early mists.

I liked making that pond; the results were so definite, and it did not have to be done over and over like the other more cyclical parts of country living. I didn't take to those, though that wasn't clear to me at the time. Most often, while Nicky puttered in the flower and vegetable gardens he made near the house, I was reading. One day, Nicky snatched a book out of my hands.

"You've always got your nose in a book. Why don't you look at what's around you, or play with the animals, or help me with the garden?"

I was astounded. Ever since I had first learned to read, books had been my constant companions, bringing me pleasure, comfort, excitement and escape through many hours which might otherwise have been lonely or boring, Through them I could imagine lives larger and more varied than my own. And not only that. In my family, my reading had always been regarded as a virtue and won me praise for keeping myself so quietly and cheerfully occupied. A few summers earlier when I spent hours absorbed in a book, Edith Schuyler had worried that I might be lonely, but until Nicky's outburst I never thought that my reading might exasperate anyone. The fact that it bothered Nicky left me stunned and speechless. To placate him, I put my book down and joined him in a bit of weeding but grubbing in the soil couldn't compete in interest with Scarlet's misguided longing for Ashley Wilkes.

That summer I also read *War and Peace* and *Anna Karennina,* working my way through the classics with determination. For more appealing reading, the library offered armfuls of historical novels, long intricate family sagas, Gothic romances, and novelized retellings of myths and legends. Whatever cultural improvements I was aiming at, or whatever ambitions I was encouraged to acquire, I was learning avidly from all that enthralling fiction about the real mission and life for women—to capture, captivate, and enchant men. *Gone With the Wind, Tristram of Lyonesse, Forever Amber, The Black Rose,* and still and again, *Jane Eyre* and *Wuthering Heights.* Love and passion, even unto death.

I was especially drawn to the stories of women at the edge of society, sultry young women who could lure men to destruction. I liked the movie *Black Narcissus,* in which the very English Jean Simmons, dipped in dark make-up and wearing a sari and a jewel in her nose, slithered across the screen into the desires of a young prince and spoiled his bright future. Then there was my persistent love for Carmen whose story seemed to become my own, though I couldn't say why it moved me so profoundly. It began with the opera, a boxed set of records which I had received one Christmas, with Rise Stevens in the title role and Robert Merrill as Don Jose. I followed the libretto word for word as the music swept over me, and I played the opera over and over. The story of the fiery gypsy outcast, tormenting one man, attracting another, stirring up such love and passion that it had to cause her death, that story transfixed me. I followed it through whatever variations I could find. Nicky and I went to see dark French movie version at the Thalia Theater in New York. Bizet's music was background to the husky French speaking voices, and the sub-titles added emphasis. Carmen dealing her cards, *"L'Amour . . . La Mort. Encore. Toujours . . . La Mort."* Dark clouds, ominous glorious music. I loved that film.

188 | MARIANNE GILBERT FINNEGAN

Glen Ford and Rita Hayworth also attempted a glossy Technicolor version of Carmen but I rejected it as too pretty and clean. Dorothy Dandridge in *Carmen Jones* was better, but not as good as the opera.

Then the whole saga was transposed and transported to the American west. Though I didn't identify the recurring theme, I was spellbound all over again by it as the horse opera *Duel in the Sun*. Jennifer Jones as Pearl Chavez, the sultry half-breed girl, became my idol. Gregory Peck as Lewt McCanles, the dark humorous amoral brother was a perfect foil. Even Joseph Cotten as Jesse the "good" brother had some appeal, his thrilling voice contradicting his pallid virtue. The film was a feast for all my emerging senses and reverberated through my fantasies.

Pearl Chavez was "the desert flower, quick to bloom, and early to die," wanting a haven, a home, respectability and acceptance in the white Texas world, but betrayed by the heat of her dark Indian blood and destroyed by the passions it aroused. I wanted to look like her, to be her, to recreate myself in her image. I sought and found low-cut Mexican blouses. In Greenwich village, I bought a large copper coin, had it drilled and strung on a chain to wear around my neck, like the medal given to Pearl by Walter Huston, "the Sin-killer." I don't know what made me seize on Pearl Chavez, the new-world descendant of the gypsy Carmen, but these women were in some morbid way my ideal alter egos. Both outcasts of mixed blood and uncertain heritage, they compelled attention through their beauty and sexuality. Prevented from entering the white world, they could at least captivate and destroy a small part of it. Not, of course, without being destroyed themselves, but to me their destruction was hard to distinguish from triumph. For me also, the theme was love and death. Pearl Chavez embodied sex appeal and the power it could bring, a power so strong that men would fight over her to the death. I was transfixed by the story and especially by the final scenes in the movie when Pearl, fatally wounded in the exchange of gunfire with her outlaw lover Lewt, painfully dragged herself across the rocks and crags of a barren landscape to die in his arms. *"Toujours . . . la Mort."*

And while I was cultivating love and destruction, Nicky was growing nasturtiums and corn, caring for small animals, bringing things to fruition in the real world. He would call me from the yard to put in some seeds or help with the weeding, hoping I'd gain some affinity for the soil. I liked seeing flower buds unfold, small green undefined nodules turn into shiny tomatoes, cucumbers or string beans, but I thought it was easier to buy food in the store. I didn't find animals all that interesting either. Ducks, geese, goats, piglets, chickens, a cow, a horse, whatever animals claimed Nicky's attention in whatever season, I watched his care for them politely. He even spoke with zest of buying a pet monkey to keep in his Greenwich Village flat for company during winter months in the city. To me that seemed an unattractive idea; why did we need more company than each other? In Woodstock I stroked whatever young animal seemed to want stroking, hated to see any creature in pain, but was basically unmoved by animal behavior and bored by their incessant care and feeding. Certainly I was not promising material for a country life.

Probably because we were so young, Nicky and I, we didn't need to think about how different we really were. We liked each other's shyness and independence. We weren't at ease with typical American teens and we liked the security of being independent together. Of course we were bound by sexual excitement. But though we came to spend most of our time together, we were not the same. I was bookish, dreamy, and urban; my head was full of words and fictional characters. He was practical, inventive, attuned to the cycle of growing things and seasons. He wasn't in love with language as I was; but he was far more capable in the natural world. Whereas I loved to look at and dream over the countryside, he loved to shape it and make it bring forth its bounty. I liked the life in Woodstock mainly because it contained Nicky and his family shielded me from the charged atmosphere of my home. He loved it for itself. I remember his pleasure in the red and yellow nasturtiums he had planted, his pride in the chicks and goslings he'd hatched in an incubator, and his happiness each autumn when we brought bushels of apples from the farm to the cider mill to have them crushed and strained into juice, till all the air and the ground and even our clothes and hair were drenched with the smell of apples. That was happiness for him; he was in tune with his world.

Who knows what we would have made of it, of each other, if we'd had more time, more years to find out who we were or would become. Perhaps I would have frustrated him with my restlessness; perhaps he would have bored me. But I remember once I saw him ride Bart's Palomino across the hillside, his legs a little too long for grace, but in harmony with the horse's motion. He was my hero then, blond and supple and young. I don't want to glamorize him after all this time, it would be too easy to do. He was just an appealing boy who might never have achieved anything remarkable. But he was gentle and kind and no matter how objective I try to be, I do not think there was darkness in him.

By 1947, two years after the war's end, the hostility between the United States and the Soviet Union in Europe penetrated into domestic American politics. America grew convinced that the Russians were seeking to expand their empire and dominate the western world. To avoid this possibility Congress approved the Marshall plan, the sustained effort of American aid that helped to rebuild and strengthen the countries of Europe. Yet Americans still feared Russian nuclear attacks and subversion of their institutions. The young people I knew felt alarmed and disillusioned at the speed with which everyone found a new enemy to fear. Our hopes of peace after the end of the war were all too quickly replaced by talk of Soviet sneak attacks, of bomb shelters, civil defense drills, and worries about radiation.

The fears of communism escalated when the House Un-American Activities Committee was formed to ferret out communists and communist sympathizers in government, business, or other sensitive positions. The Committee began its hearings with the Hollywood movie industry which was known to have a good number of foreign writers, directors, and actors. During its first year, the Committee indicted ten film industry people who refused to cooperate or give up names of others. In fear, Hollywood itself created a "blacklist" of alleged communist sympathizers who would not be hired. Over the next decade over three hundred writers, directors and actors on the blacklist were refused work and had their careers ruined.

My family and their friends watched these developments with mounting alarm. They had lived through the early Hitler days when Jews and artists were excluded from work and denied the rights of citizens. To see the beginnings of similar attacks and exclusions here in America during the 1940s seemed an ominous re-enactment of their earlier experiences. (They could not help drawing parallels either then or during later crises in America such as John F. Kennedy's assassination, the investigations that followed, and the later machinations of Watergate. As each of these events unfolded, they reminded refugees of similar former German episodes and signaled for them the dangerous slide toward political catastrophe.)

During that second summer with Nicky I began to realize that his friends, those young adults of nineteen or twenty whom I so admired, had their own insecurities. Even for them there were discrepancies of age and knowledge, and gulfs of experience they couldn't cross. One Sunday afternoon we gathered at the Big Deep, the spot where the stream that meandered all through Woodstock widened and deepened. It was the largest natural swimming hole in the area, close to the road so that it served as a popular gathering place for young people in the summers. Rock ledges formed cantilevered shelves over the curving stream banks and provided natural platforms for sunbathing and picnicking. Woodstock "natives" and tourists mingled there, though often in separate groupings. That Sunday, Nicky and I went there with a group of his friends from high school days. Their high spirits set the mood; with everyone laughing and a lot of horseplay in and out of the water. But at one point, Nicky drew apart and climbed over the ledges to another young man, sitting off to one side. He looked pale and somewhat older, and he sat quietly in the sun without making a move to swim. They sat together for a while, then Nicky returned, quite subdued. "That's Gareth Glenn," he said, "he just got back."

In answer to my murmured questions, he explained that Gareth Glenn had been a few years ahead of him in school, graduating during the war. He had gone into the Army and been a soldier in real wartime combat where he had been badly wounded. After a very long stay in a military hospital, he had just come home to Woodstock. We were all silent for a while, trying not to stare. Later that afternoon, when Gareth stood up and turned around, I could see the long red scar on his back and when he walked back to the path, he limped. I wondered how it must feel to come back to a summer swimming hole and exuberant teenagers with such wounds on one's body and God knows what scars on one's soul. I saw, too, that the young men I looked up to were themselves in awe of that other level of experience which marked Gareth Glenn like a brand and set him apart, perhaps forever.

Then, one afternoon just at the beginning of the fall semester at Columbia, Nicky fainted in class. Nothing like that had ever happened to him before and we thought it might be the start of a flu since he mentioned dizziness and a sore throat. But these faint warnings did not lead to flu and did not go away. They were clues that something else might be wrong and eventually led to tests, treatments and procedures that changed our lives completely.

The first diagnosis, the only one I ever heard officially, was of a tumor in Nicky's throat. Radiation therapy was prescribed and for that Nicky entered New York Hospital, a gleaming medical palace of wide corridors and impressive technology. As the weeks passed, Nicky grew alarmingly thin under the treatments. One side of his chin was swollen and stained by a rust-colored burn. He had no appetite, was constantly nauseated, slept most of the time. I went to his hospital room for several hours every afternoon after school and on weekends. I brought him what news I could of the world outside his hospital room, but he soon couldn't maintain real interest in anything beyond his own stricken body. He talked little but my presence reassured us both because it maintained our continuity. Mostly, I read or did my homework at his bedside and then left for my subway ride home in time for seven o'clock supper. Sometimes I ate with the Van Dorns. It was my junior year in high school. We all waited for Nicky to get better, but it seemed a slow process. To keep him company during daytime hours, his family and I began to schedule our hospital visits in alternating shifts. After every radiation dose, the doctors held brief conferences with Piet or Berthe in the hospital corridor. They claimed the tumor was shrinking. On days when Nicky seemed stronger and could sit up for longer periods we were sure of a turning point, the beginnings of an upward arc of recovery. On days after treatments he was weak, nauseated or fretful, and then our hopes were put aside. The months crept by.

After the war ended, my mother was able to stop her daily commute into Manhattan. Friends had introduced her to Kate Bernhardt, a lovely stylish woman who was editor of the *Vogue Pattern Book* and also worked for *Harper's Bazaar*. Kate soon became a good friend. She admired Elke's stylish clothes and when she learned that Elke had herself designed and sewn most of them, Kate arranged for contracts with the couturiers who advertised in the magazines and pattern books. Thereafter, Elke made woolen coats and suits that appeared in glossy full-color magazine pages to illustrate fashionable clothing that could be made from patterns. Elke sewed at home, traveling into the city only for fittings and to deliver the completed garments. Pleased as she was to avoid the long daily commute back and forth to work, she was not good at pacing herself during her assignments. Every few weeks she brought home a parcel containing a pattern, a bolt of fabric along with designated threads and trimmings, all selected by the manufacturer. With satisfaction at her newest commission, she showed me the materials—beautifully soft camel's hair wool for a coat, or a salt and pepper tweed for a suit. Then she put the bundle on top of the bookcase in the living room and left it there for two or three weeks while she enjoyed the freedom of having completed her previous assignment. She went shopping, visited museums and art galleries, had lunch in town with friends, read books, and sometimes even sewed clothes for herself and for me at a relaxed pace. But one day during each commission, I'd hear a gasp and a moan as she looked at the calendar and noted with horror that the first fitting was scheduled for the following week.

At that point, rushing about in her see-through nylon peignoir and silver mules, she swept everything off the large Queen Anne table that served as dining table, desk and sewing station. She unfolded the fabric and started to pin and re-pin pieces of tissue-paper pattern to the wool, fitting the pieces close together to save fabric, turning them to follow the weave. In the next days, she cut and basted pieces together and the nearer the day of the fitting loomed, the more intense her concentration, the longer the hours, the more frantic the pace. Often she summoned me to stand in for a tailor's dummy and try on the curve of a shoulder, the lay of a collar. Something was always wrong, had to be ripped out, re-pinned, re-fitted, sewn again. With each re-doing, Elke grew grimmer and more anxious about the approaching deadline. As she worked, she muttered to herself, "*Trottel*" (idiot), "*Nein, nein, es ist zum kotzen*," (No, no, it's hopeless!). As the fitting day approached, she worked later and later, eleven o'clock, midnight, and beyond, hunching over her work like a coiled spring, sewing as fast as she could. Sometimes, if a sleeve persisted in bunching, or the darts in a jacket refused to lie flat, she had to ask for a postponement of a fitting or a completion date. Even so, the last day or so, she worked till dawn. When the accursed garment was finished at last, she was a drawn trembling wreck.

One morning when I woke up, I found her still at the sewing machine pulling out the last basting threads of a lovely cherry-red suit. She looked up at me, squinting over her glasses, her face unusually flushed.

"I'm just finished," she said in a faint voice. "But my head hurts. I think I'm getting a fever."

I put my face against her cheek. She felt very hot. The suit was to be delivered that afternoon but she was clearly in no shape to make the trip.

"You want me to take it?" I offered. "I could drop it off on my way to the hospital to see Nicky."

"No, you couldn't. You wouldn't know where to go." But the idea took hold. "Maybe I could telephone to say you were bringing it . . ."

"And you could give me the directions, and go to bed where you belong."

So it was decided and I carried the carefully boxed suit on the IRT down to Seventh Avenue and Thirty-Fourth Street and walked a few blocks through the crowded sidewalks of the garment district to the designated address. I took a dingy elevator up to the studio where the cherry-red suit would be photographed on the model it had been fitted for. An underfed young man emerged from behind a gaggle of cameras and lights as I carried my box into the large barracks-like room. He greeted me by pointing to a curtain across a doorway at the back. "You can change in there."

For a moment I wasn't sure what he meant, then realized he thought I was the model. Me! Enormously gratified, I explained that I was just delivering the suit and left it with him, but as I returned to the subway and continued on my way to the hospital, I floated in pleasure at being mistaken for a real model. It meant

I was no longer just a pretty teen-ager, I looked like a grown-up. And not just any grown-up, a model! The compliment was ample reward for having done a favor for my mother.

Each time, she made the whole process of completing a tailoring commission a trial by ordeal. When the color photograph later appeared in a magazine, with her suit or coat looking ever so elegant on a model slim as a greyhound, then Elke could take pleasure and pride in her handiwork, but only in the aftermath, never in the doing. Yet aside from the final week of each commission when her obsessed frenzy seeped through every room, she preferred the work at home to her former jobs. Even though she couldn't manage her time well, it was hers to manage. She was earning money now not as an employee but as an independent craftswoman and that brought her a little closer to the self-directed work of artists whose talents she so admired.

But not yet close enough to satisfy her ambitions. She wanted more than working with her hands. She wanted to work with her head, to be creative like my father with whom she was in endless competition, or to be intellectual and brilliant like her friends Hannah Arendt and Heinrich Blücher. Elke was full of thwarted and confused aspirations. Sometimes, she wanted to be known for her wit and beauty. She spent hours on her clothes and make-up and saying she hoped to be like Ninon de L'Enclos, the famous French courtesan who captivated lovers until in her seventies and achieved wealth and influence through the men she attracted. Then she would scrutinize my appearance and strive to make me more fashionable. At other times, she was happy that I was taking Latin, learning about Greek mythology and reading Shakespeare at Hunter High School. She always regretted that her formal education had been inadequate and incomplete and tried to persuade me to pay attention to her frustrations.

"You've got to have a profession," she warned me. "It's the only security. You have to think about what you want to do and prepare for it. It can't just be marriage and babies. You'll be trapped; you won't have any independence or respect without a profession of your own."

In these warnings, she was at least twenty years ahead of her time, but the culture didn't support my mother's concerns and I saw them as having little bearing on my own future. All I wanted was for Nicky to get better so that we could have the life we hoped for. Marriage and babies was what I wanted and I was sure that would be enough to make me happy. As an afterthought I decided that if I wanted more someday, I could always be a writer.

Though I had seen my father concentrate on his writing and composing day after day, I assumed that his talent had always been fully formed. I had no idea of apprenticeship in a craft, nor did I conceive of an artist's continual trial and error, or the need for practice, practice, practice. And I didn't think much about my future beyond vague expectations that when I was ready, inspiration would strike like lightning from above and I would write, if not the great American novel everyone was looking for, at least an important one.

The next spring, Nicky was discharged from the hospital. He wasn't quite cured, the doctors gave us to understand, but he had reached the point where he couldn't tolerate more radiation. By then the skin on his right cheek and throat was dark brown and crusted, and his body was emaciated. Perhaps he would feel better once the treatments stopped and he was able to eat again. Surely, he would begin to recover when he was in his home back in Woodstock. Nicky himself was deeply glad to be going home, convinced that there he would begin to find his way back to health. It was inconceivable that he wouldn't.

Annie went to Woodstock to open the house and get things ready for his arrival. The rest of us drove there in a borrowed station wagon, with Nicky lying on a mattress in the back and me curled up beside him. Piet drove. Berthe, beside him on the front seat, kept turning to look back at Nicky to smile at him and reach to squeeze his hand, biting her lips with worry. The ride seemed long. Outside it was still cold enough to hold patches of snow here and there in the woods along the highway. Once back at the Woodstock house, we bustled about helping Nicky upstairs to his own room and making him comfortable in bed. That night, we were all relieved to be done with the huge efficient hospital and we hoped that it had helped him.

He did not get better. He spent little time out of bed and Edith Schuyler arranged to have a hospital bed brought in so he could shift position more easily. She came every other day to bathe him, take his temperature, and check his progress. When school ended and the summer began, my third summer with Nicky, I returned to stay in the upstairs room I had come to think of as my own. Down the hall, in his room with the shades half drawn, Nicky lay weak and disfigured. Home and the peace of the country were not restoring his health. Our hopes changed to inchoate prayers for a turning, a miracle.

Then Woodstock saw a dynamic new arrival. Dr. Giorgio Amanti came from afar, respectfully summoned by the family to examine Nicky. He had been preceded by leaflets, letters and testimonials announcing his remarkable cures. For a great sum, he agreed to treat Nicky with his new healing drug. Dr. Amanti was a solemn stocky man, with dark compassionate eyes, and a deep Italian-accented voice. Carefully, he outlined the course of his cure by which, over several weeks, the contents of a series of little phials would make Nicky well. We sat around the big kitchen table, plying Dr. Amanti with sherry, coffee and little cakes, hearing that marvelous voice rail bitterly against the medical establishment which bungled their technology and prevented cases like Nicky's, and even far worse ones, from being healed by the remarkable drug he had discovered. Nicky would get well, "with the Almighty's help," Dr. Amanti assured us, dark eyes glowing, and we all sipped sherry with fervor.

For two weeks he stayed in town at the Van Dorns' expense and came faithfully every three days to administer the injections himself. Nicky seemed stronger, eager to assist in his own recovery. After that, Dr. Amanti was called onward to other stops on his life-giving mission. Before leaving, he entrusted to Edith the schedule of remaining injections for the next four weeks. He prophesied noticeable improvement in the fourth and fifth week of treatment, and then again after the full series of injections had been given and absorbed by Nicky's body which would then return to health. Dr. Amanti was available by long distance telephone calls through the fourth week. Then he could no longer be reached at the number he had given, or anywhere else.

It took me a long time to fathom what had happened. For years I thought that he believed in his own cure and was distressed when it failed. Those large warm eyes, that compelling Italian voice. Later, when I realized what he was, part of me remained incredulous. I could not, still cannot, see how anyone could deliberately exploit the desperate hopes that hover around the dying. He knew, of course, that the surge of hope and energy brought by the initial promise of his "cure" worked to make patients seem better and stronger at first. He knew when hope alone could no longer maintain that brief vigor, when suspicion and questions would begin. By stages, he carefully increased the distance between himself and those keeping vigil. He knew when disappointment would set in, when hopes would fail, and he was sure to be gone by then, as inaccessible to anguish and outrage as if he had never existed.

X

***

Leaving Woodstock

The long summer wore on. Aside from a local Woodstock doctor, Edith Schuyler and myself, only his family saw Nicky. He was too frail and disfigured for company. Bart and Sylvia came occasionally for quiet visits, but they talked with Piet, Berthe, and Annie in the kitchen and never came upstairs to Nicky's room where I sat by his bed. The long ordeal made my jealousy of Sylvia seem trivial, beside the terrible point. Whatever Sylvia had done was now weightless whereas I, in the shifting of balance of time, had become family, at Nicky's side for all the world to know. There was no more talk of making other friends, no more cautions about settling one's affections too soon or too exclusively on one person. My parents worried about the strain of the long illness but could not ask me to desert him, and the Van Dorns were glad now that I was there, glad that Nicky still had his girl.

I turned seventeen that summer. Things had changed with me, almost imperceptibly but steadily since the time two years earlier when Nicky and I began. In that beginning I worried about his being so much older and so much more assured. The four years between us seemed a huge span and the girls of his age seemed so much more complete and more desirable than I at fifteen. I had been desperate then to be older, to look slimmer, taller, more sophisticated, and to speak easily with wit and charm. Not knowing how to do these things, not understanding that Nicky loved me for my particular self, I had feared all the beautiful girls and all the smooth young men, and had clung tightly to our shared privacy. Gradually though, without my knowing it, I myself became smoother, sleeker, more sure. I grew accustomed to the whistles of workmen in the city streets, the glances of men when I entered rooms. My new beauty made me restless, coming as it did in the long sad time when Nicky grew steadily weaker. He looked at me, when he could get past his own pain, with sadness and envy. Though he admired the bloom of my health and strength, it was flagrant difference between me and all he could no longer meet or be. Sadness and unspoken dread wore away at us as I tried to stay close beside him.

But the unused energy of my youth was there, too, always there. Out of that energy, despite itself, came one of those moments when inside the receptive brain a camera's shutter seems to open, register an image, and keep it forever, apart and distinct from the ordinary passage of events.

I can still see the leaves of the arbor rippling in the sunlight as I stood one morning in the living room looking out at the terrace. I wore a new Mexican blouse with bright embroidery. With the image of Pearl Chavez in mind, I wore it low around my shoulders. Upstairs Nicky was asleep in his dim hushed room but here, where I stood, warm sunlight flooded over me. In a half-trance, I didn't move when I heard the front door open as Piet, Annie, and the two little dogs clattered into the house.

"Ou est la Petite?" I heard Piet ask in hall, using the hushed tone we had all taken on to avoid disturbing any sleep Nicky might get. Then he stepped into the room where I stood. I turned toward him a little, smiled, and then put my hand up to the antique copper coin on its chain around my neck.

"Do you like my new blouse?" I asked.

He came to stand beside me and put his arm companionably around my waist as he had often done when we looked at the fields or out over the pond at the farm. It was a paternal gesture, familiar to us both. But this time, as we stood quietly, he looked at my bare shoulders and slowly moved his hand upward from my waist to my breast. I did not move, scarcely breathed, stayed within the circle of his arm. Sunlight. Sunlight everywhere, all around us. Slowly, softly, he stroked my breasts. Then suddenly he stopped, kissed me quickly on the cheek, and told me briskly that I looked very nice. Then he left the room. I stayed there as I had been, in stunned unthinking bliss, the sun warm on my shoulders, the coin warm at my throat.

In the months after that, I would go with Piet on made-up errands in the car, or for walks in the fields. Each time, for a few moments, he would touch my breasts, kiss me, lightly at first but, in time, he kissed me fully on the mouth. No more than that, he never removed my clothing. And as for me touching him, that was unthinkable. His body seemed unknowable, far removed from me by age and dignity; the barrier of his clothing was impassable. I wasn't even interested in seeking him out, wanted only those moments when his hands were on me, a trancelike suspension of thought and action that seemed to last for hours. I remember lying back on the meadow grass in the high field behind the house, with him sitting up beside me. We would talk little, feeling the peace of the afternoon. Then he'd turn to lean over me, as I knew he would, to stroke my face, my shoulders, my breasts, and I'd look up through half-closed eyes at the sun making his hair a fleecy nimbus around his worn face, and the blooms of Queen Anne's Lace swaying over us like white stars in the blue-gold day.

I don't know why he wanted that and no more. Perhaps the needs of his age and my youth fitted together in this soft pleasure that held us rapt, but sought no higher pitch, no resolution. It took us away from the imminence of death and took nothing away from others. It made no claims for itself, did not seem to ask more than we gave it. We both continued to know that I was Nicky's girl. When we returned to the house after our excursions, I'd go straight up the stairs to Nicky's room to see how he was, to get him what he might need, and to read in the armchair by his bed.

Strangely, I didn't feel that I betrayed Nicky. I never worried about it. So long as he lived, and even after that, I was at his side. I stayed by his side until he died, that much I can say in my defense. I knew I loved him, knew I was his girl. It was only later that I no longer knew who I was or to whom I belonged.

How old was Piet, really? I'll never know. Berthe was fifty-five when Nicky died, Piet was older. Sixty? Sixty-five? If I could see him now, I could estimate his years better than I could then when I knew none of the time-lines of aging and could see only the results. Nicky and I had been together for two years and during that time Piet and I had grown friendly and easy with each other. We were good companions. The other part, the sexual current between us, came only later when Nicky's illness had gone on for a long time. It made another bond between us then, hidden and warm, somehow not exclusive. During Nicky's long illness, those intervals became a hidden fund of energy, a time when the body could assert its secret life, its own elemental opposition to death.

On the morning of August 24, 1948, I went by subway from Riverdale to the Court House in lower Manhattan. The Bureau of Immigration and Naturalization decreed that I should now individually be sworn in as an American citizen. Until that time, my status had been attached to that of my parents. They had applied for citizenship soon after their arrival in this country and after the mandated five year waiting period they and I, as their dependent child, were granted citizenship in 1945. No national affiliation was more valued; no document more sought after than an American passport. For my parents, as for countless others who had fled from persecution, the citizenship papers and the passport signified both freedom and safety. An American citizen had rights—freedom from persecution by foreign governments, the right to privacy and freedom from oppression by any government powers, freedom to travel, freedom of speech and of peaceful assembly—and these rights if threatened would be defended by the American government. When my parents and I became American citizens, they felt relieved and protected. By 1948, however, my inclusion in my parents' status was no longer automatic. As a young adult, I was required to declare my own intentions and wishes regarding my nationality.

For me there was never the slightest question or hesitation. I felt myself to be American and not for a moment would I have chosen to be anything else. And so I waited with several others in the Court House until a government official arrived to induct us into citizenship. We lined up before him, raised our right hands as instructed, with the expectant hush slightly marred by the jangling of my five silver bangle bracelets. The official read the oath; we repeated it after him, swearing our allegiance to the United States of America and renouncing fealty to "any other kingdom, state, or potentate" (a phrase I found compelling enough to remember ever after). It was a solemn moment, oddly removed from my activities and concerns at the time. Though my official new status did not affect my daily life, it did provide me with convenient documentation. Henceforth, whenever asked for identification, I no longer had to produce a document explaining that my Berlin birth certificate had been destroyed in the war, nor did I have to further explain why said document listed my birth name as Marianne Winterfeld. Now I possessed a citizenship paper which correctly identified me as a naturalized United States citizen with my American name of Marianne Gilbert.

During that same year of 1948 we were hearing more about relatives in Europe. With the war over, my parents were gradually able to receive regular news about family and friends left behind. I heard about my little German cousin Barbara who was seven years old and had lived in circumstances very different from ours. Early in the war, the German government had sent women and children out of Berlin to escape the bombing raids. Barbara, then a baby, and her mother, Elke's youngest sister Irma, were evacuated to Czechoslovakia. Irma's husband was in the German army but served in Finland throughout the war and saw no action. After the war, the family was reunited and subsequently relocated by the Allies to Bavaria. They were among four million refugees from the east, many fleeing from the Red Army. They were quartered in small towns and villages where their numbers soon exhausted food supplies, clothing and other provisions. The Bavarian farmers strongly resented having refugees quartered in their homes, especially Prussians whom they had long disliked. There were no jobs for them and very little money.

Irma had to beg for food. In letters to my mother, she called it "hamstering." She went to the farmhouses and asked for food at each door, till she got enough to make a meal for the family, like a hamster getting a little bit here and stuffing it in his cheek to save it, then a little bit more there, till he gets enough to eat.

When the war first ended, transport and communication systems around Berlin were in ruins and civilian travel in or out of the city was not possible. But by 1948, at least in the western-occupied sectors of Berlin, the post-war conditions of extreme shortages were getting somewhat better. A massive effort on the part of the Allies helped to supply the city with essential food, fuel, medicines, and supplies toward rebuilding housing. In that year, Irma took her little daughter to see her family in Berlin. To get to the city, they had to go through the Russian sector. The Russians didn't allow people to cross the land they held, but people secretly crossed anyway to see their families. Irma described how she and little Barbara walked along a country road to cross the border at night. Every time they saw the lights of a car in the distance, they ran to the side of the road and crouched in a ditch till it passed. Irma tried to make it seem an adventure for Barbara and told her that if they were ever stopped, she was to say, 'We're going to see our grandmother.' People believed the Russians were sentimental about family, especially mothers, and Irma hoped that was true. She did not tell Barbara the other stories about the Russians, about the brutality and the rapes after the war that had terrorized the defeated Germans.

They weren't caught and Barbara didn't have to use the phrase that her mother had put into her mind like a charm to ward off capture. They succeeded in reaching Berlin. For the first time in years, Irma saw her mother, Hedwig, and her sister Lotti and spent two weeks with them in their apartment.

During their visit, the Russians banned all ground traffic in and out of West Berlin, cutting off essential food and supplies. This blockade made Irma and Barbara's return trip to Bavaria impossible by either train or car. The Americans flew them in a cargo plane back along the air corridor between Berlin and West Germany. It was Barbara's first flight, noisy, uncomfortable in makeshift hammock seats, and wildly exciting for a child. It was also one of first flights in the heroic Berlin Airlift.

After the war, Russia had clamped down on the countries under Soviet control in Eastern Europe, wanting to demonstrate the strengths and benefits of the communist form of government. According to Stalin and the communist leaders, this would only be possible if the emerging communist economies were protected from the corrupting influence of western capitalism. As Winston Churchill noted the progressive sealing off of the Eastern bloc, he memorably termed it an "iron curtain" descending across Europe.

The growing contrast between the rebuilding of western Europe and the stagnation of the eastern countries was nowhere more evident than in the two Germanys, and the focal point of that contrast was Berlin, the divided city deep within Russian occupied territory. While other borders could be closed with guards and barbed wire, Berlin with its city-wide networks of streets and public transport lines provided an easy entrance point for the thousands of people who kept fleeing from east to west, desperate to get away from Soviet oppression. The Russians began to look for a way to stem the tide. In March 1948, they began to interrupt rail, road and water transport in and out of Berlin. By June, they closed all Allied traffic through their zone, thus sealing off the city's American, British and French sectors from the rest of Germany. By blockading essential transport of food and supplies from the West, the Soviets hoped to drive the Allies from the city and out of East Germany. Instead, the Allies responded by refusing to leave Berlin. To save it, they created the famous *Luftbrucke*, an air bridge across which they flew tons of food, medicines, coal and other materials needed to keep the threatened sectors alive. Their determination and support gave heart to the people of West Berlin who stood firm, enduring hunger, cold, and intimidation rather than give up and be absorbed into the Soviet bloc. The Berlin blockade and the response of the Allies in the airlift marked the beginning of the Cold War. From then on, the western nations would think of the Soviet Union, rather than Germany, as the enemy.

My family watched the day-by-day success of the airlift intently, knowing how vital it was. Even after the blockade ended, my mother prepared and sent packages to Berlin every few weeks through CARE, an organization that provided transport and delivery for homemade packages or prepackaged vital food-stuffs for people in Europe and England. Lotti wrote to say how much they appreciated each package and my mother sent whatever she could. A special shelf in our kitchen cupboard served as storage space for the packets and cans intended for mailing and we always had a supply of brown wrapping paper, pieces of saved string, and customs forms ready for making up the next package.

The long separation from her family was hard for my mother. "I haven't seen my mother for ten years," Elke lamented. "She's been through so much, and she's getting old. I'm afraid she'll die and I won't see her again. And Lotti, too, she's lost everything. I wish I could go there, but it's not possible now."

Meanwhile, in Woodstock Dr. Amanti had faded out of reach and the summer drew to a close. In Nicky's room, on that hospital bed, he and I made love for the last time quietly while the family was downstairs. That afternoon was the last time he had strength enough to raise himself up over me. I can still see the medicine bottles and tubes, the glass with the thermometer glinting in a sliver of sunlight, the blue and white striped Kleenex box, and his pale ruined face looking down at me as he braced himself and moved in me, apologetic, grim, trying to reclaim an essential element of life's ground. I can feel the too-fragile weight of him as he spent himself, sank forward onto me, and my arms circled too easily around him. We did not either of us expect another time.

By early September he was frighteningly weak and had trouble breathing. In dread and despair, his parents arranged for an ambulance back to the city to the last hospital.

The last hospital was not like the first. In the last hospital, the hallways were narrow and dimly lit, the rooms were worn and furniture and curtains were dingy. They didn't have shiny mysterious medical equipment. They got patients when the bright shiny equipment had failed. Nicky was brought there in September, struggling for breath. Over the months his voice had grown muffled and hoarse; swallowing was a torment. The doctors did a tracheotomy to clear a passage in his throat, and began intravenous feeding to restore some strength. From then on he could no longer speak but he did rest easier. For a while he was able to write short messages on paper, but soon that became too great an effort. He made his needs known by signs and glances.

It's hard to describe what he looked like then. Once during that last summer, even before the inroads of the final weeks, Nicky caught sight of himself in a mirror and fell back in shock and horror. After that, we made sure to have no mirrors of any kind near him.

Always, he lives for me in two such different ways. First is the way I still find him in the few photographs I have. Old as these are, I can fill in the colors of life. Nicky, tall, young, healthy, with clear blue eyes, an unruly shock of blond hair on his head, with tiny blond points of light on his arms. There was still much of the gangly grown-too-fast boy about him, with adulthood not yet quite achieved. But I think he would have grown into a strikingly handsome man.

During his last year, the other image I can't help but also see, gradually imposed itself. Toward the end, the body is skeletal, the tendons drawing into the fetal position of prolonged pain or disuse. Radiation treatments have left the hair patchy and drab, and burned a huge crusted wound onto the side of the face and throat, a wound that never heals. The eyes are dull, the poor face with its burned skin is swollen on one side, more and more as the weeks go by, so that the mouth is distended and can no longer close, and the features are misshapen and grotesque. A heartbreak to look at; a nightmare to think that he might know.

As his lungs filled with fluid, a machine like a medical vacuum cleaner to clear his lungs was wheeled into his room. Nicky's parents could not bring themselves to use it and summoned a nurse when it was needed. Annie and I learned to do it ourselves, making less of a stir for him. It wasn't hard. It meant listening to his breathing and, when it became too clogged, removing the filter from the metal tube in his throat and probing down into the opening with the machine's little nozzle so that it could suction matter from the windpipe. Not hard to do if one wasn't squeamish. I could even feel grimly glad to be able to pull the poisonous sludge from the sick body. Nonetheless, one couldn't help but know how deeply diseased the whole organism had become and because Nicky now needed almost constant monitoring, his parents decided to supplement the hospital's nursing staff. They summoned Edith to come from Woodstock to be in charge of his care.

Yet he was still Nicky. Since he could no longer speak or

write or move freely, he seemed for the most part to be wrapped in a thickening cocoon of illness and weakness, ever more distant and isolated. But his intelligence still glimmered forth; he could still invent. We devised new forms and signals of human connection. Pressures of the hand, blinks of the eyes, small nods or shakes of the head became signs to replace words. With me, he even managed to create a code. Slowly, with one finger, he could trace the letters of short words on the palm of my hand. I would say each letter aloud, then say the whole word as soon as it became clear to me. I don't know why but I was the only one who could do this with him. He tried with the others, but they couldn't decipher his intentions past the few beginning letters, too sad or too nervous to trust their own abilities to understand him. He became agitated and fearful when his signals could not reach them and stopped trying. I gradually became interpreter for the small messages he accumulated. Each afternoon, after my classes, when I came into the hospital room I was greeted eagerly by his mother or whoever was at his bedside that day. My coming opened the lock of silence that held him fast. We would spend the initial period of my visit clarifying and explaining his wishes and the questions that had arisen in my absence. In its own dreadful way, that became the daily routine. It seems one can make a routine out of anything.

But it was terrible to see, to live through. Like all terrible experiences subsequently recalled, one doesn't know how they were endured, or why one endured them in what seem like distinctively peculiar ways. Both the experience itself, and my own self in reaction, appeared unfamiliar and extreme. Some time in those last months I lost the unthinking innocence of waiting for Nicky to get better, and one morning I woke up feeling clenched at some brink, wondering how much longer I could stand this suspension of life. I was young. My mind and body were full of energy and curiosity. Without my watching I had grown up and become all those things I had wanted to be, but Nicky hadn't been able to wait for me. I was impatient to see, to do, to go, and

I could hardly find the bright vital boy I had loved in the frail sick figure that had lain so long in suffering. Each day I went to school, went to the hospital, visited the Van Dorns, returned to my home at evening, and waited and watched. The sad routine seemed to stretch before me like a desert, bleaching and parching out all the flowing springs of my youth. Without thought for anyone else that morning, I prayed just for myself, "God, let it be over. One way or another, let it be over in three months."

My prayer was answered.

On November 11th, in the late afternoon of a gray Armistice Day, I sat alone beside Nicky's bed holding his hand. He had looked up at me when I came in and then seemed to relax into a light sleep. Berthe had gone home to get some rest before returning that evening. Edith, who had come on duty the previous week as a private nurse for the evening hours, was having coffee in the hospital cafeteria. The room was quiet except for Nicky's breathing which was uneven, noisy with phlegm. I thought about disengaging my hand and using the suction machine to help him, but he lay quiet, not struggling. Pauses came between breaths. The pauses lengthened. Then quietly, without tremor or sign, the next breath did not come. His breathing simply stopped. I kept looking at him, waiting for it to resume, not sure if death could come so quietly. Then I rang for a nurse. In a few moments, Edith came in. I looked up at her and said, "I think something's wrong." As she moved swiftly toward him, I let go of his hand.

She felt for his pulse, put her hand on his chest to find a heartbeat, then put her face down, her cheek near his mouth, her hand still over his heart, and waited a few seconds. then she shook her head a little and I knew he was dead. "He's gone," she said softly, and I nodded. I hear her words down through the years. Even then in the odd quiet and hugeness of that moment I was grateful for her gentle decorum. Of all the ways the fact of his death might have been spoken, her way was at once unexpected and right for me in its gravity and its simplicity. "He's gone."

I was with him when he died. That has always been a solid satisfying thump of fact. It means for me that I was really there, stuck it out to the end. When the vigil ended, I saw its end, verified it past all conjecture. No one else was in the room. His death belonged to me. He gave it to me alone, into my hand. When he slipped down, out of this world, it was me he left. And me he has stayed with.

I make it sound like a reward. Well, it was. It was better knowing, seeing it, being there, better than coming too late. Having waited and watched so long, and then having him die in one's absence, all over and done with just in those few moments when one had succumbed to fatigue or listless hunger, that was far worse. I know that. I saw Berthe, his mother, who had not seen him die, never quite believe it, never again able to stop looking for him.

The hospital called the family. Berthe was the first to come, distraught and anguished because she had gone home, might have held him back, had not been with him at the end. She felt his forehead, his body, stroked his hair, his arms. "He is warm," she said, wanting the verdict reversed, imagining signs of life. She wept steadily and, through her weeping, wanted to know everything about his last moments. I told her, and again told Piet when he came in. Annie and Edith were down the hall making necessary arrangements for the next few days. Doctors and nurses came with words of pity and comfort. A nurse covered Nicky's face with a sheet. After a time, we left. There was no longer any reason to stay in that room. There was no longer anything to keep us there.

As we came out into the street, we felt the cold, and clung closely together as we started walking. Then Piet suddenly stopped, flung his arms up, then lunged into a doorway, sobbing. "I don't know what to do," he gasped. "I don't know what to do." He broke into a fit of harsh coughing and fumbled for a cigarette and Berthe and I patted his back and his arms. "I wish I could do something," he tried to explain. "Anything, just to feel better.

Kick a cop. Anything." It was so unexpectedly absurd that right then, in the midst of everything, we laughed, all three of us. Grief so extreme is disjointed, even ludicrous. Under its crushing weight, all Piet could do was give vent to defiance on a small boy's terms. When he quieted down, the three of us linked arms and walked on, not speaking more. The wind was sharp, getting somewhere inside to be warm seemed enough of a goal.

When we got to Piet and Annie's small Jones Street apartment, we sat numbly at the painted kitchen table. After a while, Annie came in and made some tea. We drank it, passing sugar and milk carefully in the blankness. None of us quite knew what to do next, if anything needed to be done. Over the tea, we began to talk a little about Nicky, how his suffering had now ended. Then I told them about the previous afternoon. Because Nicky had died so soon afterwards, it became full of meaning for me and for the others too. The memory, in the context of the surrounding pain, was like balm.

The afternoon before he died, for the first time in several days, Nicky began to spell letters into my hand. Slowly, weakly, he spelled the word A-P-P-L-E-S. I wondered if he could possibly want to eat an apple or even imagine that he could. He looked at me, saw I was puzzled, and went on spelling letters one by one. C-I-D-E-R, then a pause to rest, then M-I-L-L. Then I understood and squeezed his hand. "I remember," I said. "Taking the apples to the mill in the fall." He nodded and closed his eyes in satisfaction. I kept holding his hand, grateful that through some obscure mercy in the midst of his suffering, he could escape back to the pleasant days of his growing up. The cider mill in the woods with the bright apples crushed into fragrant pulp, the crunching sounds of the presses, the brilliant autumn hillsides, all the busy outdoor errands of his boyhood—that was where he escaped to and could visit again even on the day before his death. The idea that his last thoughts were pleasant helped us all, a small talisman against bad dreams.

When I returned home to Riverdale later that evening, I

learned that Edith had telephoned my parents. They had worried about me as Nicky worsened, but had not known how, or if,
they should intervene. Certainly they would have wished me to
have the good times of youth rather than witnessing illness and
death, but they had respected my commitment. Now they were
waiting up for me. My father hugged me and stroked my hair in
wordless sympathy, and my mother sat with me in my room and
listened while I told her about Nicky's last hours. She asked with
particular concern about Berthe, imagining another mother's grief
at the loss of her only child. My own feelings were confused. The
strong young Nicky I had loved had been gone for a long time
and I was relieved that the siege of his illness and dying was
ended. But when I tried to picture a future without him, it loomed
bleak and empty.

A few days later Nicky was buried in Woodstock in the old
cemetery on a hill close to town. That day, it rained all morning
long. The rain continued throughout the funeral service in the
chapel, and was just beginning to taper off as people in dark
winter coats under black umbrellas gathered at the graveside.
The minister read from the Bible and spoke a few words as we all
stood by. I saw Bart and Sylvia, Carl and Edith, other friends of
the Van Dorns, not all of them known to me, and a few school
friends of Nicky's, looking cold and miserable. I was grateful
they had come. It seemed right that Nicky should have many
mourners at his funeral. He deserved it; he had been such a
marvelous boy. Then the service was over. Slowly, people came
to hug members of the family and began returning to their cars.
The days before had been so busy and now, suddenly, everything was over. I couldn't quite believe it, felt as if I hadn't really
said good-bye.

I told Piet to take the others home, that I wanted to stay there
a while longer and would walk back to the house later. But he
guided Berthe and Annie into the Schuylers' car and then came
back to wait with me till I was ready to leave. One by one, the

cars drove out of the cemetery gates. It grew quiet. There was no one about. The rain had stopped but the sky was still dark with rolling clouds. I liked the turbulence, it seemed right that heaven should object to Nicky's death. I took Piet's arm and we walked slowly along the lanes between the graves, letting the quiet countryside gradually remind us of Nicky's love for the hills and fields of his home. In a while the sky became a bit lighter as the clouds thinned and, here and there, a few streaks of sunlight slanted down. It didn't signify anything, we knew that, but it made us feel a little better all the same. And he was grateful to me, Nicky's father was, for having wanted to stay there and make possible that small respite from grief.

In the weeks that followed, feelings of all sorts errupted, as if we were coming out of a long numbness where all feeling had to be carefully wrapped up in order to endure the days and not burden others. One day, I was stunned to hear someone use the word "cancer" to describe Nicky's illness. Only the word "tumor" had ever been used in my presence or in Nicky's while he was alive. He had a tumor in his throat. Perhaps at that time, the very word "cancer" alone seemed sufficient to hurl spears of death and people avoided it to spare our feelings. When I did at least hear it, though, I felt betrayed and stupid. It explained everything I had watched Nicky live through, every turn in that steep dark descent. Nicky and I had traced all that pain, trying to reverse it again and again. People recovered from tumors, we believed. But not from cancer. I had groped downward with Nicky without understanding, as if blindfolded. They, the adults, had allowed us to live through it all, had depended on me to endure it with him, but only as a child would endure, trusting, bewildered, and duped. They had enfolded me in the experience, but had swathed the information and the intelligence by which I might have comprehended it.

Perhaps they themselves didn't know, or couldn't face or name the knowledge they held. Perhaps I had not been brave enough to ask the right questions. Nevertheless I was angry and hurt. They had let me go on thinking that Nicky had a tumor in his throat, was dying from that tumor, which to me had seemed incomprehensible, like a man dying from a bee sting.

Several weeks later, the Van Dorns drove to Key West to spend the winter. They could face neither their usual familiar winter routine in the Village, nor the house in Woodstock that held so many memories of Nicky. On impulse, Piet thought that new scenes might help; they packed and were gone. Despite all my ties to them, I was relieved.

One hears on all sides now, sad tales of abuse, not just violence but coercive or subtle forms of sexual abuse of children or teenagers. I was never able to see what happened between Piet and myself when I was seventeen in those terms. He did not abuse me. We were in collusion. Erotic pleasure was the one candle flame of joy we discovered in a world too much filled with ordeal, fading, and grief. If Nicky had not died but had regained health and energy, the intervals when Piet and I sought each other out probably would given way and ceased. Without thought or rancor, we would simply have moved past them. At least that's what I think now. But after Nicky died I did not know what to make of the hidden awareness between us. We had been partners through the long watching but, though we shared some of the gestures of love, we were not lovers. I don't know how he thought of me in that limbo time, but I couldn't think of him that way. Love for Nicky had both held us together and kept us apart. Now Nicky had left us alone: Piet and me, and of course Berthe consumed by her own loss, and Annie who would have given Piet anything to help him through this time. I felt linked to them all by what we had come through together, but I feared what might yet happen between Piet and me. Every day after school I still took the subway downtown to the Village and spent the afternoon just as I had when Nicky was alive. But he was gone and so was my main reason for going there. I was also starting to picture myself going to college, forming new friendships, meeting new young men. None of that could happen if I stayed so close to the Van Dorns. Not knowing how to express my interest in a future without Nicky, I alternated between feeling stifled and then guilty for my disloyalty. Then when the family departed so suddenly for Key West, I regretted the loss of the affectionate companions who had so long sustained me. My days seemed empty and I didn't yet know how to fill them. I still mourned for Nicky, I missed Piet, and was often lonely. Even so, I breathed deeply, as though I had been released into the open air.

XI

***

The Return

I seldom saw my cousin Thomas during our first years in America. He was eight years older than I and usually away on his train trips during occasions when our families got together. Upon his discharge from the army in 1946, while I was engrossed in my life at Woodstock, Thomas had enrolled at City College of New York with the support of the G.I. Bill. There for the first time in his life, he had friends and even a few love affairs. He and I became better acquainted during the winter of our senior years, his at college, mine at high school.

One evening around Christmas, about six weeks after Nicky's death, my parents persuaded me to join them on a visit to my aunt and uncle. The Van Dorns were in Florida but I was still accustomed to being in that family where everyone's feelings of bereavement were similar to mine and we expected little beyond the comfort of each other's presence. After a short time at my aunt and uncle's house, I found I couldn't yet join in the holiday spirit or the usual animated family talk of music, books and politics. I whispered to my mother that I was leaving early to go home by bus and hoped that the others would understand. As I slipped out to the hall closet to put on my coat, Thomas followed and offered to drive me home.

We drove through Van Cortland Park and in the enclosed darkness of the car, we began to talk. I told him about Nicky, he told me about an "older" married woman of twenty-six at C.C.N.Y. With her blessed good counsel, Thomas had learned to overcome his appearance and his shyness. She helped him to see that though he was no beauty, he was nice, funny, and smart and that those qualities could appeal to women if he gave them a chance. We continued talking and driving that evening, past my house and up the Henry Hudson Parkway. In the next weeks, we saw quite a bit of each other, went to movies, to museums, and for long drives, talking all the way. He was very good to me, sweet and understanding and real. The eight year difference between us which had loomed so large when I was a child no longer mattered and we went from being cousins to friends.

Unhappy as he had been as an adolescent, Thomas told me he never worried about being a *Mischling*, nor had he thought that having a religious affiliation would help his isolation. He did worry about being perceived as a "greasy foreigner" among the young American males he had encountered at his first high school and in the army. This was not a problem at City College of New York which welcomed a cross section of the city's ethnic populations and was dominated by Jewish immigrants or their children.

Thomas never became a candidate for love at first sight, but with a number of young ladies who gave him second thought, he managed quite well.

"I always sit next to the prettiest girl in the class," he told me, "and she's always in love with a football hero or a basketball star who treats her badly. She talks to me because I'm fat and look so safe," he gave a wicked chuckle.

"Then what?" I asked.

"Then we go for coffee so she can tell me all about how mean Bill or Joe is to her, and I listen and pat her hand. And she says I'm so understanding. And we start going for coffee after every class and pretty soon Bill or Joe isn't so important and I turn out not to be so safe after all."

Thomas's clear enjoyment of his college years at C.C.N.Y. persuaded me to apply for admission there for the following fall. After four years at an all-girls high school, I was eager to experience co-ed classes at least for a while. At that time, a Bachelor of Education was the only degree C.C.N.Y. offered to women. I didn't plan to become a teacher, therefore I intended after the first two college years to return to the all female Hunter College for a liberal arts degree.

In the meantime, I was enjoying my final term at Hunter High School. I had not been involved in most school activities during my years with Nicky, initially because of "going steady," and then of watching over his long illness. For a long time I had been serious beyond my years; now I was released into teen-age pastimes and silliness. With fits of giggling, I competed in the "Miss Hunter High" beauty contest and was declared runner-up. In the senior play, a pastiche of Snow White, I slithered across the stage as a glamorized wicked step-mother. With a friend who dated a West Point cadet, I cut classes to see him march on days when there were parades on Fifth Avenue. I started twice-weekly ballet lessons at Carnegie Hall which were enlivened by the young actors and musicians who studied there.

Then, just before my graduation in June of 1949, my parents announced plans for a major change in our lives. In the United States the anti-Communist crusade of the House Un-American Activities Committee was gearing up to blight hundreds of careers in Hollywood and on Broadway. Meanwhile, the entertainment industry in Europe was reviving. Berlin remained a divided city without the resources to support film or theater production, but Munich was thriving. My father had been trying to please American musical tastes for ten years with no success. Though he had become fluent in English, he couldn't really write songs like an American. Only his native language released his facility for word play that could join cleverness with deeper feelings. And now with the war over, while American theaters remained closed to him, opportunities awaited him in the German speaking countries of Europe. Robert and Elke decided return to Europe for a one year trial period.

"We won't live in Germany or Austria again after all that has happened, but Zurich is close by," my father explained. "And if things work out I can make some decent money again."

"We want you to come with us," my mother urged. "We'll start out in Switzerland, and Daddy will get in touch with the people he knows in theaters and films. Maybe after a while you could go to the Sorbonne in Paris. Wouldn't that be exciting?"

It was a lot to take in. I couldn't respond right away, feeling more alarm than enthusiasm. To give myself some time I said I'd think about it. It seemed that my whole life was changing. After my graduation, the girls I knew in high school would scatter to their separate futures in other places. Nearer to home, everyone I had been close to was gone or about to go. Nicky was dead and the Van Dorns were in Florida. My cousin Thomas was heading for graduate study in oceanography at the University of Chicago. Now my parents, too, were leaving. It was hard to see my future.

I was registered for C.C.N.Y. for the fall. Now I tried to imagine attending the Sorbonne instead. I pictured myself wearing a beret and going to bistros. Living in Paris certainly sounded glamorous. But it was also frightening. The French I spoke as a toddler had sunk back into my unconscious and I had only three years of high school French. Because we spoke English at home, my German had remained childish. If I went to Europe, I would have to learn to express myself in those languages, and leave English behind. That would be leaving behind an essential part of myself. I thought, spoke, dreamed and read in English. And how could I become a writer in languages that by now seemed foreign? How would I feel day by day in Paris, in a foreign country with foreign ways and with nothing familiar? Here where I was accustomed to everything, my parents stood out as different, not quite sure of American ways, never fully at ease with the language. There, our positions would be reversed with me having to learn new customs in clothing, in books, in music, in talk, even in flirting. All through my teens, I had hated being a novice at anything because it made me feel clumsy and vulnerable. In Europe I would be a novice at everything.

I wasn't sure I was brave enough. My parents were brave. My father had faced many dangers, my mother had not hesitated to stay with him even when being married to a Jew placed her in danger too. They had feared for their lives; they had struggled through years of poverty to make a life in a new country. How could they understand my lesser fears? Now they were ready to risk returning to a Europe forever altered by the war that had displaced them. But however changed, Europe was their home and however much they had lived through, they themselves were still Europeans, whereas I saw myself as American. I didn't know anyone in Europe and would have to depend on my parents as I had as a child. This prospect seemed even more precarious than facing Europe.

Throughout my teens I had been aware of the strains in their relationship and often felt like a pawn caught up in their competitive moves. In addition to their own tensions, their unspoken expectations weighed upon me. I sensed they were hoping for their unremarkable daughter somehow to burst forth with a work of genius. I too wished for genius to strike, but it hadn't so far. "You have to be independent," my mother had cautioned throughout my teens when I failed to see beyond the era's dictum that I should marry and have babies. "You have to have a profession," she insisted. "You have to be able to make your own way." And though she urged me to have a profession, she had no idea of what it should be or how I should get it. Of course, I wanted to be a writer but the idea of years of training to become one didn't occur to me. Though I had my father as a model, I hadn't availed myself of his knowledge or his talent. I had rejected piano lessons which might have brought access to his musical gifts, and my early admiration for my father's lyrics was obscured by their being in a language I was trying to leave behind. So I didn't manifest the interest in his craft that might have induced him to encourage me. In truth, I hardly knew who I was or could become but I did know that I couldn't find out in my parents' company.

Most disturbing of all, however, was the idea that if I went to Europe I would be an immigrant all over again. It wasn't travel I feared; but dislocation, a dislocation that might turn out to be permanent. I had worked hard to fit into American ways and I could neither imagine settling overseas for the rest of my life, nor picture returning here after years at the Sorbonne. I saw myself forever suspended in a desolate space between two continents.

I couldn't face it. At eighteen I felt ready to embark on independent adulthood but only here in this country whose ways I had learned and whose language was my own. I remembered my mother's repeated saying, "You have your life, and I have mine." How those words used to thrust me into unwanted separations. But now, when my mother wanted me with her and I had to make a choice, I finally thought she had been right. My life was distinct from hers. My life, the life I wanted, was in the United States. I had grown up here and here I would stay.

Once I had made my decision, I told my parents that I would not be returning to Europe with them. We discussed it several more times till finally, when they were sure I knew what I wanted, they accepted my decision and began to work out the necessary arrangements.

My personal feelings of dislocation were trivial compared to the large-scale human dislocations left by the war. A vast repatriation movement under Allied supervision had begun even before the war's end to expedite orderly transfers of people. This was a monumental effort when the post-war refugee total rose to over twelve million people. A majority of the displaced persons were gradually able to return to their homelands but there were still over a million who were unwilling to return. Many were refugees from countries of eastern Europe under Soviet domination. Others were Jews didn't want to live again in Germany, Austria or Poland since those countries held memories of persecutions, suffering, and murdered family members. After the war, help for Jews from European countries ended, and other countries restored their pre-war limited immigration quotas. In response to the worldwide barriers to Jewish immigration and despite objections from various governments, pressures for a Jewish homeland mounted. In May of 1948 the sovereign state of Israel was established, fastened onto the unwilling Arab country of Palestine, and thus generating immediate and lasting conflict between Arabs and Jews.

In the United States, President Truman's efforts to raise the quotas for displaced persons were curtailed by Congress. Nevertheless, the United States took in 105,000 Jews, more than any country except Israel. Israel received 744,000 Jews from all parts of the world but only 387,000 were from Europe.

I was only dimly aware of the large-scale international problem of displaced persons until it flashed into my own domestic situation. While my parents prepared for their return to Europe, I looked forward to living alone as a college student. I thoughtlessly assumed that I would continue to occupy the Riverdale apartment we had shared, with my parents continuing to pay the rent and my living expenses just as they always had. After all, I wouldn't cost much. In those generous days, there was no worry about college tuition at City College. For a city resident who met the admission requirements, college was free. For many years the children of poor but aspiring immigrants, gained their college and professional degrees with full support of the city or the State of New York. But while I gave scant thought to money matters, my parents faced the trip with as little financial security as they'd had ten years earlier when they embarked for America. One important difference was Robert's hope of reviving his career in Munich. (As it turned out, he succeeded. His German songs and shows became popular again and he later gained new fame and a substantial income by translating a series of hugely successful American musicals for European audiences. His ten years in America were not wasted after all.) But before that could happen, they needed cash to live on in Europe. They also needed to pare down ongoing expenses in America. Though I wouldn't need tuition, I would need a place to live and a stipend. For the next months, my mother sewed almost non-stop to earn money and they saved every penny they could from my father's royalty checks. Fortunately these royalty payments were arriving more often as his music and that of other Jewish composers was again being played in Germany.

I pictured my emancipated life as a sophisticated young woman with her own apartment while, unbeknownst to me, my parents searched for ways to subsidize the rent. Once again, as so often in their ten years' sojourn in New York, the network of their fellow refugees provided a solution. A married couple who had been living in one of the European resettlement camps for displaced persons had at last being granted permission to enter the United States. They had just arrived from overseas and needed an inexpensive place to live. My parents could help by subletting part of our apartment to the couple, a good deed which would also reduce their own rent payments. To my dismay, the arrangement was agreed upon. As my mother described the couple's flight from Poland and the conditions in the D.P. camp, I was sorry they had been persecuted, sorry they were poor, but it didn't make me any happier about the prospect of sharing my home and relinquishing my vision of unfettered independence. Living with my parents was bad enough, I thought, but at least I knew them. Now I would be sharing the apartment with middle-aged strangers, and not just strangers, refugees. Would I never get away from refugees? I pleaded, I protested, but the decision was firm.

Then came a time of sorting through belongings. Our apartment was crammed with stacks of clothing, china, books, papers, and personal items—some to be left behind, some intended for storage in the Schuylers' barn in Woodstock, and some to be packed for the trial year abroad. When all the stacks had been dispersed, the time for departure was at hand.

In September of 1949, Robert, Elke and I rode to a Manhattan pier in a taxi with luggage in the trunk and strapped on the roof, just as it had been ten years earlier when we came to America. Then I had been almost eight years old; now I was eighteen. This time I would not be crossing the ocean with them as they sought to restore their lives in Europe. I was coming to see them off at the pier before embarking on my own American future. Filled with excitement, we walked up the gangplank together and boarded the *Ile de France*. Trans-Atlantic travel was still mostly by ship in those days and the crossings meant five or six days of pampered idleness. I was charmed by the snug staterooms and awed by the public dining rooms and lounges glistening with chandeliers, polished wood and damask. Paneled wood walls glowed along what seemed like miles of corridors on multiple levels. Stewards escorted arriving passengers or hurried to staterooms with farewell tributes of flowers and champagne. The atmosphere was that of a huge elegant party. The luxury liner was not only far more sumptuous and larger than any hotel I had seen, but it also held the thrill of voyaging to distant lands. During our repeated hugs of farewell I was almost sorry I had refused to join my parents on this voyage, Almost but not quite. Even though I'd have to share the apartment, I would be free to come and go. I would go to college; I would meet boys; I would have adventures. I was about to be an independent young woman in the exciting city of New York. When the final good-byes had been said, I pattered, in shoes like ballet slippers, down the gangplank, through the long pier building until I reached the street. Outside in the sunshine, my spirits soared. Henceforth, I would be on my own.

GE